THE Wingman

A Novel

MEG ROSENTHAL

For our darkest parts that deserve a little color.

ISBN: 978-1-966343-12-7 (hard cover)
       978-1-966343-13-4 (soft cover)
Rosenthal. Meg
Edited by: Melisa Graham

Warren Publishing
Charlotte, NC
www.warrenpublishing.net
Printed in the United States

PRAISE FOR *THE WINGMAN*

"The Wingman *is the perfect blend of heart, humor, and healing. With sizzling chemistry and emotional depths, Archie and Talia's story is an unforgettable ode to second chances—you'll devour it in one sitting and then wish you could start all over again.*"

— ALISSA DeROGATIS, author of CALL IT WHAT YOU WANT

"*Witty, tender, and filled with heartfelt hope,* The Wingman *is a vibrant celebration of friendship, resilience, and the intricate beauty of relationships in all their messy complexity. With an artist's touch, Rosenthal navigates heavy topics with grace and sensitivity, painting a story that reminds us that sometimes the most beautiful masterpieces—and the happiest endings—begin with your best friend.*"

— KALYN FOGARTY, author of *What We Carry* and *Everything's Still There* (Alcove Press)

"*A charming, fast-paced romance that examines how mental health impacts relationships,* The Wingman *will keep readers turning the page to discover if Talia can be forgiven for hurting the person she loved by trying not to hurt him in the first place.*"

— SARAH CREECH, author of *Season of the Dragonflies* and *The Whole Way Home*

"*The Wingman is a beautifully-woven story of friendship, love and the promise to carry each other through bad time—not stay on the sidelines. Throughout the book, the relatable characters felt more like friends.*"

— MEREDITH RITCHIE, author of *Poster Girls*

Whereof what's past is prologue;
what to come, in yours and my discharge.

–WILLIAM SHAKESPEARE, *The Tempest*

AUTHOR'S NOTE

When people ask me what this book is about, the simple answer is street art and depression. But it didn't start out that way.

This book's origin story started with an idea: What if there were two friends who were always meant to be something more? And what if, in college, they were each other's "wingman" every time they went out? And what if, after the female love interest leaves town after college, she is back suddenly, two years later?

In August of 2019, I approached colleague Elisabeth King with this idea and the opportunity to write this cute romance with me. We met a few times to plan the book, splitting both the perspectives and the timeline. After a time, development of this iteration slowed down, and I asked Elisabeth for the opportunity to take the story over. With her permission, I began rewriting in February of 2021 and finished the new manuscript in January of 2023. During this time, I also gained access to Talia's perspective and the inner workings of her mind. In my head, the first brainstorm saw Archie as the main character, with Talia in a supporting role. But this version of the story posed a new question: What if there was more to Talia's Manic Pixie Dream Girl front? What if it was all a facade?

It is worth noting that this book does contain heavy subject material as a result. In these pages lie themes of mental health, suicide ideation, and attempted suicide. But there is also humor, hope, and a HEA. And while this story is a work of fiction, these themes can be very real. If any part of this book resonates with you, please know you are not alone. It is my goal that the final version of this book serve as a reminder to all that there is often more to the story than what's seen on the surface.

I hope you laugh, and I hope you cry, and I hope that if there is any semblance of an artist in you, you don't ever stop creating.

Your voice deserves to be heard.

Meg

PART ONE

ARCHIE

PRESENT DAY

When I answered the phone, the ghost's voice was painfully recognizable. "Are you still single?" the ghost asked.

Even though it had been two years since she'd taken my calls, which I'd stopped making long ago, I would never forget the sound of her voice. I couldn't, because I had memorized her voicemail—*Thanks for calling! I'm obviously not answering the phone, so don't leave a message!*—as well as her last words to me before college graduation—*I'm grateful to have met you here. Thanks for memories. And the pancakes.* As if that were the most memorable thing she chose to walk away from when she left.

"Talia?" I asked anyway, knowing full well that even though her name tasted foreign on my tongue, the haunting voice on the line did indeed belong to my former best friend.

She sighed heavily. "Who else would it be, Archie?"

My stomach somersaulted when she said my name.

"How am I supposed to know?" I asked. "You haven't called me in ... forever." The last word was a hoarse whisper, nearly caught in my throat.

"Has it been that long already?" The lilt in Talia's voice feigned surprise. "Time sure does fly when you're having fun."

"Fun," I repeated. "Is that what it's been since you left Oregon? Fun?"

"Depends on your definition of it, I suppose. But I repeat: Are you still single?"

My mind was whirling as if my whole universe was a soda can that had been shaken and tilted on its side, counting down the seconds until it would explode. Much like I imagined my head was about to do.

"Um," I said, rather stupidly. "I wasn't. Now I am."

"Really?"

Regaining some of my composure as the surprise of her call began wearing off, I couldn't help but scoff. "Is that shock at the fact that I was in a relationship? Or that I'm single again?"

"I mean, I guess the latter. You can be quite the catch. I would have thought you'd be snatched up by now."

I took the phone away from my ear and hit it against my forehead a few times, trying to beat some sense into my brain. I took a deep breath, then said, "Not enough of a catch, I guess."

She paused. "Sorry about that."

This was absurd. Both the conversation and the fact that Talia Scott was on the phone with me again after nearly two years of actively ghosting me. It was nothing short of ludicrous. I couldn't decide if I wanted to scream in fury or cry tears of joy. I cleared my throat instead.

"Is that why you called? Just to belittle my singleness?"

"No. Well, maybe." She took a deep breath. "Actually, I'm glad you're single. I'm single too. Can you be my wingman again?"

Stomach. Dropped. Gone.

Two years since Talia Scott had up and left my life. Two years since I had heard her voice. Two years since she had asked me that question.

"Be your … what?"

"You heard me. I need my wingman back."

"I'm still in Oregon," I said. "You are … I don't even know where you are." I never knew where she had gone after she left. Hollywood, Vegas … somewhere exotic and amazing probably, just like she was.

"Wrong again, Arch. I'm back."

"You're … *back*?" I squeezed my eyes shut at the hurt I could hear in my own voice.

"Wow, you got really smart after graduation, didn't you?"

I ignored her jab. "You're in Oregon. Right now."

She clicked her tongue. "Bingo. What do you say? Are you in, wingman? For old times' sake?"

After she had left, there was nothing I wouldn't do to be Talia's wingman just one more time. But now, two years later, after all the time I'd spent repairing the gaping wound she left behind from tearing my heart out, I wasn't so sure.

"I don't know, Talia."

"Oh, come on," she pleaded. "Just this once. I … I miss you."

I took the phone away from my face and cursed colorfully. After a steadying breath, I replaced the phone and said through gritted teeth, "Fine. But you owe me big-time."

"I know I do, Archie. I know."

TALIA

SIX YEARS EARLIER, FRESHMAN YEAR

Bridgeport College was supposed to be my phoenix moment. A symbol for how I had died and rebuilt a new life for myself. A new state, a new school, and a new me.

And all that newness started with a choice.

Or better yet, a correction.

My RA led me up the stairs to find my room number in the freshman dorm. On the outside of the door, written on colored construction paper, was my name: Natalia. A matching green slip held the name of my new roommate: Kathryn.

I paused at the door, dropping the first of my bags on the floor. "Is it okay if I change my name here?" I asked as I looked at my name written in swirling penmanship and told my first lie in my new town. "I usually go by my nickname."

The RA, whose name I remembered was Becca, beamed. "Of course!" And she flourished a black marker from her pocket, prepared for this occasion.

The girl really was kind. I wondered what it must be like to have so much kindness inside of you to just give away freely.

I took the marker, offered a thin smile, and crossed out *Natalia*, wanting to leave that part of my identity behind. I wrote *Talia* instead, in thick black block letters. Just Talia.

I went to hand Becca the marker back, but she shook her head. "Keep it. I made name tags for Welcome Week, but you're going to have to change that too," she said sheepishly as she handed me the card.

"I appreciate you taking the time to have everything ready for me," I said as I took the name tag from Becca's outstretched hand. Propping up my knee, I hunched over to scrawl my new signature. Once my name was written again, I pocketed the marker and clipped the name tag to the bottom of my jeans I had cut off into shorts before I left Mount Pleasant, South Carolina.

"Does everything you do have to be that extreme, Natalia?" my mother asked without looking up from her needlepoint when I set the scissors back in the kitchen drawer and threw out the denim scraps. "As if choosing a college that is three days of driving away, you're going to leave behind half your wardrobe as well?"

"I'm thinking about a tattoo when I get there too," I answered.

"Your father won't allow it."

"Considering he's too busy to drive me out there himself, I guess he won't see it."

"You know your father's work is what's paying for this education you seem to be throwing away."

"It's fine. I'll spend my allowance on sketchy motels on the way there."

"Use the credit card," she said, ending the conversation. I harrumphed. I always kept one of her credit cards on me in case of emergency, but I vowed, then and there, to instead use the cash I had been saving whenever possible.

"You said your parents were traveling?" Becca asked innocently, bringing me back to the present. "And they weren't able to come help you move in?"

I gave her that same small, tight smile, the only one I seemed to have stored in my arsenal. "Yeah, but it's okay. I don't have that many things."

"Do you need any help?"

"Not really," I said. "I'm fine. But thank you."

"If you change your mind, just let me know! I'll be making my rounds," Becca said. She handed me my keys, and with a cheery wave, she turned to greet the next group of parents coming up the dormitory stairs.

I turned to look at the door again and took a deep, steadying breath. With a slight jiggle of the key in the lock, the door sprang open. My roommate, Kathryn, must have been rather organized and prepared, as her half of the room was already neatly unpacked, while mine looked skeletal. I tossed my bag onto the empty twin bed before backing out of the room and closing the door quickly behind me.

I jogged back down the stairs, needing to move my car from the drive-up space to the actual parking lot behind the dorm. I took in the view as I drove. The campus was just as pretty as it looked online, which was a blessing considering I had never visited before move-in day. It was far away, emphasis on *far*, and it had an accredited art program.

And most importantly, the college was settled in the little namesake town of Bridgeport, Oregon, home to a popular art blog called *The Digital Art Show* that I had been following since high school. It seemed like kismet when I started researching programs that would put me several states away from my hometown, and the one that piqued my interest first happened to be home to my favorite blog.

I applied the very same day. Rolling admission granted me entry and a scholarship a few months later.

There were parents *everywhere* on campus. By one building, a mother and a father were helping their kid unload their laundry, and on the next corner two fathers and their kid and their kid's friend were all lugging bags inside.

I pushed down the rock that had appeared in my throat and pulled my sunglasses from my head to the bridge of my nose. I entered the parking lot, where I found zero open spaces. I weaved my way in and out of every row, hoping a space would magically materialize. Instead, a lanky boy appeared quite literally out of nowhere, a look of shock and horror on his stunned face.

"Oh my god!" I screamed and slammed my brakes, squeezing my eyes shut, dreading the impact. My Toyota Corolla squealed, but no other sound, or thud, came.

I opened one eye. The boy was still standing in the middle of the parking lot, right in front of my hood, with the audacity to stare at me, dumbfounded. I glared at him.

Lowering my window, I popped my head out and yelled, "I almost hit you!" The boy still just stared. I hoped he wasn't shitting his pants because that would be an inconvenience for us both. "Hello?" I asked.

"You almost hit me."

"Yes, I think we established that," I sighed and pinched the bridge of my nose. But somewhere in my movement, I caught a quick flash of an open parking space behind him. "Hey, can you slide over a bit? I need that spot."

Slowly, *painfully* slowly, Boy turned to look at the empty parking spot behind him. "My mom was just there."

"But she's gone now, yes?"

"Well, y-yes …" he stammered, and that was all the confirmation I needed as I lifted my foot off the brake.

When I started to inch forward, Boy came to his senses and sidestepped out of my way, bowing in dramatic salute and ushering me into the parking space. I didn't want to laugh, so I pressed my lips together, praying he couldn't see my expression behind my sunglasses.

Boy was still waiting when I parked and exited my car.

"That was quite the introduction," he said, casually leaning his hip against the car next to mine.

I pretended to ignore him while I busied myself opening my trunk and retrieving my backpack and final suitcase.

He tried again. "I didn't get your name."

"I didn't give it," I said, probably too sharply for someone who almost ran over another someone who was actually being rather nice about the whole ordeal.

"But you almost killed me," he said. "I think that makes us automatically acquaintances."

I thought about arguing the fact that death doesn't make the best of friends, but instead, I threw one hand on my hip and held out my other in introduction. "Talia Scott."

Boy waited a few beats, and his hazel eyes crinkled as he grinned. He took my hand and shook it. Firmly. "Archie Morgan. Nice to meet you, Talia."

ARCHIE

PRESENT DAY

I really didn't have much to complain about. Life wasn't bad.

I had a job at an accounting office. (Pay no mind to the fact that it was my family's business, and I worked the front desk reception.)

I had a degree from an actual college (accounting major from the college one neighborhood over … still no CPA though).

I had a roof over my head. (I mean, I lived at home. But I did have all the freedom I could want. I just didn't have much use for it.)

And, up until just a few short weeks ago, I had a pretty awesome girlfriend too. Right up until the point when Lex had looked me in the eye and said, "I care about you, Archie. I really do. I just can't keep waiting until the day you finally care enough to do something with your life."

So that sucked.

But that loss was like finding a hole in your fourth-favorite T-shirt—it really wasn't the worst thing that could happen.

But when Talia had walked across the stage to get her diploma with the rest of the arts department and then vanished into thin air before the dean could get to the business school graduates, it left a crater in my chest.

When I couldn't find Talia in the crowd of people at graduation, I was terrified of what had happened to her. In the nearly four years that I had known Talia throughout college, she wasn't usually hard for me to find. She was always … around.

"Typical," her mother said when I sought her in the parents' section, waiting to embrace their new graduates. "Just like Natalia to disappear on her next adventure without even thanking us for flying out all this way."

Just like it was typical for Talia to resurrect herself now as if that jump in time had never happened. As if she had never left town at all. As if she had never left me.

When she said *meet me at Blue Elixir* before hanging up the phone, a big part of me wanted to be strong and tell her no. Tell her that she couldn't just expect to fall back into the routine that our friendship relied on when we were in college. Tell her that times had changed—I had changed—and because of her departure, I had to find a way to carry on, one that didn't involve pulling back into the college dive bar we had frequented as undergraduates.

But unfortunately for me, as I parked my van beneath the glowing blue signage, it looked like I would say none of those things tonight. Also typical. I double-checked the time on my phone before sighing at my own stupidity. With a quick exit and lock of my car, I pocketed my keys and headed toward the door to see Talia again.

TALIA

PRESENT DAY

Very few things in my life were predictable, mostly because I tried hard to keep it that way. But one of the things I could always count on in recent years was Archie Morgan. In a world of chaos and man-made destruction, Archie had been a reassuring constant for me since the day we met.

That being said, I had no way of knowing whether or not he was actually going to show up. I wouldn't blame him. I wouldn't have come if I were in his shoes.

I had gotten to Blue Elixir twenty minutes prior, mostly because I was too jittery to wait any longer. My old college roommate, Kathryn, was letting me stay with her while I was back in town. She was married now, but she had graciously offered her couch without second thought—and had just as easily shooed me out the door when she could hear my pacing from the kitchen.

"Get out of here. Just come back at some point later," she said, and although she was dry in tone, she never said anything that she didn't mean. Some might call her honesty harsh at times, but I appreciated her bluntness after being raised in a life of thinly veiled secrets and lies that floated through the old-money Southern country club scene I had left behind six years ago.

"You're always welcome here, Talia," Kathryn said.

I left with a quiet thanks and misty eyes, and I was still blinking away the moisture as I searched for the door through the crowd of college-aged girls in short black skirts and too much lipstick. Lucky for them, the Oregon weather had just started to warm up as spring crawled out from under the cruel month of April.

To keep myself distracted, I watched the condensation collect and pool along the edges of my cider glass while I waited, one eye still on the door.

I almost didn't recognize him when he walked in. He was … bigger.

Not in a bad way. No, in a very *good* way. Archie had always been what my mother would've called "scrawny." I might have described him as gawky. He was still lean, but the man who walked through the door bore little resemblance to the one I'd known in college. His shoulders were broader, as was his chest, but it was in the way he walked that seemed larger. He walked as if he were unapologetic for occupying space, unlike the awkward freshman I had first met. I would almost say it was confidence that provoked the change in his demeanor—that was until his eyes met mine and I saw the expression they wore.

Hard. Archie's gaze was hard, which was something I'd never imagined it could be.

His lips thinned, and he averted his hazel eyes. Stuffing his hands into the pockets of his jeans, he walked toward me.

I had the entirety of the day to prepare for what I was going to say to Archie once I saw him. I had tried on several familiar greetings, but I couldn't recall a single one at that moment.

He stopped and stood before me, finally looking up at me again. There was pain, yes, but I had to believe that the same kind soul was in there. That he was still my Archie. That it would just take time for things to get back to the way they used to be.

But I couldn't put him through that same story again.

"Hi," I said.

He grumbled and pulled out the barstool beside me. It screeched as it slid before he settled onto the chair. Lifting two fingers, he signaled to the bartender and ordered his usual, a Michelob Ultra. Nice to see that hadn't changed at least.

He opened his mouth to say something to me, then closed it again. My heart squeezed, suddenly afraid.

His voice was low, and the words rang cold when he finally said, "I deserve an explanation."

ARCHIE

FRESHMAN YEAR

"What is that god-awful racket going on up there?" I asked, mostly to myself, but it was my new roommate who answered.

"Dunno. But it sounds like a party."

I shook my head. "Seems like an excessive amount of noise for move-in day."

The new roommate, Grady, repeated, "Dunno."

I flicked my wrist to look at my watch. "I mean, it's almost dinner time. Shouldn't they have everything in place by now?" I know I certainly did. My parents had dropped me on my college doorstep hours ago, teary-eyed like so many before them. Even though our house was only thirty minutes away, apparently this was still a big deal.

"Dunno," Grady said. Again. "But it sounds like they're still moving furniture." He closed the book he was reading and laid it on his chest. "If you know what I mean," he added with a wink.

I shuddered. I didn't need my ears privy to that kind of activity if that were to ever go on upstairs.

Grady stood from his bed, placing the book on his desk. "Think we should go investigate? Meet our new dormmates?"

"Not if someone is having sex up there!"

Grady shook his head and laughed. "Dude, I highly doubt it right now. Let's go meet them." He headed for the door. "You coming?"

It was nice to feel included in his endeavor. And maybe, underneath the carefree coolness of his graphic tee and long hair, Grady just had the same desperation for friends during freshman year as the rest of us.

"Okay."

It was amazing how many doors were open, students sitting inside clustered in pairs, waiting for someone to pop their head in. Grady turned out to be that special someone. Every open door on our way to the stairs, Grady stopped and said, "Hey! I'm Grady. This is Archie. We're number 307. What's up?"

I accompanied his introduction with an awkward little wave and a quiet *hi*, then hurried to catch up with him as he moved to the next door.

I picked up on the pattern: guys' room, girls' room, guys' room, girls' room. That meant we had girls on either side of our dorm room. I wondered if my parents knew that would be the case when they agreed to let me live in the South Residence building. Probably not.

I didn't remember the names of our immediate neighbors, but when we finally made it to the stairs and to room 407, directly above ours, I remembered her.

"Talia?" I said, halting Grady as his mouth opened for his introduction. He turned toward me slack-jawed, no doubt surprised that I knew someone he didn't. The girl who had nearly run me over with her car turned from a desk in the back corner of the room, where what must have been all of her belongings were strewn across the desktop.

"Oh hey … you." She offered me a small smile, but even with that tiny tilt of her lips, I swore the entire room lit up like a disco ball in a seventies nightclub. She fished for something in her back pocket and clicked it to cut the music that was blaring.

"Archie," I supplied for her.

She tapped her palm against her forehead, remembering. "That's right. Archie Morgan, the boy who plays in traffic."

"Parking lots," I said. It dawned on me that I had never seen her without her dark sunglasses. I definitely would have remembered those big blue eyes. I could drown in them. "But yeah. That's me."

I continued to hold the pause until Grady, bless him, cleared his throat and said, "Well, I'm Grady. What's up?"

"Hi, Grady." Talia's cautious attention shifted from me to my room-mate, who leaned against the doorframe behind me. "Talia Scott." She tiptoed between her two open suitcases to get to the door and leaned to shake his hand. "How do you do?"

"Splendid."

She gave him a tight-lipped smile as well, immune to the deadpan, then turned and said, "This is my roommate, Kathryn."

"How's it going, Kat?" Grady asked, snaking his arm around me to shake hands with the other girl in the room whom I hadn't even noticed yet. I was still just awkwardly standing on Talia's messy side of the otherwise immaculate room.

"It's Kathryn." She politely corrected him and shook his hand as well. "It's nice to meet you both."

"You said you're 307?" Talia asked, locking eyes with me again.

"Um, yes," I squeaked at her eye contact. I cleared my throat. "Yes, we are."

She lifted an eyebrow. "That means we're practically neighbors."

"No, we aren't," Grady countered. "We aren't next to each other."

Talia rolled her eyes, "Trivial detail. We're close enough."

I furrowed my brow. "Well, who said that the term *neighbor* had to require a lateral adjacency? Who's to say that we can't be neighbors via a vertical togetherness?"

Grady was silent, as were Kathryn and Talia. I considered just curling up and dying right there on the spot from sheer embarrassment. *Vertical togetherness? What was that?*

Then a small grin fractured Talia's puzzled expression and grew until it stretched from ear to ear, the first genuine smile I had gotten from her. It was beautiful. Suddenly, I couldn't catch my breath.

She broke the silence. "I think we might be very good friends after all, Archie."

ARCHIE

PRESENT DAY

The bartender nodded to me as he slid the bottle across the counter. I caught it deftly in one hand, still refusing to look Talia in the eye.

She was refusing to start off the conversation, which was ridiculous since this whole reunion was her idea.

"Seriously?" I began and took a swig. The bottle clattered on the counter. "Almost two years go by without any communication, and suddenly, you pop back into town acting like nothing has happened? Talia, I tried calling almost every day, months after graduation, and you never answered."

"I changed my number," she said softly.

"Great," I scoffed. "I think that's even worse than if you had blocked me."

"I'm sorry."

"*Sorry* is not going to be good enough."

"Look, I get that you're mad ...."

"I'm not mad. I'm beyond mad. I'm livid. I'm pissed. I'm—"

"You're here though."

"I ..." I fished for the words I wished I had said to her after she left, but I came up with nothing. I had nothing to counter because she was right. I was still here. And I hated it.

Even after those first few hellish months of worry, then the anger, then the overwhelming sadness, then the solemnity of just accepting her disappearance from my life, here I was. Sitting at the bar we always went to. Right next to the girl who had nearly destroyed me.

I finally looked at her. She was turned toward me, ankles crossed on the bar stool, hands folded in her lap. Her face reflected something that looked like remorse, but the expression was foreign on her features. Her hair was about half the length that it used to be, maybe even less than that.

And she was still as gorgeous as ever with her dark curls and dark clothes and the biggest, boldest, bluest eyes framed by dark lashes.

I sighed and turned back to my drink. It wasn't any use admitting that she was right or that she was still pretty. She knew both of those things. "When did you cut your hair?" I asked instead.

"Um, not too long ago, actually."

"Hmm" was my only reply before I downed about half of the bottle and signaled to the bartender that I would need another.

"You've gotten much better at drinking those," she commented.

"You've given me plenty of reasons to practice."

"How's Addie?"

I paused, the bottle halfway to my lips. I put it back down on the napkin coaster. "She prefers *Adeline* again now that she's in high school."

"She's a junior." It wasn't a question. Talia knew. Of course, she would have remembered my little sister and kept up with her.

"Yep," I said anyway.

"Things still good at the new school?"

Talia's memory was astounding. Especially since she never remembered to tell me that she was still alive out there in the world somewhere. I grunted some sort of caveman reply in confirmation.

The second beer slid across the bar, and I caught it, nodding back to the bartender.

"Did you drive here?" Talia asked, eyeing my second drink.

"Don't pretend like you care," I said. "You still haven't even told me why you're back. I'm pretty sure it's for more than just a casual game of wingman."

She had uncrossed her legs at some point, and one of them was bouncing up and down against the footrest of her bar stool. And she was biting her lip.

"You're right," she finally said. "This is about more than that."

"So ... is there an actual reason for your triumphant return?"

"Yes."

"What is it?"

"I can't tell you."

I gave a half chuckle that sounded anything but amused. I remembered this game all too well. Talia was all-knowing in our adventures, and I was the happy-go-lucky sidekick along for the ride. It had worked well, for a time. Until it all came crashing down. Until she disappeared.

"Of course you can't."

"Look, Archie." She drew herself up a little taller in her seat. "I can't pretend like I didn't hurt you when I left. I know I did. And I know I don't deserve to be coming to you now." She reached for the napkin underneath my drink and flourished a black marker from somewhere in her pocket, as if she had been planning on needing one this whole time. She scribbled on the napkin before pushing it back toward me. "Here's my new number and where I'll be tomorrow night. Eight o'clock. I'm going to need your help with my *triumphant return*, as you put it. If you think you could forgive me, or if you're too curious not to come, I'll see you there."

She stood up and capped her marker, pocketing it again before pulling out a twenty from a different pocket. She tossed it on the bar beside me. "Put it toward your Uber home."

I didn't touch the cash or the napkin with her number and the mysterious address. I didn't even look up at her.

I heard her footsteps click away on the laminate floor, then stop. "Archie," she said, loud enough to make sure I heard. "For what it's worth, I really am sorry."

I picked up the napkin, stuffing it into my back pocket. I left the cash on the counter as a generous tip. "For what? The leaving or the lack of communication?" I made the mistake of looking up at her.

Her eyes glistening, she replied, "For letting you care so much in the first place."

TALIA

FRESHMAN YEAR

For as long as I could remember, I wanted to be an artist. My mother always said that art was a hobby and not a profession and that I should be prepared to get a real job when I was done with college. I agreed that I might need a day job while I started, but whatever I did within the hours of 9 a.m. to 5 p.m. was not going to be my career. Hence her feeling that I was "throwing away" my education when I declared an art history and visual art double major.

But I didn't feel like that when I entered the small private art building on campus. I felt like I was crossing the threshold home, way more so than I had ever felt in my old house. I picked a spot at the paint-splattered table and surveyed the other students with their open sketchbooks. I opened my own to a clean, blank sheet.

The heavy door whooshed open, and the gust of warm air lifted the corner of my page. I looked over my shoulder at the figure walking in. The kid looked familiar. I watched as his eyes did a brief flitter across the room before settling on the open chair across from me.

"Is this seat taken?" he asked. His voice was still raspy, as if he had just woken up with barely enough time to grab a coffee on his way into our 9:20 Monday morning class.

It didn't matter what my reply was. The boy was already setting his paper cup down and shrugging his bag off his shoulders.

"I don't think my antisocial personality is contagious," I replied. "But sit at your own risk."

He chuckled, then popped the lid off his cup and took a long swallow. "I'll take my chances," he finally said and gave me a playful smirk. "It's Talia, right?"

I stiffened. "Yes. Remind me of your name?"

"Grady."

"Archie's roommate," I blurted without thinking twice and then felt a rush of heat flood my cheeks. I had met them on move-in day, but they hadn't come back upstairs to my room since then.

Grady laughed again and shook his head; his black locs swayed. "If that's to be my identifier, then so be it. But yes. Archie's roommate."

"You're an art major?" I asked and wondered what Archie's major was. He didn't seem like the artsy type.

Grady took another gulp from his steaming cup of coffee. "I am," he said. "Much to my father's concern."

"Mine too!" I beamed. "My parents don't think of art as a safe career choice." My parents didn't think much of my life choices lately. Not since The Diagnosis. Hence my desire to get as far away from my hometown as possible.

"Of course it's not," Grady said. "Why else would we pick it?"

The door opened again, and Grady squinted his eyes at the harsh streak of light. His eyes were the color of warm honey.

"Morning, friends." A man whom I assumed to be our professor entered the room, although he didn't look like any professor I was expecting to see. His flannel was unbuttoned over a graphic tee that advertised some sort of rock band, and he had a navy baseball hat flipped backward on his head.

"I'm Professor Conrad. But from now on, call me Joe. And from the looks of your eager, bright young faces, this must be Introduction to Art Technique." His voice was dry with little inflection, but he didn't seem altogether unfriendly as he searched through his papers.

"All right, I'm going to call roll real quick, and then we can jump right in. I'd go over the syllabus, but it's posted online, and I'd honestly rather you guys get jump-started on the basics so we can get into our first project of the semester."

Yep. I liked him.

Professor Conrad, *Joe*, found the sheet of paper he must have been looking for and looked closely at it. He made it through the majority of the alphabet, including last name *Mitchell*, first name *Grady,* by the time he got to me. "Last name Scott, first name Natalia," Joe said without looking up.

"I go by Talia now," I said from the back of the class, which earned a quiet chuckle from Grady.

The professor lifted his gaze and an eyebrow. "Reinventing yourself?"

"Just hoping that I no longer have to hide behind the extra letters," I said.

"Well rest assured, Talia, there is nowhere you can hide in art," Joe said while marking the note on his paper. He clicked his pen shut, then looked up with a kind smile. "Welcome."

ARCHIE

PRESENT DAY

I checked my phone again, making sure I was at the right address from Talia's napkin. Saving her contact in my phone again last night felt weird. The number was different, but the name was still the same. Just *Talia*.

I looked up at the numbers printed above the door and confirmed that I was, indeed, at the right place.

When Talia told me last night that this meeting was to convince me to help her with her return, I didn't know what to expect. But I certainly hadn't expected walking into The Glass Menagerie, a literal glass building downtown usually reserved for museum exhibitions. I glanced quickly down at my sneakers, and a brief spell of anger whipped through me that Talia hadn't prepped me for what I should've worn.

"Oh, hold the door," her very recognizable voice chirped as I was opening it.

I started to cut her a hard glance, but the bitterness melted when I saw her. She was wearing a black dress. It left her shoulders bare but covered her neck and hit her legs mid-thigh. She paired the dress with black boots that covered her knees. Her dark hair was coiled at the base of her neck, with several pieces escaping confinement and framing her face. Her light-blue eyes were stark against the thick eyeliner.

"Are you going to go in or going to the gym?" some guy dressed in a suit asked, eyeing my shorts and T-shirt.

"Oh, um, s-sorry," I stuttered. I guess I forgot I was holding the door because it closed right in the man's face.

Talia stifled a laugh and looked away, smiling.

The guy muttered a few choice words that I didn't register because I was still looking at Talia as a small crowd approached the building. I was like a salmon swimming upstream, moving toward Talia against the flow of bustling people.

"Hi," she said, beaming as we stood alone outside.

"Why didn't you tell me this was where we were going?"

She didn't miss a beat. She just stepped around me and reopened the door, gesturing for me to go through. "Because then you wouldn't have come."

I took one more look through the door at the glass walls and the shape of paintings hanging inside the building. An art show. Or a gallery. Or a museum. Maybe they were all the same thing. Since I wasn't in the art program like Talia and Grady had been, I certainly didn't know the difference. Regardless, Talia was partly right. I wouldn't have *wanted* to come.

I mean, I probably would've come anyway.

But she didn't need to know that.

I looked at her as she stood next to the open doorway looking like a gothic goddess or something.

"You could've at least told me to wear my nice shoes," I grumbled as I walked through the door.

It was kind of amazing that, inside an all-glass building, I could still manage to get lost in the maze of the artwork.

After Talia had closed the door behind us, she told me that she was "going to find Joe" and that she would "be back soon."

I didn't know who Joe was, but twenty minutes later, she was still nowhere to be found.

I was standing in front of a painting that spanned the entirety of one back wall when someone I didn't know appeared beside me.

"It's magnificent, isn't it?" said a very pretty someone dressed in slacks and a blazer. The button-down underneath her jacket was pink, as were her glasses that she pushed a little farther up the bridge of her nose as she turned toward me, smiling.

"Um," I said. "Very. Magnificent."

The woman laughed. "Mr. Conrad is quite the visionary. Every time I see his work, my own imagination runs wild. I wonder what it would be like to live in his head."

Creepy, I thought, but I smiled politely. She didn't notice. She was looking back at the painting again.

Honestly, it made zero sense to me. It looked like a landscape from a distance—if you closed one eye and tilted your head sideways, maybe. But then there were purple waterfalls where there should've been clouds in the sky and red fire hydrants where there should've been trees on the rolling hills.

I leaned closer to the painting.

Nope. Those weren't hills. They were ears, human ears, painted green. One even had an earring that was supposed to look like a leaf.

"There you are, honey. I've been looking everywhere for you," Talia said, practically skipping up behind us, threading her arm through the space between my elbow and my side. I froze; the graze of her arm felt like a jolt of lightning. If she noticed my reaction to her touch, she didn't acknowledge it.

I made a fist with my hand tucked in the pocket of my gym shorts as Talia leaned over to the woman and said, "Pardon me, but I do have to steal him for one second. Joe is about to give his speech."

I tried to look sheepishly at the woman, but she was still ogling the "masterpiece."

"Who is Joe?" I asked as Talia whisked us away.

She kept her hand on my arm. "Joe Conrad. The artist."

"You know the artist?"

"So do you."

"What?"

"Good evening, friends!" A voice boomed through the main foyer, and I winced, turning to see the speaker.

I squinted. "Wait. Is that—"

"Yep," Talia quipped, proudly. "Bridgeport College's own director of studio art, Joe Conrad."

"He was your art teacher."

"Well, yes, if you have to put it that way."

"He's wearing a baseball hat."

"And you're wearing gym clothes" was Talia's response.

"Again, your fault," I murmured.

She continued on, ignoring me. Something she was also good at. "Plus, he always wears a baseball hat."

"Thank you all for joining us here tonight," Joe, *the art teacher*, continued. "It means so much to me to have such a great group of people here to celebrate my recent tenure position. And endless thanks to Bridgeport College for sponsoring this exhibit tonight for the neighborhood."

"Ten year?" I whispered. "What's a ten year?"

"Ten-*ure*," Talia enunciated. "Essentially, the university can't fire him."

"Oh. He's that good?"

"I think Joe is a very good teacher."

I paused. "That's a big compliment from you."

Talia looked at me and then glanced away, embarrassed.

I sighed. "I really don't get the ear fetish."

Talia withdrew her arm from mine and crossed both of hers in front of her chest. I pretended that I didn't feel the loss like a vacuum in space.

"Mr. Conrad!" someone from the crowd cried. "What can you tell us about your inspiration for your work?"

"My inspiration?" Joe asked. "Well, isn't it obvious? It comes from dreams."

"Dreams?" I whispered to Talia. "He dreams about ears?"

"It's called surrealism."

"It's weird."

Talia bit her lip and admitted, "I don't disagree."

"So why are we here?"

"Because," she said, "he told me he would help me with my dream."

Joe's voice rang out on the microphone again. "I have always been a firm believer that the biggest power we have as artists is the ability to look at our dreams as more than just colors and patterns swirling behind our sleeping eyes. I believe that it is our job, and our duty, to pry them apart with our pens and our paints and our hands in an effort to find more meaning. That is my goal with my art. To find meaning for myself, and to inspire others to do the same."

I whispered to Talia once more, "I think he's pretty brave, putting out his ear fetish for the world to see."

She shook her head and lightly shoved me.

"Mr. Conrad! I have a question for *The Digital Art Show*. What's the biggest dream you've ever had?" someone else asked from the crowd.

Talia perked up at that. "I didn't know *The Digital Art Show* was covering his exhibit."

"What's *The Digital Art Show*?" I asked.

She looked at me like I had just asked what color the trees were outside. "Only my most favorite blog in the entire world."

"Wow," Joe said, addressing the spokesperson from *Talia's most favorite blog in the entire world*. "That's a tough one, but I think it would have to be …"

I tuned him out. "What's your dream, Talia? The one he's supposedly going to help you with."

"I mean, he's already done his part," she said without taking her eyes off Joe. "And I can't tell you the rest yet. I need you to agree to help me first."

"But it has to do with why you came back?"

She nodded.

I shook my head, suddenly angry again. This was such a Talia thing to do—plan some elaborate scheme, dragging me alongside her with little to no information. And it was such a typical Archie response to just go along with it, simply because she asked me to.

"No," I said. "No more games. I'm not agreeing to anything else until you tell me what you're actually planning."

She paused, then looked over at me finally. "Haven't you ever had a dream, Archie?"

She looked almost sad, with a twinge of hope and an ounce of worry behind the question. And I had that fleeting desire that used to drive too many of my decisions in college—to do things just because I wanted to see Talia happy.

I stuffed my hands into my pockets. "How honest do you want me to be?"

"Brutally."

But I wasn't going down this road again. I couldn't. Not after I had poured myself into a friendship that she had chosen to discard. I turned toward the glass door, not able to be in the art space a moment longer.

Before I fell out of earshot though, I turned back to make sure she heard me.

"Talia, my dream used to be you."

TALIA

PRESENT DAY

I didn't want to listen. I didn't want to hear him say it. I didn't want to feel the crippling guilt that clutched at my heart and drew its claws through my stomach at Archie's affirmation that I had indeed broken a piece of him when I left.

But he would never truly understand why I had to leave. Why I couldn't stay any longer, leaning on him, *relying* on him to get by in my daily life.

Staying wasn't fair to him—that was what I told myself for weeks after I left. It was my turn to protect him from the darkness living within my brain. And that mantra worked for a while, until my resolve finally broke and I came crawling back.

But I couldn't unhear the hurt in Archie's voice as I walked toward his parents' office building the next day.

I had thought about calling him after he left Joe's exhibit last night. I stayed just long enough to give Joe my congratulations before heading back to Kathryn's place, knowing I deserved the emptiness I thought I'd grown numb to feeling.

I also thought about giving up and resolving not to keep pushing Archie to join me.

But I kept reminding myself that he did show up. Twice now. Even when he shouldn't have. I could swallow whatever pride I had left and pay him a visit over what I hoped would be his lunch break.

I finally found the sign at the top of the extended multiuse building downtown that read Morgan Accounting & Tax Firm. Drawing my shoulders a little more square, I pushed open the door.

A tiny chime whispered through the lobby, but it was otherwise quiet, save for the rhythmical tapping of computer keys behind the front desk.

If Archie noticed me walk through the front door, he didn't acknowledge anything as I walked toward him.

"When did you get glasses?" The question escaped my lips, breaking the silence. He never needed them in college. Maybe it was part of his new aesthetic, complete with a button-down and slacks that I had also never seen him wear. His brown hair was tamed into submission too, unlike the unkempt mop I used to know.

I pressed my lips tight and waited for his response.

Archie lifted just his eyes to peer at me over the black frames but gave me no other reaction. His long fingers continued their tapping. "They're blue-light glasses. Nonprescription."

I nodded and looked around the office. It was plain, just a few leather chairs and bare walls. Sunlight illuminated the space.

Archie's tapping paused as he sighed. "What do you want, Talia?"

I held my own hands together and ran my right thumbnail against my other palm. "Do you want to go get lunch together?"

"Lunch," he repeated.

I pressed my nail a little deeper. "Well, yes. You do eat lunch, don't you?"

"I usually pack it."

"I'll buy," I offered.

Archie sighed, deeper this time with more tiredness in the sound. "I don't need you to buy me lunch, Talia. I would prefer if you just told me what you needed me to do this time around instead."

I glanced at the thin red mark on my wrist and then slipped my hands into my back pockets. "Just come with me."

I didn't miss that Archie's eyes had followed my hands. He chewed the inside of his cheek before saying, "Fine. Let me leave a note."

He plucked a pen from the cup on his desk and left a yellow Post-it note on the computer screen. Unfolding his body from the chair, he walked around the desk, past me, and opened the door. "Are you coming?"

I bit back the firm retort I had bubbling in my throat and just nodded instead.

"There's a deli on the next block we can go to," Archie said.

"I remember."

The city looked just the same as I had left it. The sidewalks were wide with people eating on the patios we passed. Colorful signage lit up the shops and boutiques on the first levels of the buildings while open balconies and rooftops weaved throughout, holding the city's nightlife venues that lay sleeping in the afternoon sunlight. But the best part of town was all the green space incorporated between the buildings and walkways and the sculptures scattered in the open spaces.

My favorite sculpture was made of recycled metals. It was featured frequently on *The Digital Art Show* as a tourist destination. It was meant to be a mermaid of sorts with sharp, spindly tentacles blowing behind her humanoid body as she gripped the edge of a brewery's roof overlooking a traffic intersection. Spanning over twenty feet long, the kids thought it was terrifying. The local artists thought it beautiful.

I thought she looked like the personification of pain.

"So what have you been up to, Archie?" I asked, desperate to find a way to break the tension in the air.

He scoffed. "Same old, same old."

"Why are you single again?"

Archie stiffened. "Long story. Where have you been?"

I paused. "That's also a long story."

We reached the door, and Archie jumped ahead to open it. "Try me." And I thought he almost cracked a hint of a smile before it vanished again.

We fell in line behind an older couple to place our order. "I've been to a few places," I said. "I really liked Florida."

"What's in Florida?"

"Miami."

"Hi, welcome to Millie's Deli." The girl behind the counter smiled at us. "What can I get for you two today?"

"I'll do a turkey and cheese melt," I said. "Thank you."

"Um," Archie said and scanned the menu above us that he had surely read a thousand times. "A Reuben please."

"Got it," the girl chirped. "Would you like drinks too?"

"Yes, please," I said.

"Perfect. And will these be together or separate checks?"

"Separate," Archie said at the same time I said, "Together."

He cut me a glare as I fished money from my pocket. "What? I told you I was buying." I checked the total and left twenty-five dollars on the counter. "Keep the change."

"Thank you!" the girl said sweetly. "Here are your cups. Good to see you, Archie."

My stomach clenched. Of course they knew each other. This was Archie's town.

"You too, Kendall," he said and swiped the cups.

I gave the girl, *Kendall*, my thanks and followed Archie to the fountain drink machine. "Is that your ex?"

"Nope," Archie said and lifted one of the cups to the machine before asking me, "Same drink?"

"Yes," I replied. "I'm impressed that you remember."

He filled my cup: no ice, half Coke, half Diet Coke. "Of course I do," he said and handed me the drink to put a lid on. "It's weird."

I laughed, just a little bit.

We sat down at a small table against the wall, facing each other. Archie looked mildly uncomfortable as he shifted in his seat before he crossed his arms on the table's surface and gave up trying not to look at me.

Instead, his eyes pierced mine as he asked, "What were you doing in Miami?"

I swallowed. "Mostly bartending."

He furrowed his brow. "You moved to Miami after graduation to be a ... bartender?"

I bristled. "First of all, the money wasn't bad. Second, I was actually in Austin first."

"Oh, is that where they teach you how to bartend or something?"

"I mean, I learned there on a different job." I bit my lip and forced out part of the truth Archie deserved. "I was trying to visit as many art districts as I could after graduation."

Archie was quiet and dropped eye contact with me, choosing to stare at a corner of our table instead.

The silence strung between us was snapped by a waiter bringing our sandwiches. "Reuben and turkey melt for the happy couple."

"Not happy. Also not a couple," Archie grumbled and took the trays from his outstretched hands.

When the waiter left, Archie said, "So let me get this straight. You took off, on your own, telling absolutely *no one* of your whereabouts, leaving the rest of us to worry ourselves nearly to death over your disappearance, just so you could go on a self-guided, cross-country art tour?"

I could see from Archie's perspective how shitty that was. But he didn't know the whole story of why I had to leave. "To be fair," I said, slowly, "my mom did find me. Once." I pushed that bubbling memory and its emotions back down beneath the surface.

"What do you mean she found you? You were lost?"

"I didn't think so, but maybe she did." To quell the panic fighting to surface, I changed course slightly. "I did send Kathryn postcards."

Archie bit into his sandwich. When he swallowed, his voice was bitter. "So you kept up with Kathryn this whole time?"

"Loosely," I admitted.

He paused. "What about Grady? Did he know?"

Grady and I were close when we were in college, mostly just because we shared all the same classes. But where my mediums tended to stay in two dimensions, Grady could build his art.

41

I had seen Grady exactly once in my two-year hiatus from Bridgeport. And that visit had been far from planned.

Besides that one and only interaction, I hadn't told Grady anything. It wouldn't have been fair to ask Grady to keep secrets from his best friend, so I left both of them in the dark.

And Grady never asked where I had been or where I was going.

For that, I was grateful.

But I shook my head to Archie. "No. He didn't know either."

We ate silently for a few moments before Archie asked in a pained whisper, "Why did you do it?"

I wanted to tell Archie everything. I really did. I just couldn't. I didn't know how. "That's an even longer story."

"At least tell me why you're back then. Why now?"

That much I could muster. I took a deep breath before saying, "I've been to almost all of the cities I had on my wish list by now, studying their art. I want to leave my mark on all of them too. And I thought it was fitting to go back and have this town be my first."

"Leave your mark? What, like your art?"

"Precisely."

It was kind of fascinating to watch the gears in Archie's mind work behind his expression as the pieces fit together. "So your plan is to go on another whirlwind tour and use what you've been studying on your own to create your own art pieces?"

"I'm jumping on the street art bandwagon."

"As if it's just a casual thing to do," Archie said, mostly to himself. "You're going to leave again, is what you're saying."

It wasn't a question, but he waited for a confirmation anyway.

"Yes," I whispered.

I knew Archie, and a desperation to hold on to the past would always guide his present choices. I would never understand that mindset myself, but I knew why he felt that way and how it led him to ask, "You said you needed my help?"

Something inside me fluttered. "Yes," I said, this time with more conviction.

"I can't believe I'm even considering this." Archie sighed and pinched the bridge of his nose before letting his hands fall to his sides. "What are we going to do?"

ARCHIE

FRESHMAN YEAR

By the third week of college, I had started to fall into a steady morning routine. I would get up and trudge to the communal bathroom to fight for a shower. And by fight, I don't mean with my fists because, let's face it, that wouldn't have gotten me anywhere. I fought by using time to my advantage, like setting my alarm twenty minutes earlier than I needed to get ready for my morning class. After the shower conundrum, I would swing by the coffee shop to grab a bagel and a mocha on the way to Quantitative Business Methods I.

What wasn't part of my normal morning schedule was running into Talia Scott sitting on the middle step to the coffee shop, earbud in one ear, eyes closed, her back leaning against the concrete slab behind her.

My heart leapt to my throat, and I stuttered in my step. "Talia. Hi."

She opened one eye, and recognition flared in it enough to open the other. She took out the one earbud and strung them both over the back of her neck. "Is it everything you thought it would be?"

I paused. "What do you mean?"

I had seen her a few times since we moved in. I mean, the school was small, so it would've been hard not to, especially when it was mostly freshmen who frequented the Welcome Week activities at the start of the semester.

There had been several occasions when I sat on my bed, listening to the music coming from our ceiling, and had lengthy conversations in my head trying to convince myself to walk up and talk to her again. Unfortunately, my opportunities to have Grady as backup were few and far between. He rarely spent time in our room except to pass out late at night. I was always gone before he woke up.

Talia stood up from the steps and tugged at her shorts to straighten them. "College. Has it lived up to all of your hopes and dreams?"

"I mean … I guess so? It's different, but it's supposed to be, right?"

"You don't seem confident about that."

I furrowed my brow. "Well, what about you? Has college lived up to your dreams?"

She didn't hesitate. Nor did she elaborate. "No."

"I'm sorry about that."

Her gaze shifted somewhere far off. "You shouldn't apologize for things that aren't your fault."

"Sorry," I said again because I didn't know what else to say. I resisted the urge to check my watch, feeling as if too many minutes had ticked by to order my breakfast and still make it to class a solid ten minutes early. Part of me didn't care though.

"Are you hungry?" Talia asked.

"I mean"—I gestured to the door behind her—"I was on my way to grab something before class."

"Oh," she said and looked at the glass frame behind her. "Sorry about that."

I did one of those sharp nose exhales that you do when you're scrolling through your phone and find a funny meme. Not quite a laugh, but close. "You shouldn't apologize for things that aren't your fault."

She finally cracked a grin, and my chest inflated at the sight.

"I guess old habits die hard," she said, but she was still smiling.

"And look at all of the guessing in that cryptic statement."

She rolled her eyes. "I'm going to get breakfast at the diner down the street. Do you want to come?"

"Why?"

She flushed. "Why not?"

What a move, Archie. I scolded myself. "I just mean … why … me?"

She looked around at the empty walkways. "Who else am I going to ask?"

Right. Maybe I was just convenient. Maybe she was lonely. Nevertheless, I said, "Okay."

Her entire being lightened. "Really?" Then darkened again. "You have class."

Shit. I did. I made the split-second, completely irrational, and perchance detrimental decision to my academic career. "I'll skip."

She lifted an eyebrow and asked with a note of skepticism, "You will?"

"Yes," I said, and to prove it, I started walking toward the street. "You coming?"

She half smiled in response. "Yep. The other way though."

I thinned my own mouth. "Right."

Not even twenty minutes later, at the same time my math class was supposed to be starting, Talia and I both had stacks of pancakes towering in front of us.

"So," I said as I cut through my carefully layered pancakes, "why did you pick Bridgeport College?"

"Because it was far away," she said in between thick, syrupy bites. "And had a good art department."

"You're an art major?" I asked stupidly. Of course she was; she just said so.

"Art history and visual art double major."

I nodded, then paused. "Far away from where?"

She set her fork and knife down while she chewed. "Small town deep in South Carolina."

"Wow," I said, visualizing where Oregon and the East Coast lay across a map. "That is far."

"Sometimes I still don't think it's far enough."

She sliced into her pancakes again, not offering anything else.

"Well," I said, working to fill the silence, "I'm from here. I mean, not *here*, here, like this diner, but here as in not too far from ... here."

She lifted her eyes and smirked.

I continued my ramble. "And I'm an accounting major ...."

"I know."

I cocked my head. "You what?

"I know you're an accounting major."

"How?"

She shrugged. "I mean, I kind of assumed. I know you have that intro class around this time, so that's how I knew where you would be this morning."

She knew? Maybe I wasn't the only one that had been paying attention. And if she was waiting for me to pass by the coffee shop on the way to the business school building, maybe it wasn't just a coincidence that I was the one to accompany her on this breakfast excursion.

She looked up from her pancakes and caught me still looking at her. "What?" she asked sharply.

I shook my head, but I couldn't stop the smile from spreading across my face. "Nothing. Why did you want to get so far away from small-town South Carolina?"

She narrowed her eyes. "You've got an awful lot of questions for the morning."

"I'm just making conversation." I was still smiling.

She chewed silently for a few moments. "It's complicated."

I placed my fork and knife down and crossed my arms. "We have the time. You already peer pressured me into missing my class today."

"You have the backbone of a spaghetti if you give in to peer pressure that easily."

I chuckled, shaking my head.

She placed her utensils down as well. "What color are your eyes?"

Damn, she knew how to throw me. Her train of thought was more like a derailed roller coaster. "Not really brown, not really green."

"That's what I thought."

"My little sister actually once told me that they were like mossy mud. She has them too."

"I think they're nice."

"Thank you. But you're evading my question about why you ended up in the middle of Oregon."

"So you've noticed. Any other siblings?"

I sighed. She was impossible. "Nope. Just me, Addie, Mom, and Dad."

The waitress came up to clear our plates. "Separate checks. Thank you," Talia said with a polite smile.

When there was nothing more between us other than a few crumpled napkins, Talia propped her elbows on the table, resting her chin in her palms. "I can't stand stagnancy."

"Stagnancy," I repeated, rolling the word around on my tongue.

"Correct. It would sound cliché to say that I needed a change, but I needed to leave, you know? Sometimes you just need to go somewhere else, just because you can. And you know that if you don't, you'll just be … stagnant."

"Totally," I agreed without knowing the feeling, since I obviously had not ventured very far away in life.

"That's the simple answer as to why I left small-town South Carolina," she said. "I didn't want to stay stuck."

"Stuck how?" I pressed, trying to understand more of the enigma surrounding this girl.

The waitress returned with our checks and waited while I pulled my credit card from my wallet and Talia flourished a few bills from one of her pockets.

"Stuck in societal confinements and expectations. Or trapped," she said as she watched the waitress walk away. Her voice got small. "I didn't want to be trapped anymore."

ARCHIE

PRESENT DAY

An art project. Talia whisked herself back into town for a bloody art project. I wished I could say that I was surprised, but in a way, I understood. If she was going to go on an elaborate journey leaving her mark on the towns she crossed, it made sense to begin in the place that started it all.

Yet part of me wanted to cling to the hope that there was more to her return. More than just the new address she left me with after lunch. More than the promise to see me later that night. More than just another mission.

I hoped for a reason that I was the one she called asking for help.

I slugged back the last of my second beer at Al's Tavern, the bar that Grady and I *normally* went to, and slammed the bottle back on the counter. I figured two beers was enough courage to break the news to him too.

"Talia's home," I said with zero inflection in my tone.

Grady, in his usual nothing-in-a-hurry way, swirled the Jack and Coke in his glass before asking, "Talia? As in *the* Talia who vanished seemingly into thin air after we graduated and snapped your fragile heart into a million pieces?"

I thought about flagging the bartender for just one more drink—to be able to make it through this night as her art assistant—but thought better of it. I still needed to drive to meet her. I rapped my knuckles against the polished wood. "The one and only."

"For how long?"

I shrugged, a little stab in my chest as I considered his question. I hadn't thought about how long she would choose to grace us all with her presence, or when she might leave again. "Who knows?"

"Where is she staying?"

I hadn't thought to ask her that. She really had a way of messing with my head and making all rational thoughts evaporate. "Don't know. Don't care."

Grady chuckled. "Sure you don't."

I glared at him. Grady had been there. Grady had known us both. And no matter what I told him now, no matter how cool I played off her return, we both knew I was lying to myself—as if this weren't careening my boring little life toward another potential heartbreaking disaster.

"When are you going to see her?" he asked because he knew me well and knew I couldn't stay away.

"Supposed to meet her in twenty minutes."

He sipped the rest of his drink slowly. When it was empty, he sighed. "You know I like Talia just fine. But you and I are bros, Arch."

The corner of my mouth lifted into a half smile. We weren't always close in college, but in our postgraduate days, Grady had become one of my best friends. He was the type of loyal person not many people deserved. Some days, I didn't think I deserved him either.

Grady shook his head. "Just be careful, man. I'll kick her ass if I have to pick up the wreckage from her tornado a second time."

TALIA

FRESHMAN YEAR

A month in college had passed, and I still hadn't heard from my parents. This fact was apparent only because Kathryn's parents sent her three care packages—per week.

"Where are you from?" I asked her one day as she was unboxing the latest treasure. I realized I had been a pretty shitty roommate to not know her story. But in my defense, she didn't know mine either. She had never asked.

"Boston."

My heart fluttered as I sat down on the edge of my bed in front of my desk. "That's on my bucket list to visit one day."

"It's okay. Nothing special," Kathryn replied as she folded up her box, prim and neat. Her dry tone pricked the balloon swelling in my chest at the fantasy of visiting as many places as I could one day.

But honestly, anywhere was better than where I had come from.

I was pulled from my travel reverie of cityscapes and long stretches of highways by a tentative knock on the door.

"Door's open," Kathryn said with the same lack of inflection in her voice, just a few notches louder.

I watched the door creak open to reveal Archie Morgan standing sheepishly.

"Archie," I sputtered and, in a swift moment without thinking, asked, "What are you doing here?"

He stood tall enough for me to wonder what life must look like when your messy brown hair almost touches the average door frame. His hands were coming in and out of his pockets, fingers curling closed, then unfolding again as if he couldn't decide what to do with them. He finally smoothed his palms down the legs of his pants and said, "Hi, Talia. Hi, Kathryn."

"Hello, Archie," Kathryn said in the same monotone and resumed putting her box away.

When neither Kathryn nor Archie said anything else, and Grady wasn't there to buffer both of their awkwardness, I asked Archie again, "What are you doing here?"

His eyes shifted around the room, nervous. "Um, I was just wondering if you wanted to maybe hang out? Again?"

Part of me was impressed—even after our impromptu diner excursion the other day—that Archie had the balls to walk himself up to my door and ask for a repeat of some sorts. Neither Archie nor Grady had ventured back up the stairs to visit since the very first day. Even though I had class several times a week with Grady, our conversations usually only revolved around our schoolwork.

Another part of me wanted to grin at Archie's offer.

I shut down any warm fuzzy that tried to surface and said, "No."

"No?" Archie repeated, and I felt bad. It wasn't his fault that I couldn't afford the risk of always saying yes.

"No," I said again and turned to my open laptop on my desk. "I have to do homework."

"But it's Saturday," Archie said. "Shouldn't you have done your work for the week?"

"We can't all be rocket scientists like you," I snapped.

"Accountants, actually," Archie mumbled, as if I had forgotten.

"Same thing." I brushed him off. "Maybe next time."

I didn't dare look at him, but I heard the disappointment in his voice when he said, "Okay. Sure. See you around."

Then he closed the door gently behind him.

"What was that about?" Kathryn asked when his footsteps were no longer audible in the hall.

"Nothing," I said. "Just don't want to give him the wrong idea."

"He was asking to hang out, not for your hand in marriage."

She didn't understand, but I didn't have it in me to try to explain it.

"He seemed nice," Kathryn said as she sat down to open her own laptop.

"That's the problem." I shut my computer and rested my head on my arms. "They usually do."

ARCHIE

PRESENT DAY

Icut the engine on my van and peered out the front windshield at the figure illuminated in my headlights. She was crouched near the ground and dressed in black from head to toe: black beanie, black scarf, black jacket, black pants, and black boots.

"Isn't it technically spring now?" I asked as I got out of the van. "I think wearing a scarf is against the rules."

Talia stood up and unwound one length of scarf from her face. "It's still cold outside though." She tucked the scarf right back around her chin before mumbling through it. "Plus, it helps my stealth."

"Helps your stealth," I muttered, looking up at the building behind Talia. Even in the dark, I could make out the rough outline of its unique architecture. From the traditional red brick exterior, I knew we had to be somewhere associated with our old college campus. "What is this place?"

She cracked the seal on a five-gallon bucket of paint. Cautiously pouring white paint into a tray, she said, "When the inside is finished being gutted and rebuilt, it's going to be a new workshop building and showcase studio for Bridgeport's art department."

"Why is it so far away from the school?" I asked.

"Why do you have so many questions?"

"Why don't you give me any real answers?"

She snapped the lid back into place on the bucket and stood up. Her blue eyes flashed amid all the black material. "The arts program is hoping that this will be more of a community engagement place to encourage local admissions."

Not really one of the answers I was desperate to have from Talia, but she did answer my first question. I tried another. "What exactly is the plan here? Besides painting. Obviously."

"Vandalizing," she said as she dipped a brush into the thick white goo. She winked at me. "Obviously."

"Talia," I chided through my teeth, "we can't just *vandalize* one of Bridgeport's construction zones." Did this girl really think I was going to go through with this?

She laughed. "Relax, Arch. It's not technically vandalism if you have permission."

"You asked permission?"

"I will at some point." And with that, she slashed one broad white stroke of paint against the red brick, marking it as hers.

I shook my head and sat down on the curb, surveying the damage she continued to inflict on the walls. It was a methodical chaos, just like Talia. There was a steady rhythm to her strokes and turns of her brush that made the whole process seem mesmerizing as she covered the wall in splotches of white.

"Can you get me a ladder?" she asked without turning back to me.

I paused awkwardly, having been mesmerized watching her shoulders move and stretch beneath the black fabric. "Yeah. Yeah sure."

I wrestled the pop-up stool she had next to her pile of materials and set it beside her. She still didn't acknowledge my presence. And I didn't retreat. I crossed my arms instead. "Talia," I whispered, my voice straining against my tight throat. "Look at me a second."

She turned her head in my direction and lifted her blue gaze from beneath her lashes. Her expression was one of irritation—I'd disturbed her work.

"Yes?"

I didn't falter this time. "Why are you really back?"

She held my eye contact with a steely gaze, but I could almost make out something else entirely. Was it all for show?

She finally gave in. "Can you hand me the small can of black paint?"

"No."

She glared at me, then went to retrieve it herself. "Why is this not a good enough answer for you?" she asked, gesturing to the wall. "You know art has always been my passion. You know that this is something I've always wanted to do. Why isn't that enough for you?"

She was clawing at the can, trying to pry it open to no avail. I reached out and plucked it from her grip. Taking my pocketknife from my jeans, I popped the lid with one flick of the blade.

When she reached for the can again with rage in her eyes, I stayed the course.

"But why here, back in Oregon? Why now?" *Why me*, was what I didn't ask.

"Why not?"

I groaned and gazed at her pile of supplies. If I wasn't going to get the answers I wanted, *needed*, from Talia, I might as well take the frustration out on anything that wasn't her. I grabbed one of the extra brushes and loaded it with the black paint. Then I started to mimic Talia's strokes on the brick. The black marks looked more like punches.

"Easy there, tiger." I could hear the smirk in her voice without turning around. I harrumphed but lightened the pressure on the brush anyway.

Several moments passed as I continued to paint haphazardly. Talia had stepped away, cleaning her brush in a bucket of water. "That's not half bad," she said from behind me.

"I don't really know what I'm doing," I said, stopping to actually look at the paint job.

Talia came up beside me and held out a hand. "May I?" she asked.

I handed over the brush, and she climbed the small step stool to adjust some of the lines I had made, mixing the black with the white already on the wall to make several shades of gray.

"Is that a nose?" I asked.

"It will be eventually," she replied softly. The quietness in her voice made me pause, wondering what was going on in her head as she worked. Eventually, I found my way back to the curb and sat down once more.

She continued to paint until I could start to make out the outline of a portrait and the beginnings of facial features.

"Do you remember that time on Halloween freshman year when we dressed up like wizards and tried to get into the club?" Talia asked with her back still turned to me.

I raised my eyebrow, thinking about all the adventures we used to have. "Yeah. Complete with robes and long beards." I paused. "Or when you made me drive the getaway car when you stole the road sign for Harbour Street."

"Or when we would just get in the car and drive around this city, getting lost in the maze of streetlights."

"Until there were no streetlights because we had ventured too far."

"And you could never find your way back without GPS because you have the directional skills of a broken compass."

"That's just rude," I said. But I still smiled.

Talia stepped away from the wall, dropping her brush in the bucket before she sat down beside me. She was close enough that I could've brushed her arm with mine. I wrapped my arms around my legs and leaned my head against my knees instead.

"I think we have to wait for these layers to finish drying before we can do any more," she said, still not looking at me.

I nodded, wondering how long that might be.

"Want to go back to Blue Elixir?" she asked. "Celebration drink for the beautification of bricks?"

I thought about saying no. I really did. "Sure" was what came out instead. When it came to Talia, my self-discipline was a negative twelve.

"Archie"—she looked over at me, several thick curls of hair shielding her face—"I really did miss you, you know."

Fireworks, or some other sort of catastrophic explosion, erupted in my heart. Tears started to well in the backs of my eyes. I broke our eye contact so she wouldn't see, but that didn't stop me from melting as I said, "Come here."

The strain on her face faded into relief as she tucked herself into my side and I wrapped my arm around her. It was everything I had in me not to bury my face in her dark hair. It still smelled the same, like oranges and flowers.

I just held her while she clung to me, the years between us slowly fading away. I finally admitted to her what she had always known.

"I missed you too."

ARCHIE

FRESHMAN YEAR

"We need to get you laid," Talia said, barging into my room one night after the first month and a half of school had passed.

I looked up from the video game on my TV. "Excuse me?"

She plopped down on my bed, sprawling on top of the covers, shoes and all. "I repeat: We need to get you laid."

"I didn't know that could be a mutual need," I muttered to myself and turned back to the game.

She plucked my controller out of my hands. "Archie," Talia said, towering over me while I sat cross-legged on the floor. "We're friends, right?"

I looked up at her, confused. We had seen each other a handful of times in passing and always stopped briefly to exchange pleasantries, but Talia and I hadn't spent much more real time together since she had me skipping class and eating pancakes at the start of school.

Or since she had rejected my offer to hang out again.

"I think so?" I answered.

She glowered for a moment, then said. "Just humor me while I'm real here. The second month of school is nearly over. And I haven't seen you go out once. Or bring a girl home. Or be around any girls besides me."

"That's not true." I bristled and reached for my controller again. She held it out of my reach. "Abigail is my lab partner."

"Abigail"—she set the controller on top of my TV and shut the game off—"has a girlfriend. She doesn't count."

"You've been watching me?" I asked.

"Paying attention. And if I'm being honest"—Talia took a deep, steadying breath—"I haven't gone out much either. So I'm proposing a solution."

"I wasn't aware I had a problem," I said, standing directly in front of her so she had to look up at me. "And what do you know about needing to get laid?" I asked.

She crossed her arms over her chest. "I know enough. I'll bet more than you do."

Her intent stare told me not to argue with her. Even though I hadn't *explicitly* thought about it, her confidence and willingness to attack life made her seem like the type of girl to have experience.

"How are you so sure about that?" I asked anyway.

"Please, Arch. Everything about your behavior since getting to college screams *virgin boy*. It's time to make you a man." She turned on her heel toward the door. "You and I are going out tonight. Together. And I'll be your wingman. Be ready at eleven."

TALIA

PRESENT DAY

I missed you too.

Archie's admission continued to ring in my ears as I got into his passenger seat. I hadn't thought twice when we stood up from the curb and hopped in his van, just like we used to. We never drove mine when we were in college. He had always offered his.

"So," Archie began once the engine was running, "what have you been listening to while you've been gone?"

I reached over and plucked his phone out of his hands, then paused, biting my lip. "Can I play you my new favorite song?"

"Well, you already have my phone."

"I mean, yeah, but I could just play you a top forty hit. I'm asking if you'd like a window to my soul instead."

He tilted his head in my direction and lifted a brow, ever so slightly. "You have a soul?"

I punched his shoulder. "Asshole."

Archie chuckled as I typed it into the search bar.

A violin struck a singular strong chord and echoed throughout the van. A piano picked up the tune. I let the phone fall into my lap and closed my eyes as the lyrics came in slowly.

The world breathes in watercolor
The days bleeding into each other,

The colors having no beginning or end,
The people: fading in and leaving again.
Archie broke the reverie I had slipped into. "What song is this?"
"Shush."
The chorus came in.
But what if it was all an experiment?
Someone else's grand design—
To lie, to cry out Love
And claim it was just an accident?
The soft violin continued to echo in the van. "It's by Shady Oasis," I said. "I found them while I was gone."

Archie just listened as we drove to Blue Elixir.

"What's it about?" he finally asked.

I shrugged, my eyes still closed. "I've tried to look it up, but I think it's supposed to mean something different to everyone. There's no one real meaning, supposedly."

"Can you start it over?" Archie asked as he slowed for a red light on the empty street.

I opened my eyes. "Really?"

He nodded but didn't look at me. His eyes were narrow, focused only on the road. His brows were drawn tight, as if he were hunting for a meaning behind the lyrics.

I picked up the phone and started the song over.

The same haunting tune built between the doors of the van. The tension was palpable in the air.

When the first verse finished, Archie said, "I think it sounds rather existential."

"I think it's a good example of how people who don't see the world in black and white have a hard time rationalizing why things happen."

"You mean like things being described as gray instead of black and white?" Archie asked.

"Yes," I said cautiously. "But no. It's a song for those who rationalize in color."

"Is that what you do?" he asked, innocently.

I thought about how easy it would be to just agree. Instead, as the song faded out, I answered his question quietly, "I wish."

All the ones who cared enough
Where were you when it got tough?
What if the ones who loved enough
Strung their hearts and secrets up?

"I know why you wanted to come here," Archie said as we stood in line to get into Blue Elixir. "You still need my help as your wingman."

He said it in a joking tone, but there was a bitterness deep beneath the words.

"Yes," I said. "I'm really hoping to find the great love of my life while playing cornhole and having philosophical conversations over domestic beer."

He shrugged as we shuffled ahead in the line, long since immune to my incessant deadpan sarcasm. "I wouldn't think cornhole. Surely it would be at the pool tables."

I elbowed him lightly against his ribs. "Care to join me there first?"

He grumbled, "If we ever get in. This line is ridiculously long."

"It's always been long, Arch. It's like you've forgotten," I accused.

He waited for a beat before saying in a low tone, "I don't forget much."

We shuffled forward again.

I couldn't help but ask, "Did you still come here? After … college?"

"Only since you've dragged me back here yourself. Grady and I usually go to Al's. That's where I was with him before I met up with you tonight."

"So you've been avoiding Blue Elixir?"

"It's too crowded for my taste."

I was sure that was part of the truth, but I doubted it was the only reason.

A few more steps. I could see the open door now and hear the faint pulse of background music fading in from the bar.

"Talia," Archie began, "I know you're probably not ready to talk about why you left. But can you promise me that you'll tell me at some point?"

It was the most levelheaded he had been with me so far, and the calmness from him washed over me like a drug. I didn't know why he chose to calm the harshness in his voice now.

Regardless, I melted. Even though promises didn't last, and hiding truths was how I survived the past several years, I said, "Yes. I promise."

We didn't say anything else until we reached the front of the line and the bouncer wordlessly asked for our IDs. We handed them over, and I swore there was a hint of judgment as he passed them back after checking our ages.

Which was dramatic—we were only twenty-four.

Archie made a beeline for the bar once we were inside. "What are you drinking?" he asked over the noise.

"Surprise me," I replied and looked around.

I hadn't really taken the time to take in the scenery the last time we were briefly here. Not much had changed. Other than the bar itself, the space featured several pool tables, benches, and a side door that led to the backyard, fully stocked with cornhole games and a fire pit.

Blue Elixir was great.

And looked exactly the same as it did two years ago.

Archie appeared at my side again, now standing closer than he had dared earlier.

I didn't mind.

"For you," he said, handing me a pink drink complete with a sour rainbow candy on top.

"What is it?" I asked, skeptical but accepting the drink anyway.

"I have no idea. I pointed at you and said that you wanted to be surprised."

"Seems like this new bartender doesn't know me well at all," I muttered and tentatively took a sip. It was sweet. Incredibly sweet.

"Pool?"

"Pool," I agreed.

Archie touched the small of my back lightly once, gesturing for me to go down the three steps to the pool tables first. I tried hard not to think of a time when he would have willingly held skin-to-skin contact with me; I tried not to think about how much I missed it.

That wasn't fair to him. I was the one who made the decision to cut ties when I left.

I quickly made my way down the stairs, putting distance between Archie and me that I didn't think I needed again until I realized I wasn't breathing properly. I inhaled deeply and found an empty table farther back. In a hurried zigzag, I weaved around the bar's other occupants, trying not to bump into too many.

Archie followed in a much more casual manner.

By the time he got to the table, I already had the balls racked and was chalking my cue.

"When's the last time you played?" I asked with my back still turned to him. I only knew he had arrived from the sound of his footsteps. They were heavier than you would think for a guy that used to be so skinny.

"Last Tuesday," he replied and set his beer down on the high-top table.

"I'm a little rustier than that," I admitted.

"Probably doesn't matter anyway," Archie said. He picked a long cue from the rack and picked up the chalk I had set down on the corner of the table. He dared to wear a small smirk on his face when he said, "You'll still whoop my ass anyway."

I allowed a small smile in return. "We'll see about that. You break first."

"No ladies first?" he asked with a raised eyebrow.

"Consider it my gift to you. Sink a few for me."

Archie broke the triangle of balls with a force I didn't know he had in him.

"Wow!" I said and leaned against my cue. "You've obviously been practicing."

"Here and there," he said, but his brows were furrowed, focused on the stripes. He lined up another shot and sank it easily.

"If not here," I began, "where have you been shooting?"

He stalked the table and found another straight shot. "Grady's apartment complex has a pool table."

I didn't reply. It was kind of surreal to think that the people I had once been friends with now had these whole other lives I didn't know about. Because I wasn't in their lives anymore. Archie finally missed a shot and leaned back from the table. "You're up, solids."

"Yeah, I figured that much since that's the majority of the balls left on the table," I muttered and prepared for my first shot. I found one that looked easy enough and leaned down on the table.

I struck the cue ball and sank a red solid.

"Nice shot!" Archie said and clapped me on the shoulder.

I turned my head to gloat, but he kept moving until he was directly across from me. With smug charm, he leaned his forearms on the edge of the table and said in a tease, "I bet you can't do that again though."

"Oh yeah? Watch me."

Archie righted himself and folded his arms across his chest, which made his shoulders look even bigger. "I'm waiting."

A female voice cried out right as I had my cue drawn back to fire.

"Archie!"

My shot missed gloriously as vague recognition swirled in my gut. I remembered that voice.

I looked up and saw a girl we both knew from college.

Nope. *Girl* was the wrong identifier. She looked scarily attractive. She was still pretty, just sharper. A woman, refined.

"Um, hi," Archie said with none of the suave gusto he had just displayed. His fingers fidgeted against his pool stick and his hazel eyes flicked back and forth between my studious gaze and her polished beauty.

Said beauty drew Archie in for a long hug.

"How have you been?" she asked.

In her defense, the question sounded sincere. But I had decided a long time ago that I just didn't like her on principle.

"Good." Archie's voice had a crackling quality to it as she released him from her embrace. He cleared his throat and repeated, "Good. I'm here with Talia, actually. Do you guys remember each other?"

Archie gestured toward where I was standing, and I watched her eyes follow until they landed on me.

"Lex," I said without giving her the chance to speak first, "you're still in town."

"And you're back," she said, but there was no malice behind the words. Just frank observation. "Welcome." Her eyes trailed along the scene before she smiled at me. "Glad you found your way back to my ex."

Ex. *Ex.*

Lex was Archie's ex-girlfriend.

Of course she was.

"Talia and I aren't together." Archie nearly tripped over the words. "We're just here. Together."

"Right," I said, a waxy smile molded to my face. "Just friends." *Because,* I thought, *we never seem to really be together.*

ARCHIE

FRESHMAN YEAR

Naturally, Talia had a fake ID. I did not. They let me into the bar anyway since Talia gave the bouncer some ridiculous sob story claiming I was her cousin who had just been diagnosed with a terminal disease that limited a person's ability to become sexually attracted to anyone, resulting in lower testosterone levels and self-confidence. Possible side effects were depression and death.

Part of me fully believed the bouncer just wanted to shut her up by letting her in, but I also think he found Talia cute based on the way his eyes watched her chest as she was telling her tale before waving us through.

After they finally let us through, Talia made a beeline to the bar and immediately ordered us drinks.

"So the trick to picking up a girl at the bar is—" She reached over me to grab another lime. I was careful to keep looking at her face as she leaned forward. She squeezed the lime into her bubbly drink and continued. "The trick is that you have to find the right target."

"Target?" I repeated.

"Maybe that's the wrong word." She picked up her glass and took a long sip.

I swirled my bad-tasting beer around in the bottle. "It's objectifying."

"But you know what I mean," she said, exasperated, and replaced her glass back on the bar, completely missing the napkin coaster the bartender had put out for her. "You want to choose someone that you find attractive, ideally. Someone that looks unengaged for the evening."

I nodded, understanding. "Someone alone, probably."

Talia cut me a hard glance. "You're never going to find anyone alone in a place like this. Most girls, like me, are smart and know better than to brave the bar alone." She picked up her drink again. "It can be risky if the guy turns out to be a douchebag."

"I'm not a douchebag," I said, defensive.

"I never said you were, Arch. You're a good guy." Talia downed the rest of her glass and patted my shoulder. "Which is why you need help here."

"But you just said that girls didn't like douchebags. So shouldn't they like the good guys here?"

"Theoretically. But douchebags usually have some game. Good guys … it's debatable. They're just nice."

I stared down at my beer. "I'm so confused."

Talia flagged down the bartender again and ordered us both refills, even though I still had half of mine left. "It's okay," she said and thanked the bartender with a sly wink. "That's what a wingman is for."

Without being inconspicuous about it, Talia started swiveling her head like an owl, looking around at the crowd.

"What do you think of her?" she finally asked, jutting her chin toward somewhere in the back.

"You're going to have to be way more specific than that," I said without bothering to turn around.

Talia grabbed both of my shoulders and turned my body in my chair. "Twelve o'clock now. Red hair. Long legs. Laughing at some fake joke to get your attention."

I pulled my shoulders back out of her grip and faced forward. "Way to be subtle," I grumbled, then in a much more *discreet* manner, turned to look at the girl again. Sure enough, there was a beautiful girl in the corner, looking shyly over our way. I suddenly got very interested in my drink in front of me again. "She's okay."

"Okay?" Talia exclaimed. "She's *hot*, Archie! Think she goes to our school?"

I shrugged. "Maybe. This is a college bar. And we are the closest college."

"Don't be a smartass," Talia hissed and punched my shoulder. "I think you should go talk to her."

"I don't know," I said into my drink. Not looking at the girl. Not looking at Talia.

"I'll help you," she said standing up. "Come on."

"What are you doing?" I asked, suddenly tense.

Talia rolled her eyes. "Only being the best friend in the entire world and helping you on your way to manhood. Now come along. We're going to talk to your future lover."

I watched as she strode confidently in the direction of the other girl. "Unbelievable," I muttered and chugged the remainder of my drink. I followed, begrudgingly.

"Hi!" Talia said, charisma bubbling from her wide smile. My urge to kick her in the shins suddenly evaporated. With just one flash of a smile. It was annoying.

"Hey," the girl said cautiously and obviously confused, but she was smiling nonetheless.

"I just had to come over here and tell you that I absolutely love your sweater." Talia gushed in a form that was way too saccharine for her normal tone, but I didn't bother pointing it out. Instead, I took note of this supposedly amazing sweater. It was white, a ballsy choice, I thought, to wear at the bar. But it looked soft.

"Thanks," white-sweater-girl laughed. "Gotta love a good Target run."

"The kind where you forget what you went in there for and end up spending all of your money on everything except the shampoo you actually needed?" Talia asked.

She laughed. A pretty laugh. "That would be the one."

Talia laughed too, a deeper, less calculated one. "I'm Talia, by the way. And this is my cousin, Archie."

I resisted the urge to roll my eyes at the cousin angle again, but I guessed it was one of her tricks to ensure this chick knew we weren't together or something.

"It's nice to meet you both." Her eyes flitted briefly to mine before ducking away with a shy smile. "I'm Lex."

Talia looked pleased with the exchange so far and was still smiling pleasantly at Lex. She subtly delivered a sharp jab to my rib cage and cleared her throat.

It was then I realized I was still looking at Talia instead of the girl she had dragged us over here to meet.

"Um," I said, turning to Lex. I pinballed a few phrases around in my mind, trying to find something to say. "First time here?"

Talia let out a laugh that quickly turned into a violent fit of coughing that sounded anything but natural as she excused herself to go find some water, leaving me alone with Lex.

As it turned out, Lex did go to our school, and she was in the dorm right next to mine and Talia's. And that white sweater she was wearing was, in fact, soft. I felt it brush against my chest later that night when she was tugging it over her head and tossing it onto her floor.

"So you and Talia aren't really cousins, right?" She was straddling my lap as I lay back on her bed.

"Ah, no. Not really. How did you know?"

"Lucky guess." Lex leaned down and gave me another slow kiss. "And your face kind of gave the whole thing away."

"Remind me to never play you in poker," I said as I settled my hands against her bare waist. "That whole thing was her idea. As was coming up and talking to you. She knew I wouldn't have had the guts to do it on my own."

Lex smiled, biting her lip before saying, "That's really sweet of her." And she kissed me again.

At some point my shirt joined hers on the floor.

But when her delicate fingers sought the button on my jeans, I had to wrap my hand around her wrist. She looked up at me, her wide eyes full of questions. They were a beautiful shade of brown. Not blue.

And suddenly, I couldn't look directly into them. I couldn't be there any longer. I kissed her goodnight, mumbled, "I'm sorry. I had a great time," and hurried out of her room. I cursed both myself and Talia as I walked back home alone.

ARCHIE

PRESENT DAY

It was weird seeing Lex again.

It wasn't like I had been avoiding her on purpose. It was just a happy coincidence that I didn't have to see her if I only divided my time between home (where she didn't live), work (where she didn't work), and Al's Tavern with Grady (where she was no longer welcome, post breakup).

But that didn't matter. Because here I was, feeling like an idiot once again standing between the girl who ripped my heart in shreds and the one I wished I had given it to instead.

Even though we had met when we were freshman, Lex and I didn't start dating until the middle of the winter after graduation.

And it was entirely Grady's fault.

"I think a rebound could do you some good for the lost love that was never really yours," he had said on the night I smoked my first joint with him—okay, half, and even though we split it, I still counted it.

"If it wasn't mine, then why does the hurt feel so real?" I asked.

"Cut it out," he said. "You're not a damn poet. Give me your phone."

A couple of texts later—without the proper punctuation I was known for—Lex Carver agreed to meet me for a drink that weekend. And shortly after our first few dates, Lex declared us to be in a relationship because it made sense that, if we were seeing each other on the daily, we might as well put a label on the situation. And I didn't have a good enough reason to disagree with her.

But now, being wrapped back up in the cloud of confusion that Talia always brewed, I couldn't help but wonder how much easier it would've been to love Lex instead.

"How have you been?" I asked and leaned on my pool cue, trying to ignore the daggers I felt Talia throwing my way.

Lex tossed her auburn hair over one shoulder. "Good. Busy with work. My manager is having me train the new recruits this season, so that should be interesting."

She worked as a digital marketer at a mass media company. I never really knew what that meant her job was, even when we were together, but she had landed the entry position right out of college and had been climbing the corporate ladder ever since then. All I knew was that she always "had a lot of meetings."

She liked to tell me this whenever I had a video game challenge scheduled with my online friends. I think it was a power move, which she didn't need to pull because we all knew she held the majority of it in any room she walked into.

"That's exciting," I said, but anyone could tell the enthusiasm was strained at best. "Congrats."

"Thanks," she beamed, and the smile she threw at Talia next was dazzling. "What brings you back, Talia?"

Talia sighed. "I've been sent by my superiors to gather intel for their efforts in overthrowing the patriarchal regime. Sources say their secret lies in dive bars and the egos of pool tournament champions."

If Lex was at all fazed, she didn't let it show on her features. "Must be some job you hold."

"I freelance."

"Well, keep up the good work," she said and turned to me. In a softer tone, she said before leaving, "Good to see you, Arch. I hope you're doing well."

My eyes flitted over to Talia as she was hunched over the table, letting her pool cue slide between her fingers, intent on practicing her strokes. Her expression was contorted into some concentration face that was so terrifying it was almost humorous.

"Yeah," I said, doubting if I had made the right choice for my own sanity in accompanying her tonight. "I'm doing fabulous, Lex."

After Lex left the side of our table, Talia insisted on playing three more rounds of pool, even though she continued to lose. With every loss, her temper got shorter. I could tell not by the words she spoke (because there was very little talking happening on her end) but by the thrusts of her shots and the sharpness in how she moved around the table.

Talia didn't like to lose. She didn't like things she wasn't good at.

Her silent treatment continued until I finally called it quits around midnight. "Do we need to go back to the scene of the crime at all tonight?" I asked.

Talia turned to me, the look in her blue eyes cold, detached, and devoid of feeling. "No. I'd like for you to take me home now, if you don't mind."

I scoffed, taken aback by the bluntness of the request. "What am I, the cab of this mission?"

Talia picked up her cue and replaced it on the wall rack. "Forget it. I can call my own."

"Stop," I said and reached for her wrist as she tried to slip past me. "I can take you home," I said.

She gave me a curt nod and tugged her arm free from mine before pushing past me to the exit without another word.

I blew out a breath and counted to three before I followed her. The abrupt snap of her attitude was a mainstay of her personality in college. She was passionate, in more ways than one, and it seemed like she had yet to outgrow that habit.

I followed her out the door.

"It's not really fair for you to come storming back into my life, Talia, and then get upset that it's not playing out the way that you wanted it to." My tone was calm. Even.

"I don't give a shit what you do, Archie," she snapped. "Or who you've been doing, for that matter."

"Is that why you're in a pissy mood all of the sudden?" I asked, stalking after her as she stomped to the car. "Because I dated Lex?"

"No." She spit out the word as if it tasted sour.

Talia had her back turned to me, one hand on the door handle, waiting for me to unlock the car. I made my way beside her and leaned my back against the car, looking out into the parking lot.

"Unlock the door," she said.

I crossed my arms. "If you ask nicely."

"Nice isn't really in my vocabulary," she said, but she spun to face me.

I searched her eyes, her face, her lips pressed tightly together, and everywhere I looked I found a wall. There was no use pressing her tonight. I would never win when she chose to shut down.

Talia had long ago taught me when to retreat.

"Where are you staying?" I asked and clicked the unlock button.

Her eyes flickered. Almost as if she were shocked that I receded so quickly. Almost as if she were disappointed that there wasn't more of a fight.

Her voice was small. "With Kathryn."

I shouldn't have been surprised that she had chosen her old roommate to crash with for this adventure. I knew where Kathryn lived. She had a house in the suburbs with her new husband, Andrew. We didn't keep up, but I saw her in town every so often. Her postgrad life seemed so … normal. Like a poster board for what "being an adult" should look like. Not like living at home and working in a family company, still wondering what you were going to be when you grew up.

"Okay," I said and walked away to the driver's side door.

I had my seat belt buckled and key in the ignition before she even opened the door.

Talia was silent the whole way to Kathryn's house. And even though her body thrummed with tightly sealed energy in the seat next to mine, the silence echoed in my chest, and I felt like I had lost her all over again.

NATALIA

ON DEATH AND DYING

I was eleven the first time I thought about dying.

No, that's not true. I had thought about death when my mother first taught me what it meant to "pass on," and no, it didn't mean the same thing as passing the butter down the Thanksgiving table. My mom tried to explain that there was a Heaven with a capital *H* where my little pet fish was going to go swim in a little pet pond "Somewhere Better" where he could float upside down all the time if he wanted to. Just not in her house.

"But where could be better than here with me?" my six-year-old self asked through snot and tears, not really understanding that the road to this next life supposedly existed as a slip and slide down the toilet bowl.

"You'll understand one day, Natalia," my mom said as she washed her hands in my bathroom sink, "that there are places far better than here."

Her voice had been bitter, like the red wine she always had at dinner. I knew what it tasted like because I had snuck a sip once. I never forgot the bite of it as I coughed and sputtered afterward, trying to hack up the burning sensation in my throat.

But when I was eleven, I thought about death, not in what it meant as a place where Goldilocks could swim upside down, but instead, I wondered how I might get to Heaven one day too. Would I go in a carriage drawn by white horses like a princess? If so, would there be a parade of the townspeople who might miss me? Maybe my parents would attend too. Or would I be swept away quietly, in the dark, alone, with no grand gesture or farewell?

The latter felt more real when I was in the bathtub one night and could hear the shouting from the living room beneath me; the sound carried up the stairs in shrill cursing and idle threats. The words my parents threw at each other were daggers, slick in venom. I slipped my head beneath the surface of my bathwater and stayed there, where I couldn't hear the fighting. I couldn't hear anything. The world felt numb. Peaceful.

And I wondered how long I could stay there, floating in that tranquility, before I swam upside down too.

PART TWO

TALIA

SOPHOMORE YEAR

The week before Halloween during sophomore year of college, I marched myself down to room 307 and kicked open the door, literally. The door thudded against the adjacent closet. Grady wasn't in the room, but Archie looked like he had just jumped out of his skin.

"What the hell, Talia?" he yelled.

"I've come to solicit your aid in a quest."

"That's how you come around asking for help? Busting things open?"

"Got your attention, didn't it?"

He grumbled. "A knock and a *please* would have also worked."

I turned my back. "Are you coming?"

"Coming where? I'm doing homework," Archie said, gesturing to the papers and notebooks strewn across his bed.

I sighed. Not much had changed since our first year of college. Archie was still the same perfect schoolboy. "Would you like me to ask someone else?"

He paused. "No, I guess not."

"Then hurry up," I said and started walking toward the stairwell.

There was a flurry of papers and books as Archie packed up his things. "Wait up!" he called.

"Can't," I replied. "The ghosts don't wait for anyone."

"Ghosts?" Archie panted as he ran behind me to catch up. "What about ghosts?"

I leapt down the stairs, two at a time. "We're going ghost hunting. You know how the old auditorium is named after one of the early donors? One of the seniors in my sculpting class told me that Connie still haunts it."

He stopped at the top of the stairwell, but his voice echoed down after me. "You know that's probably a load of bullshit, right?"

I looked over my shoulder. He had thrown on a hoodie before chasing after me, and the hood still shrouded his face. He would look eerie with the hall light illuminating his silhouette if it weren't for the crazy curls jutting out from behind his ears.

"You said *probably*. So you agree there's a chance he's right."

Archie shook his head and jogged down the steps to meet me at the landing. "He's *probably* wrong though. You don't even strike me as the type of person who believes in ghosts."

"Why's that?" I asked and led the way out of the dorm stairwell into the cold night air.

Archie trailed behind me. "You're smart. Surely you know that ghosts are just figments of your imagination."

I stuffed my hands into my pockets, thinking that I probably should've brought a heavier coat before I was overcome with the idea to take Archie ghost hunting and bolted out of my room. "Do you not believe in imagination?"

My steps were short and quick. Archie's were long and slow, but we kept even ground cover as we made our way to the Constance L. Weber Auditorium. "I deal in facts and numbers," Archie huffed. "And things you can see."

"What about things you feel? Do you believe in those things?"

"What, like love?"

"No, like pain," I huffed. He was kind of an idiot sometimes. "Ghosts are the result of death, which is painful. Therefore, how can you not believe in them?"

Archie's running commentary paused, but his pace didn't break from mine. "Guess I never thought of it that way."

"Therefore …" I said as we climbed the concrete steps to the front door. I gave the huge handle a tug, using all my body weight. It creaked open, begrudgingly. "We are hunting this bitch."

Archie sighed deeply, resigning himself to the task at hand. He shrank his lithe body through the gap in the door. "And what do you intend to do with *this bitch* when you catch her?"

"Easy," I said and let the door fall shut behind me. We were plunged into darkness. "Interrogation."

I could hear the rustle of fabric, and then the flashlight from Archie's phone sprang to life, directed at my face. I squinted.

"Why are you interrogating this poor unfortunate ghost?"

"Sport?" I shrugged, then patted Archie's chest. "But that's the spirit, my friend."

I plucked his phone from his hands and picked the path through one of the backstage halls toward the stage. Bridgeport had just finished its second play of the semester. The spring shows moved locations to the newer theater, while all the fall semester shows were run out of this building. I guessed they hadn't cleaned up from *The Addams Family* musical yet, as props and boxes littered the hall.

"Now the legend goes that sweet old Connie actually was a student here back in the day. She was a theater major and starred in the majority of the school plays," I said as I made my way through the maze. "Connie was quite the drama queen and demanded the attention of the audience when she performed. So much so that after her death, her family donated the money to build this auditorium in her honor. It's believed that her ghost still comes back to pinch those who are too loud during shows."

"Where did you hear that story?" Archie asked, tripping over a stray box.

We reached the end of the hall, and I fumbled with the latch to the stage door. "All the art kids know it."

He didn't say anything while I struggled to unlock the door. It finally gave under the weight of my shoulder when I rammed it. I tumbled onto the stage, righting myself just before I face-planted. I thought I heard Archie chuckle behind me.

The stage was vacant. No props, boxes, microphones, nothing. Just the linoleum floor that looked like a sheet of black ice.

Beyond the stage, the auditorium was softly illuminated by a faint glow from the sound box above, but there wasn't enough light to make out anything other than the rough shapes of the seats.

"Where to now, oh wise ghost hunter?" I heard Archie's sarcastic tone behind me. The echo was eerie. Chilling.

I kept my eyes trained on the space where the audience was supposed to be, trying to make out the individual outlines of each chair. "Might as well start checking out the crowd."

"What crowd?" Archie asked as I made my way across the stage. Even though I had picked out my quietest sneakers for this expedition, the sound of them squeaking against the stage was distractingly loud.

"You don't see them all out there?" I asked innocently.

Archie's steps behind me stopped for a second and then continued. "That's not funny, Talia."

"I'm not trying to be funny." I sat down on the edge of the stage in an unceremonious plop onto my ass. I gave Archie his phone back and swung my feet a few times before saying, "I'm hysterical."

I jumped off the stage, finding my footing with ease. Archie followed and landed with a loud thump. Everything about him was moving incredibly conspicuously.

"Do you want to take the right side? I'll search the left," I offered, if only to give myself some distance from his noises in the dark.

"No," he said simply. "I don't even know what I'm looking for."

"Clues," I said. "Anything that seems to indicate any level of paranormal activity." I went to stride away, then stopped. "But don't use your phone flashlight. The ghosts will scatter like dust. Like they were never even there."

"Probably because they weren't," Archie muttered.

"I'll meet you back here in ten!" I whisper-shouted as I was already walking away.

More light curses came from Archie's direction, but I hustled, putting a good distance between us as I weaved in and out of the rows of seats. I sifted through leftover debris from the show. Apparently, the student cleanup committee had some work to do.

I pocketed a program and stacked a few paper cups together as I made my way around the entirety of the left side of the theater but hadn't found any remarkable treasures. As quietly as I could, I creaked open the door to the lobby and slipped through.

Slightly disappointed, I figured I could go help Archie scour his section, so I ran through the lobby, bouncing lightly on the balls of my feet. I opened the door to the right side with just as much stealth as I had managed through mine.

The auditorium was darker when entering this way. Here on the back wall of foldable seats, hidden from the glowing light on the floor above, it was like we were in a cave.

Which is precisely how I managed not to see Archie when I swung a leg over the row in front of me to hop down, kicking his shoulder.

"Ouch!" Archie shouted.

"Ah!" I screamed and lost my footing, flailing over the back of the seats and falling in a heap with one foot still caught in the air.

Archie's backside cushioned my landing, but his voice was sharp. "Are you freaking kidding me? Talia, you scared the hell out of me!"

"First of all ..." I grunted, trying to sit up. He groaned as I was basically sitting on him. My elbow landed in his gut as I tried to right myself. He must have been crouched down looking under the seat or something. "Using the word *freaking* is so lame. We're alone in a haunted auditorium. If there was ever an appropriate time to yell the word *fuck*, it would be now."

"You're a fucking nightmare," he said as I finally managed to crawl off him.

"That's better," I said and sat cross-legged on the floor, trying not to think about how dirty it might be. "So did you find anything?"

Archie glared at me. "Of course I didn't."

I shrugged. "That's a shame."

Archie adjusted himself so that he sat with his back leaning against the seat, his legs folded up awkwardly around him, but he didn't respond.

We were quiet as we sat there, silence from the stage roaring in my ears. My arm was pressed against his; neither one of us shifted.

I finally broke the tension in a whisper so soft I didn't know if Archie could hear me. "I made it up."

He responded in a voice just as quiet. "Made what up?"

I cleared my throat and stared straight ahead at the back of the seat in front of me. "The story of Connie."

"What do you mean?"

"It's not real," I said with a sigh. "None of it was real. I told you a story that wasn't based on facts or numbers about someone that you couldn't see, yet you still believed it."

I couldn't tell if he was angry or just confused, but I continued, "Everyone says they don't believe in ghosts until you give them a story. But what if there wasn't a story to go along with the ghost? No one would remember."

"You mean to tell me this whole quest was basically pointless," Archie stated, flat, with no emotion.

"I guess so," I said, and my voice fell quiet. "That's what I'm afraid of. Not having a story. And when I'm gone, no one will remember me."

ARCHIE

PRESENT DAY

"When were you going to tell me that Talia was visiting?" Adeline asked me the morning after I had committed my first crime—vandalism. I nearly dropped my fork.

"Who told you that?" I asked, stabbing a slice of pancake.

"Grady did." She shrugged. "He didn't mean to say it, I don't think. Just kind of slipped out while I was waiting in Ms. Hammond's office at school."

While Grady's undergraduate degree was in art, he'd shifted gears postgrad and applied for a master's program in clinical mental health counseling with a certificate in expressive arts therapy. He landed his spot in the program at the top of the interview group and then got his internship at Adeline's school. He was the smartest one out of us all. And maybe the only one who appeared to know what he was doing.

But apparently, he was not smart enough to keep his damn mouth shut around my little sister.

"Talia? Talia Scott?" My mother asked, surprised. "Now that's a name I haven't heard in a few years."

"She's that one friend of yours that skipped town after you guys graduated?" my father asked as he swiped through the morning news on his iPad. Which was a little bit ridiculous because I knew he remembered her too. We all did.

"She's back," I said with little inflection, wiping the corner of my mouth with one finger. "But I figured it wasn't really worth mentioning since she's going to be leaving again shortly."

"When does she leave?" Adeline asked earnestly. Her eyes were wide, almost too large for her face as she stared at me. "I want to see her."

"No, you don't," my father and I said at the same time. I didn't even need to look up at him. We both knew why.

"Yes," Adeline began slowly and firmly, "I do. Mom, can you please reason with the men of the household? I'm seventeen years old and fully capable of making my own decisions about the people I choose to see."

"Not when those decisions require me to track down Talia and bring her to you," I said. "Her number changed, remember? You can't get in touch with her without me."

"That's actually an excellent idea, Archie," my mom said, picking up what I assumed to be her second cup of coffee for the day. "If Addie wants to spend some time with Talia, how about you both go to the school and join her for lunch?"

I stared at her, dumbstruck. "Surely you're joking."

"I think it'll be good for everyone to see one another again," my mom said. "Especially now."

Now that Addie is better was what she didn't say, but we were all thinking it.

A heavy pause filled the air, and no one tried to fill it.

"So it's settled."

Again, my dad grumbled, but he didn't argue. "Whatever you'd like, dear."

She beamed. "Great! I'm going to head to the yoga studio. I can't wait to hear how everyone's day goes."

My appetite shriveled. I picked up my half-full plate and carried it to the sink. My dad started asking Addie about her classes or something, and their chatter shrouded my mom's whisper in my ear.

"She's strong, Archie," she said. "She'll be fine."

"I don't think she needs anything that would remind her," I said in a hushed tone.

My mom reached up to pat my shoulder. "It's been years, Archie. Your sister is ready."

TALIA

SOPHOMORE YEAR

"Why does it have to be so cold outside?" I whined. I blew warm air between my bare hands as Archie and I waited in the line outside of Blue Elixir.

"Maybe because you chose a school in the Pacific Northwest," Archie deadpanned. "Or maybe because you refuse to buy a pair of gloves."

"Thank you, Captain Obvious," I grumbled.

"Or maybe your Southern charm got frostbite. That would explain so much, actually."

I went to glare at Archie but found him smiling in amusement. I threw a dagger at his black gloves instead. "If only we could all be as prepared as you."

The line shifted, and we shuffled forward, ever so slightly.

"It's not hard," Archie said. "It's called a weather app. Or common sense. It is the week before Thanksgiving in Oregon. I'm not sure exactly what you were expecting."

I groaned again. It was annoying how *right* he had to be all the time. I stuffed my hands into the pockets of my recent thrift store score. The oversize trench coat was perfect for wrapping myself like a human burrito while we waited outside the bar. If only it had come with a pair of gloves attached.

Archie sighed. "Here."

I looked over at his outstretched hands. "I'm not taking your girly gloves."

"I'm not giving you my girly gloves," he countered. "Give me your hands or freeze. Up to you."

Reluctantly, I pulled my hands out from my pockets.

I figured Archie was just going to hold them and hope that the slim cotton fabric would somehow seep some warmth into my fingertips. I was taken aback when he gently grasped my palms in his and raised them to his mouth.

"What are you doing?" I jerked back.

Archie was unfazed. "I was trying to be a gentleman and warm your hands up, but if you want to continue being difficult, that's your choice."

The line moved forward again, and I felt someone push impatiently at my back to walk. I shot the stranger a glare but stepped forward into the small empty space in front of me. I looked back to Archie, and he was looking at the line in front of him, zero expression on his face.

After an awkward pause, I said, "Fine." I flipped my hands in front of me, outstretched.

Archie didn't move. Without changing stance or posture, he said, "I believe that magic word is *please*."

I hated when we both knew I was in the wrong and it was up to me to fix it. My voice was small when I spoke. "Please."

His smile was small, not smug, just there as he turned to take my hands once more. "Don't worry," he said. "I'm not conspiring to suck on your toes or anything next."

The laugh in the back of my throat was unexpected, but it crackled and pulled up short as Archie lifted both of my hands to his mouth. His lips parted, and he only barely grazed my palms against them. Slowly, ever so painfully, excruciatingly, incredibly slowly, Archie blew hot air against them.

I was aware of everything. His hands cradling mine, his lips against my skin, the line behind us, in front of us, everything except the cold night air. Forever had passed when Archie finally drew back and released his light grip on my wrists. Nothing was in his expression to give away what he was thinking.

I, on the other hand, could not stop thinking about how that was one of the most innocently sexy things to have ever happened. I didn't know Archie could be sexy. And I didn't even think he was trying.

It was wild—and terrifying—to admit.

And thank god the line decided to speed itself up. I turned to face forward, mumbling something along the lines of *thanks*, which sounded so lame, even to me. In approximately two more minutes, we had closed the gap on the space between us and the bouncer. I handed him my not-so-real ID, and he handed it back without a second glance.

"Good to see you again, Talia," he said.

"You too, Steve," I said and dashed through the open door, not waiting for Archie behind me.

ARCHIE

SOPHOMORE YEAR

I must really have a way with girls if just a simple hand-holding has Talia bolting away from me. Except it wasn't just holding her hand. I knew that. I'd crossed a line when I brought her palms to my mouth, no matter how innocent the gesture. But the weird part was that it didn't seem weird at all in my mind. It seemed perfectly normal, natural even, to offer her some sort of comfort like that. And for once in my life, I had tried to take a page from Talia's book: Don't overthink things and just act on impulse.

And look where that got me. Alone at the bar. My wingman had flown away.

Not knowing what else to do, I went to the bartender and flagged down what was slowly becoming my usual order.

He slid me a Michelob Ultra as I shifted in my barstool. "Where's your friend?" he asked.

I looked behind me once, to make sure he was talking to me. No doubt he was talking about Talia. "Somewhere in here," I replied.

"Surprised she's not joined at your hip like normal," he said, then turned to his next customer.

I didn't reply. It wasn't worth telling him he was wrong. It was me who stuck to her.

In the few minutes I sat alone, drinking my beer, I realized I didn't care so much for going out to Blue Elixir every week the way Talia seemed to.

If I didn't have her company, the draw wasn't so big for me. Watching all the groups of people mingle together, dissipate, then fall back together in clumps, made me realize how alone I was without Talia by my side.

I briefly wondered if I would ever actually tell her that.

Or if I would make any other friends.

"I found my target for the night."

Probably not.

I turned to Talia as she clambered up into the empty stool beside me.

"Who is this poor, unfortunate soul you've located?" I asked.

She finished situating herself on her barstool, and a beer magically appeared before her with a wink from the bartender in our direction. Her grin was impish in response.

"Hmm, about eight o'clock. Tall. Blond. Broad. Almost like a young Leo DiCaprio but hits the gym morning and night."

"Interesting," I said and casually stretched my back in my seat so I could get a better look at this guy. Unfortunately, her description was spookily accurate. And I had the briefest moment of awkward eye contact that made me feel puny and insignificant.

I turned back to face the rows of liquor on the back shelf and sighed. "What do you want me to do?"

Talia took a deep slug of her beer before slapping it on the counter. "So here's the plan …."

As if I ever doubted that she had one.

"I think we should cause a scene."

"A scene?" I couldn't hide the panic in my voice. "What kind of scene? Like a fight?"

Her face brightened. "Exactly! I'm thinking I want to try channeling my inner damsel-in-distress vibe and have that knight in shining armor—or flannel—come to my rescue. Maybe you and I are dating, and suddenly, I caught you cheating, and now I'm humiliated, and we fight about it right here at the bar. I think I can cry on command pretty believably."

"Are you serious?" I whispered, my voice hoarse. "No. No way. I'm not playing that role for you."

"Oh, come on, Archie," Talia whined and clung to my arm. "Please? I can't do this without my wingman. He's gorgeous. And for some reason, I think that plan could really work."

"Yeah, I'm sure it would. You'd probably get laid, and I'd probably get my nose broken by a stranger defending your honor that was never actually in jeopardy."

She just looked at me, her eyes wide.

It almost worked. I didn't like disappointing her.

Instead, I picked up my beer. "No. I'm not doing that. Just go shake his hand and introduce yourself. He's already been looking over here."

"Really?" Her tears magically dried up, and her expression perked.

I rolled my eyes and took a deep slug. "Yeah." I turned to take one more glance at the guy. His eyes were still flitting back and forth between his group of friends and Talia.

I set my empty bottle down on the counter and signaled for another. "Go ahead. I'll be here. You don't need me." I caught the bottle that the bartender slid my way. I raised it toward Talia in a salute. "Trust me."

She pursed her perfectly lined lips. "Fine." She wiggled forward in her seat until she could easily hop down in one little jump.

I stayed very focused on the neck of my bottle while she adjusted her clothes. The dark amber of the glass rippled under the faint light of the bar. I turned it slightly and caught a distorted reflection of Talia on its surface. She almost looked nervous.

I resolved not to watch her walk away. I almost got away with it too.

That was until a soft touch of her hand on my shoulder pulled me from my fierce staring contest with my drink.

"But you're wrong, Archie," she whispered, and in that moment, I swear I lost the ability to breathe. "I do need you."

As she withdrew her hand and walked toward the other guy, I closed my eyes, cursed her lies, and was left with the only thing I could do—wish they were true.

ARCHIE

PRESENT DAY

I clocked out of work early and told Stacey, one of my dad's other assistants, I'd be back from lunch late. There wasn't much argument from her.

I pulled out from my spot on the street and started making my way toward Adeline's school. It only took fifteen minutes to arrive at the stately brick entrance. I left the engine idling to avoid getting in trouble for parking in a teacher-only space.

I checked the time on my phone, counting down the minutes until Addie was supposed to meet me. I'd texted Talia about the plans: Chicken sandwiches at the old place on South Blvd. 12:15. Addie is coming too.

She sent me a thumbs-up in response.

At twelve o'clock, the double-door entrance to the school burst open, and the chatter of high schoolers filled the campus. I looked up briefly and saw my little sister at the head of the pack, her long brown hair thrown back over her shoulders as she laughed with her friends. I was relieved that she seemed happy.

After hugs goodbye, even though they would see one another approximately fifty-five minutes later, Addie was bouncing her way over to my passenger door.

I clicked the unlock button as she approached. "Hey there, kid."

"Hey there, weirdo."

"Well, that's an incredibly rude way to address the person shuttling you off to your chaperoned lunch date," I accused, but I was smiling.

"I think it's more like *I* am the chaperone for *your* lunch date."

"Not likely," I said and put the van into reverse. I scanned behind us before I pulled out into the busy parking lot. "This was your idea, remember?"

Addie didn't respond. I glanced over at her, and she was folding her fingers over each other, repeatedly, and staring at her hands.

I sighed and reached over, covering both of her small wrists with my palm. "You're okay. She's going to be happy to see you again."

"I feel like I have to apologize," Addie said, pushing my hand away.

I was quiet for a moment. I knew what she thought she should apologize for, and suddenly, this whole impromptu lunch event made a lot more sense.

"You have nothing to apologize for," I said softly, training my eyes on the road.

"You don't understand," Addie said and turned her head toward the window.

I didn't respond. I just drove.

TALIA

PRESENT DAY

I never used to be the type of person to arrive early to things. Now for my return to Oregon, early seemed to be my middle name, and tardy was a style of the past. Maybe it was nerves. Even though I knew I would only be here for a few days, I hadn't been able to ease the clenching feeling in my gut brought on from being back.

Or maybe I wouldn't let myself sink back into what was comfortable. But that meant my old college town felt like a strange land where I was an unwelcome intruder.

Regardless, when Archie texted a place and time, I didn't have it in me to turn him down. In fact, I was elated, but I quickly pushed away the feeling. It was only temporary, after all. All of this was.

Now I sat at a corner booth in the neighborhood chicken sandwich shop where we ate lunch most Wednesdays in college, and I drummed the pads of my fingers against the table repeatedly. *Tap, tap, tap. Tap, tap, tap. Tap, tap—*

"Talia."

I snapped out of my daze, brought on by watching the cars roll by in the drive-through line. I turned to see Archie, in a blue button-down with gray slacks, striding toward my booth. The girl I vaguely recognized as Adeline was trailing behind him.

The last time I saw her, she'd looked hollow, a shell of the girl I felt like I knew through Archie's childhood stories. Now she looked taller, and it was easy to see how the two were related. They shared the exact same shade of mousy-brown hair and hazel eyes. Except Adeline's face was bright and covered in freckles, and Archie was wearing his newfound scowl.

"Hi," I offered.

Archie pulled himself up short in front of the seat across from me. With his hands in his pockets, he looked around. "Did you order yet?"

Obviously not, I thought, but the retort didn't come out. "Not yet," I said. "I waited."

"That's a first," Archie mumbled, and Adeline poked him in the back, hard. After clearing his throat, Archie continued, "Talia, you remember Addie? Addie, Talia again."

"Hi, Talia," Adeline said, her voice cautious and her smile small.

"Good to see you, Adeline," I responded, and I meant it.

"I'm hungry," Archie grumbled. "Let's order."

By the time we got our food, the tension surrounding the three of us was slowly dissipating. At least, I hoped it was. I had been picturing it to be an easy lunch with easy conversation, so much so that I hoped I was willing it into existence.

"How's postgrad life treating you, Talia?" Adeline asked as she opened a sauce packet in one clean rip. Like a Band-Aid.

"Not too bad." I managed a smile and wrestled with the foil wrapper of my own packet.

"Do you have a job?" She asked the question casually, but I didn't miss the raise from Archie's brow, indicating he was listening.

"I did," I replied, slowly.

"Did you get fired?"

"Addie," Archie chided, and she glared at him.

I stifled the chuckle. "It's okay. I quit."

"Didn't like it?" Archie asked, knowing full well what I had been doing with my work.

"I didn't mind," I said. "Just needed a change." *Again* ....

Adeline was quiet, slowly nodding to herself as she ate her chicken nuggets.

"I was moving," I added when the silence didn't magically fill itself with another one of her questions.

"Where to?"

"Not sure yet," I admitted. I couldn't help but flicker my gaze toward Archie.

"Well"—Adeline popped a nugget into her mouth—"I'm glad you're visiting. At least for a little bit."

"Me too."

"How's the artsy side of things?"

She asked the question so plainly that I was grateful. It was like it wasn't an obscene idea for my name to be associated with art. I had spent my whole life in that bubble, carefully talking around the idea of my art but never straight at it. The candid way she asked brought me back to the time of my life at Bridgeport where it was my identity, and it was okay to admit that I made art because I was safe in a space where others made art.

"I'm still artsy," I said simply.

Someone's phone started ringing at the table, surprising us all with a little jolt. Archie immediately began fumbling through his pockets until he found the phone.

"I've got to take this," he said. "I'm sorry."

"All good." I pressed my lips together in a smile, uncharacteristically nervous at the prospect of being alone at the table with his sister.

After a huge amount of shuffling on their side and Archie's exit (his phone still ringing loudly), Adeline and I were left alone.

"So," I began, tentatively plucking another nugget from my own tray, "how are you? How have you been?"

"Since The Incident or just in general?" she asked. There was no malice behind her words. She was just direct in the way she said them.

She must have noticed my obvious pause because she laughed. "It's okay," she said. "You can say it."

"I don't think I can," I whispered.

Her smile faded, but she remained open. "That's okay too. But for what it's worth, I do have something to say, if you don't mind."

"You don't have to say anything." Again, my voice was quiet. Barely a murmur.

"I do," she said firmly. "And I want to. Talia, I'm truly sorry for bringing you into something that was my own problem to deal with. I've apologized to my family, obviously, but they are kind of wrapped up in this mess that is my head. But you ..." She pushed her tray away and folded her hands in her lap, her shoulders leaning in toward the table, closer to me. She took another deep breath. "I'm sorry you were there."

I didn't know what to say. I mean, I know what I wanted to say. It was right there, burning on the tip of my tongue. I opened my lips so barely a breath of voice escaped between them. "I wanted to be there."

"For Archie?" Adeline asked.

It would have been easy to say yes. Of course I would have wanted to be there for Archie. He was my friend. He needed support. That's what good friends do.

But I had waited two years to ask my questions. I shook my head. *No.*

Adeline's smile was dry and her words laced with sarcasm when she said, "Don't tell me you were there for me. You didn't know me. You didn't know the reasons."

Reasons. Plural. Well, that was one question answered.

But again I shook my head. "No," I said aloud this time. "I was there because ..." I struggled for the words. This time, they were floating in my head, taunting me while they danced away. The thoughts in my head barely made sense, even to me. "I just wanted to know."

"Know what?"

"I don't know, maybe what it would look like? What it would ... feel like?"

"I felt nothing." Again, her tone was frank, candid. *Unfeeling.*

"It's getting better," she said. "I've started talking to someone. Taking new meds too. It helps, in case you were wondering."

"I wasn't," I said too quickly.

She nodded. "Then what are you wondering?"

I took a deep breath, and it shook the space between my ribs. "I don't know."

"Most people ask *why*."

"Then you're probably tired of the question."

"I usually just give them the same answer."

"It's probably a lie."

"I won't lie to you, Talia. If you really want to know."

At some point during this conversation, I had changed my mind. I was scared of the answers she could give me that I probably already knew. I didn't want the words and ideas floating around in my head spoken into existence. If they stayed trapped, suppressed, *suffocated*, then it didn't matter.

I shook my head no. Again. Adeline stayed silent, save for the munching on her fries.

I finally folded my hands in my lap, the rest of my appetite gone. "You're so brave."

"For which part? Putting the knife to my wrist?" She plucked another fry. "Or finding a way to live with that?"

I shrugged and shifted my gaze out of the window. "Maybe all of it."

"I was a *coward* before," Adeline challenged.

"I think it was brave to try it."

"If that's your definition of bravery, I think we're going to have to revoke your college degree," she deadpanned.

"It's braver than I've ever been," I countered. "I haven't come close, as much as I've wanted to."

Adeline didn't miss a beat. "Then you probably haven't really wanted to."

"Then what do you think I want?" I asked. It sounded whiny, even to my ears.

"To be saved?" she offered.

"No. I learned a long time ago that you don't count on others to save you. You have to want to save yourself."

Adeline beamed. "See? That's a step in the right direction."

"But which way is right for *me*?" The question sounded both philosophical and desperate.

Adeline picked up another fry. "Maybe you don't want to be saved. Just heard."

I couldn't help it. My gaze out the window trailed to where Archie was pacing back and forth outside, angrily talking into his phone.

Adeline followed where I was looking. Quietly, she said, "Archie has always heard you, Talia."

"Yeah, Archie has heard me," I said sarcastically. "He's heard me laugh, and he's heard me flirt."

Outside, Archie was hanging up his phone and stuffing it back into his pocket. He dragged a hand over his face before turning to reenter the building.

"But he's never looked deep enough to hear me cry."

ARCHIE

PRESENT DAY

According to the phone call from Stacey that had interrupted lunch, I was apparently a complete dimwit who managed to schedule two appointments for my father within fifteen minutes of each other. Little to her apparent knowledge, I had no power over his scheduling. I simply took phone calls and gave *her* the sticky notes. But telling her this only added fuel to the panicking fire in her voice. I promised to leave lunch *now* and drop Addie back at school before returning to the office.

I ended the call and paused. I didn't really want to go back in there. Who knew what Addie and Talia were talking about? Whatever it was, I didn't feel like it was my place to hear.

But on the flip side, I couldn't stand the thought of being away a second longer. It all felt complicated in a way that hadn't been this complex since college.

And when I opened the door, the look on Talia's face hit me in the gut. Hard.

She looked hollow. Haunted. *Empty.* I had seen this look before. It shocked me so badly I nearly stepped back onto the woman that was entering the building behind me. She squeaked, and I rambled an apology before composing myself enough to go to the table. Talia heard my commotion, *obviously*, and the dark expression on her face was replaced with her usual carefree smile. A smile that radiated confidence, that told the world she didn't have a bother, that she could coast through the scenes of her life where nothing touched her.

I was so used to this smile that I wondered if I'd imagined the look in her blue eyes before.

"Everything okay?" Talia asked, and if I didn't know her so well, I wouldn't have been able to detect the slight elevation in her voice.

I regretted having to leave her side. "Stacey needs me back at the office. Apparently, there was a scheduling mishap, and she needs backup."

"That's okay," Talia said. "We're just about done here anyway."

"Yeah," Addie drawled. "I guess I have to return to the hallowed halls of high school."

I harrumphed and reached for the empty trays to throw out. "You're dramatic."

Addie shrugged and rose from the booth, pushing past me to throw her own garbage out. I turned to Talia as she slowly slid out as well. "How did that go?"

"Great," she said, and I wanted to believe her. "Your sister is fantastic. Seems like she's doing well."

"She is," I said and waited for Talia to lead the way out. "She's definitely doing much better." I fished for words in my head with a line that wavered too much to catch anything that would concisely ask how Talia was doing.

I ended up changing the subject instead. "So any more vandalism planned for this evening?"

She chuckled as she slid her cardboard containers into the trash and set the tray in the stack. "Probably should at some point, if I'm going to finish on time."

"You're working on a deadline?'

"Something like that."

"Do you need help?" I couldn't believe how easy it was to offer.

She gave me a tight-lipped smile. "I'll text you later if I do. Thanks for the lunch invite." Then she turned to push open the door leading to the parking lot.

Addie was already waiting outside by my car, sunglasses hiding her features, looking more and more adult every day. I unlocked the van for her.

"It was good to see you, Adeline!" Talia called and waved to her.

"Take care!" She called back and let herself into the passenger side door, leaving Talia and me alone.

"Well," I began, "I guess I'll see you later? Just let me know if I'm meeting you somewhere."

"I will," Talia said softly. "Only if you want to."

I sighed, and my arm did this weird twitchy thing where it almost reached to do something, like pull her into an embrace. I stopped the movement, but not before my fingers had grazed the edge of her sleeve, lightly flitting over her wrist. "I do. Want to."

TALIA

ON COLOR THEORY

Color Theory was my favorite class in college. Of course we talked about the color wheel and how to mix colors and hues, tints and shades and tones. But in the latter half of the semester, Joe had us applying color in a study of what our favorite color meant to us.

My favorite color is, was, and has always been green, but that felt like too personal of a thing to admit to the class. Other kids who chose the color green to study were exploring concepts like rebirth, revival, and spring. It seemed entirely too optimistic and, quite frankly, too much pressure to put on a color I simply enjoyed looking at.

I chose red instead, and it made sense. It was the color of passion, love, and danger. At least that's what the internet was telling me.

The goal of the project was to find where and how our color occurred naturally in nature to create a mixed-media monochromatic landscape. In other words, don't even think about touching the acrylics.

Grady and I were in the class together. Unfortunately, we shared the same lack of respect for a deadline. The week before our due date found us both working in the art building after hours, the fluorescent lights flickering overhead as we tried to finish on time.

"All I can say is, thank god Joe amended his 'don't touch the art supply cabinet' rule and at least let us use *glue*." He was tapping an obscene amount of the gloppy liquid from the bottle onto his canvas. "I can't imagine the shit that would have been used to attach our found objects."

He'd chosen the color brown, and his disdain for this assignment was evident in his collection of dead leaves. *A commentary of the circle of life*, he said a few nights prior when he started collecting them. *And minimal effort.*

"I wouldn't put it past you to use literal shit," I joked, not letting my focus waiver from the soft hair-like strokes I was carefully brushing on, using a homemade paint of juiced red berries. The produce section and I had become great friends for this project. I think that's the biggest reason Grady was accompanying me, for the promise of raspberries, cherries, strawberries, and pomegranate seeds.

"Don't think I haven't thought about it," Grady said. His dark eyebrows were scrunched together as he picked at the dried bits of glue between his fingers. "It's almost midnight. How much more are you going to do tonight?"

"Well," I said patiently, "considering this is due at 8 a.m. tomorrow, I think I should probably try to finish it up."

Grady picked up the last of his leaves and carelessly sprinkled them over his canvas. "I wonder what Joe would say if I submitted this to *The Digital Art Show* and actually got accepted."

I looked up from my work. "You follow *The Digital Art Show*?"

Grady rolled his eyes. "Everyone in Bridgeport follows *The Digital Art Show*." Between his pinky and his ring finger, the only digits presumably without glue on them, he carefully balanced my last strawberry and popped it into his mouth. "Don't stay up too late, Natalia."

My hand jerked, jagging what was a perfectly straight line on my canvas. "Don't call me that."

"Why not?" he asked simply. "It's your name."

"Not anymore."

It felt like he was going to say more. When he ultimately didn't and turned to leave, giving the top of my head an awkward pat, I felt empty.

Like I wanted more of a fight. Like I wanted to keep arguing the fact that I was no longer the girl with the longer name and longer story that no one cared about anyway. But the words that would have filled my chest, the *feelings* I had left behind, didn't seem to matter anyway.

"Goodnight," I said and crushed another pomegranate seed in my palette.

"'Night," Grady said, and the door whooshed open and shut behind him.

I narrowed my eyes at the small dark pool of liquid the broken seed had created. Dark, but not dark enough to get the shade I needed to finish my painting.

I let the paintbrush fall onto the canvas. A smattering of berry juice scattered across it, Jackson Pollock-style. I got up and started pacing around the room, angry at the fruit gods for not supplying a color dark enough, angry at Joe for this stupid assignment, and angry at myself for waiting until hours before it was due to realize I didn't have the correct *shade* from nature. Just … angry.

My pacing carried me over to the scrap material garbage bin where most of the odds and ends and pieces of projects ended up. Most any material you could get your hands on landed in abstract hunks here, discarded but not trashed.

"Reduce, reuse," I muttered the mantra Joe preached about our supplies. Out of habit, I started feeling my way through the scraps, seeing if anything could be of use.

"Damn it!" I cried and yanked my arm out from the barrel. A thin trickle of blood dripped from my wrist and down my palm, coloring my fingertips in warm liquid. Some idiot must have thought a piece of glass would have been of use to someone. The cut stung, and I pressed my opposite thumb over the wound. It wasn't that deep. But it still burned.

I instinctively made my way toward the sink to run my hand under cool water, then halted, staring at my hand and the *color* seeping from beneath my thumb.

"This is morbid," I said aloud as I retraced my steps back to my palette. I hunched over my collection of reds and slowly released the pressure that bound my cut. The blood that had gathered on my wrist pooled again, and I waited for gravity to do its dirty work. A single, fat, crimson drop plopped onto my palette.

I pressed a little harder on the skin beside the wound. Another pool of blood slowly formed, and as I clenched my teeth, I was rewarded with one more drop.

But it wasn't enough. I eyeballed the scrap bin again but quickly disregarded the thought of playing with more broken glass. It didn't feel all too good the first time around, even though the sharp sting was becoming more of a dull throb by now.

I settled with my thumbnail. I never kept a real manicure on my hands, but they weren't the longest nails either. Ever so slowly, I brought my thumb to rest beside the already-opened wound. I clenched my teeth in my jaw and pressed my nail along the edge of the broken skin.

It hurt, but not bad enough to stop.

I pretended it was surgery, on someone else's hand, on someone else's body, with a proper knife or scalpel. Mind over matter. If you could convince yourself that you didn't feel, odds are, you wouldn't.

I was rewarded with a slow trickle, an incredibly narrow but steady rivulet. I squeezed my eyes shut to keep the tears from escaping. No use crying over something you chose to do yourself. I held my wrist over my palette. *Plink, plink, plink.*

I grabbed my blotting paper towel from beside my workstation and held it gently over my wrist. I would worry about cleaning it up later. I just wanted to be done and out of there.

I picked up my brush and set to work finishing my project. "Perfect," I murmured as the color brushed on just as I had thought it would.

I hoped no one would know. It didn't look like blood. Not really.

But if they did, Joe said it was supposed to be mixed media, after all.

ARCHIE

SOPHOMORE YEAR

"Archie, why aren't you paying attention to me? I'm recapping my wild night of promiscuous activities, and you don't seem the slightest bit interested in my affairs."

That's because I'm not was what I didn't say to Talia. Instead of admitting I was irritated that her affairs had left me alone at the bar last night, I said, "I'm sorry. You were saying?"

She cut into her pancakes and took another bite, talking around the food in her mouth. "I was trying to tell you about Justin."

"Who's Justin?"

"Come on, don't be like that. He's the guy you told me to go talk to last night. I'm thinking he's my future boyfriend."

I coughed at her words, spewing a perfectly good pancake bite onto the table in front of us. "What? I thought you told me you didn't date." She *definitely* told me she didn't date. Right after our very first wingman excursion. That the whole wingman endeavor was just for fun. Nothing serious. So why does she want a boyfriend *now*?

Talia made a face at my sad piece of pancake on the white linoleum table. "I don't *usually* date."

"What's so special about this guy?" There was a heat rising in my voice that I knew was probably unfair, but I couldn't really quell it. I knew what was special about this guy. I saw it with my own eyes, her instant attraction to his blond GQ looks. And the unabashed way he kept *looking* at her. He was confident, plain and simple.

She shrugged, not meeting my eye. "I don't know. I just had a really nice time last night."

She fell silent as she poked around the rest of her food.

"What? Is that really all you're going to say now?" I don't know why I continued to snap at her like that—I didn't really want to know any of those details. It just wasn't like her to clam up like this when she had a chance to show off her superiority.

"I don't feel like sharing any more with you and your bad attitude."

I grumbled under my breath, "My bad attitude."

"Archie, just because you're jealous that I've had multiple successful wingman outings and you haven't doesn't mean that you get to take out that frustration on me."

It was all I had in me to not let my jaw drop in shock. My phone buzzed in my pocket. Saved by the bell. It was my mom calling. I clicked it off and put my phone face down on the table.

"I'm not jealous that you've been more successful in participating in twenty-first-century hookup culture than me," I said.

"Well, you sound jealous."

"Not about that," I said. My phone buzzed again, and I groaned, flipping it over to read the text from my mom: Call me.

That was odd. I rubbed my thumb up and down the screen a few times, debating whether to call her back now or later.

Talia pressed on. "Then would you like to explain your juvenile behavior?"

The buzzing persisted urgently in my hand.

Please. It's Addie.

My heart leapt to my throat. "Talia, I've got to call my mom real quick."

She made a dramatic show of rolling her eyes. "Of course. Just as conversation gets personal, you find a way to evade my questions."

"Please, like you're one to talk," I snapped and dialed my mom.

She answered on the first ring. "Archie, we're in the hospital with her now. I need you to come as soon as you can."

Time felt like syrup as I walked out the door, like the thick, sticky kind that still drenched the fork I had left on my plate. It felt like it coated my throat as I repeated back, "You're in the hospital with Addie?"

The breath she drew was shaky. "Archie ..." Her voice cracked, and I heard a choking sob. "Archie, there was so much blood."

"What do you mean?" I asked slowly, but I knew. I knew things had been bad and only seemed to be getting worse during her peak middle school years. Addie was never the type to have tons of friends, just a few close ones, but over the past year, we'd mostly stopped seeing them around the house.

"Why don't you spend any time with Halen and Sarah?" my mom had asked Addie when I visited home a few weekends ago.

Addie just shrugged.

I knew Sarah's older brother. He was two years younger than me and a senior at our high school. I did some digging and called him.

"Addie and Sarah? They haven't hung out in years, man. To be honest, I didn't even realize Addie was still at our school."

Dissociation or destruction. Those were the two avenues that led to depression in young children, I would later read in a pamphlet. I knew these things, and I knew Addie wasn't the destructive type. Not naturally. Not without reason, I thought.

There was so much blood.

"What did she do?" I asked my mom as clear and steady as I could make my voice. I could barely recognize how hollow, low, and *scared* I sounded.

My mom was audibly crying on the line. "Just ... come quickly, Archie."

I hung up the phone. I walked back into the restaurant. Once at our table, I fumbled with my wallet.

"I need to go," I managed to say as I wrestled out a credit card with shaking hands.

"What do you mean *go*?" Talia asked. "You can't just leave diner dates." The hiss on the end of her words sliced the air.

The card fell from my hands, tumbling to the ground. I knelt to pick it up. "I need to go," I repeated and started walking away.

"Hey!" Talia called. "You can't leave me! Or your card, for that matter."

"Addie is in the fucking hospital, Talia!" I exploded, not caring who witnessed the reaction in the diner or how loud my eruption was.

The diner stilled, but Talia was frozen. I was on fire.

"So no, Talia, I don't really give a damn right now about your stupid diner dates or how amazing your night was, or who you've fucked most recently! My mom and my sister need me. I'm leaving."

I took my card to the register, and the woman behind the machine was already ringing up my usual.

"Are you okay to drive, honey?" she asked.

I appreciated her kindness, more than I would ever be able to vocalize, but I could only spit out, "I'm sure. I'm fine."

"I'm driving." Talia's voice appeared over my shoulder, and my teeth ground together in the back of my jaw. Her voice was quiet, soft spoken, unlike its normal brash quality. It made me want to punch something. Instead, I ignored her and walked right out of the diner as she paid her bill.

"Hey!" she called after me.

My long strides left her in the distance. Or they would have, if she didn't break into a run to catch up.

"Archie, wait for me!"

"Not this time, Talia."

"Archie! I'm … I'm sorry, okay? I'm sorry. Please let me drive you. I don't want you behind a wheel right now."

In the two years I had known Talia, she had never ever apologized. My step faltered, and she kept jogging past me.

"I'm getting my car," she huffed breathlessly as she kept running.

I didn't know how else to argue, and the will to do so vanished. Instead, I felt an overwhelming tiredness and something heavy that felt like dread.

"Okay."

ARCHIE

PRESENT DAY

It was Friday. Which meant, per our normal routine, Grady and I were sitting at Al's Tavern, each on our second round of both drinks and onion rings, playing trivia.

Well, *playing* was a term used loosely. Every Friday, for as long as I could remember postgrad, Grady and I would answer about 92 percent of the questions correctly, but never actually signed in to get points.

"It's a quirk," Grady had explained to Addie the one time she joined us and we sat at a table and had dinner instead of drinks during one of the rounds.

"It's weird. And lazy," she replied. "I could walk up and make us a team right now."

"Nah." Grady brushed her off. "Can't change tradition now. Let the mere mortals have their chance at victory."

Even if we were playing, we would've lost stupendously that night. Addie didn't join us again.

And even if we were playing tonight, the result probably would have been the same. Grady had nearly every answer several seconds before my mind had even wrapped around the question; after the first round, his answers were proving to be rather incorrect.

"Dude," he finally said. "I'm drowning here. What is going on with you? You're supposed to be a vault full of factoids in trying times like these."

"Sorry," I mumbled and picked up another onion ring. "Distracted, I guess."

Grady groaned. "What did she do this time?"

I gave a weak half laugh that wasn't worth finishing. I sighed and knew I had to come clean. "I'm still waiting on a text from Talia. I thought we might meet up again later tonight."

Grady lifted his gaze to the roof of the bar and prayed to an invisible god. "Give me the strength to once again protect this man from his own stupidity."

I laughed for real this time.

He turned to face me. "So you're telling me you're sitting here moping around, waiting on a text from the long-lost-now-returned love of your life, leaving me to *flail* around and *fail* at trivia? That phone you're staring at could, coincidentally, also *send* a text message to simply ask this fairy princess of a girl, *Where are you?*"

I blinked at him. "When did she grow wings?"

"You're being ridiculous, man. Either move on, which we all know is not going to happen, or reach out." And at the sound of the host's voice asking the next question, he turned away from me and folded his arms.

"It didn't sound like that simple of a choice in my head," I responded softly.

"Shush. I'm trying to radiate genius," Grady said, then nudged my arm with his. "Just text the girl."

I unlocked my phone and let my thumbs hover over an empty text message screen.

I tried on several of what I thought to be witty one-line openers, but I settled on **Hey.**

Then I turned my phone face down on the bar. I ordered another round for Grady and me.

When the bartender set the drinks down, my phone vibrated, and I jumped to pick it up, all too eager, which earned a chortle from my friend. I ignored both him and the flutter from somewhere deep inside of me when I saw her name at the top of my screen.

Hey was all it said.

How's the graffiti going? I typed, and before I could delete and rewrite, I hit Send.

Her typing bubbles appeared, disappeared, and flashed. Then her next message came through: **Tabled for now. Kathryn and Andrew are making me fraternize with the local townspeople. Going to the drive-in movie tonight.**

I must have been a really bad local resident because I hadn't realized the drive-in was still in operation. I hadn't been since I was in high school, probably.

I didn't know you consorted with commoners.

I hung out with you.

Ouch. Not tonight, apparently.

The host started calling out the winning teams as I reread that last text. It sounded whiny. And a little desperate. And unfortunately, I didn't regret sending it in the slightest.

Her text bubbles appeared and disappeared once more before her new message sat glowing at the bottom of my screen: **Feel free to join us. Kathryn has preapproved your company. I just didn't know what your plans were tonight.**

You didn't ask.

You're right. Let me start over. Would you like to go to the drive-in tonight?

Her sarcasm and irritation leaked through the spaces between her words.

I don't know. I'll have to check my very busy nightlife schedule.

You're probably with Grady. Bring him too. See you in 30.

I think it was that confidence, that directness, that drew me to her originally and left me not wanting to disappoint her. I felt the same tug now. It pulled me to the edge of my seat.

"So Grady," I began, which earned a pointed look from my friend. "How do you feel about a drive-in movie?"

"Sounds romantic. Like a date. But you're not my type."

I just stared at him. He stared back.

He sighed. "You know, I never really liked this little wingman game of yours."

"Just this once," I implored, which really wasn't fair because of course he wouldn't like it; Grady didn't need a wingman. Between us, he was the Maverick.

"You don't need me to go," he said.

"Maybe one day I won't."

"But not today?"

"Not today."

Grady reached over and finished my drink before I could. "Of course not."

TALIA

PRESENT DAY

They brought Archie's van.

Their record timing in approach meant that my assumption had been correct—Archie and Grady were already together.

I had been sitting up from my seat in the bed of Andrew's truck, watching for them to pull in. I saw Grady in the front seat, and his trademark locs bounced as Archie hit the same pothole Andrew had discovered when we entered the drive-in parking lot.

"Archie's here," I leaned over to tell Kathryn.

"Did you tell him where we were parked?" she asked without looking up from her phone.

We had arrived early to find a good spot in the center of the field, but Kathryn told Andrew to park his truck diagonally, ensuring a spot could be made beside us when the rest of our party arrived. It earned a few grumbles of discontent from the other drivers that pulled in, but apparently Andrew and Kathryn were regulars, and no one was going to complain.

"No," I said. "I figured we were going to make a game of finding each other."

"I certainly will not be." Kathryn shifted in her makeshift sofa she and Andrew had set up in their truck bed. They really were drive-in movie experts. The bed of the truck had been converted into a lounge complete with an air mattress, pillows, and a thick outdoor-type quilt.

"He'll find us," I responded and wiggled down beside her once more. He usually did.

"Don't get too comfortable," Kathryn shook her head. "You're getting evicted to straighten the truck and get in Archie's car."

"First, where is Andrew? Second, why am I getting into Archie's car?"

Kathryn shifted again. "Andrew is getting snacks. And you're getting into Archie's car because if you don't, that completely defeats the purpose of inviting him."

"You invited him," I said.

She pretended to look innocent. "Did my fingers ever touch your keyboard?"

"No, but it was your idea when I told you he texted me."

"You were already thinking about it."

I bit my lip. "Maybe. But you and Andrew probably just want the truck bed to yourselves." That was certainly an easier explanation than the matchmaker she obviously thought she was.

Her face broke into the briefest and smallest of smirks. "I wouldn't complain."

I finally sat up and started to clamber out of the bed of the truck. "Fine. I'll flag them down *and* leave you two to hold hands conspicuously under the covers."

"*Under* the covers?" I heard Andrew's voice over my shoulder. "Now that sounds scandalous."

I hadn't met Andrew until this trip. I had heard about him from Kathryn through the postcard correspondence we had kept up since graduation, but Andrew hadn't gone to Bridgeport. Rather, his *job* had transferred him to Oregon, and they had met through the firm where Kathryn interned during law school.

But he was nothing like what I had pictured when Kathryn described him as a big-time divorce attorney. He was older than her, but Kathryn was the grown-up of the relationship, and Andrew was *goofy*.

He had a wide, almost silly smile, and a full beard that matched his dirty blond hair. And he was wearing a red flannel. He looked like a lumberjack.

Plus he owned a *truck*. In the *city*.

"Can't take away all of the South from me," he had said when we first met a few days ago and realized we were both originally from the same region. He thoroughly defied all my preconceived notions about him.

I jumped down out of the truck bed and took the large popcorn out of Andrew's arms, snagging a few pieces before I handed it to Kathryn. "Good timing," I told him. "You can straighten the truck now. Archie and Grady just got here."

Andrew willingly obliged and opened the driver's side door. "You went to college with them?"

The history Archie and I shared was so much more complicated than that, and it was mildly deflating that the entirety of our past could be boiled down into that one small sentence. "Yes," I said and raised a hand in greeting as Archie's van came around the turn. We locked eyes through the front windshield, and something in my core heated. I quickly pushed the feeling down and capped it. "We did go to college together."

"All of us," Kathryn added, munching on her popcorn. "So strange to think that after all this time, we came back together again."

"It hasn't been that long," I said softly so that no one else heard.

"They live here though, right?" Andrew turned on the engine, and the truck roared to life. "Why haven't we hung out with them before?"

Kathryn's eyes flitted over to mine. The unspoken weight of her brief gaze made me appreciate her constant presence in my life, no matter the physical space between us. "Archie and Grady are Talia's people," she said simply, as if that were enough of a reason. "But I've always liked them fine."

Andrew pulled the truck forward, then back again, this time lining up a perfectly perpendicular parking space to the large screen at the front of the field. "Well, I'm excited to meet your people," Andrew said to me before handing me a small pack of Twizzlers from his jacket pocket.

Kathryn must have told him they were my favorite, a fact she knew from our time living together.

"You could make the list of my people if you keep this up," I told him with a wave of the Twizzlers.

Archie's eyes met mine, and he gave me the briefest of nods as he slid in beside Andrew and turned off the van.

Grady's door opened first. Much like Archie, he also seemed bigger since the last time I saw him. There was a small pang in my chest at the thought. His smile was sincere when he emerged from the van, arms outstretched.

"Natalia Scott," he said slowly, voice and smile still deep.

I didn't bother to correct him on my name. Instead, I all but threw myself into his warm and still-familiar embrace. He felt solid, good, and real. "Hi, Grady," I said into his chest and didn't let go.

I felt the chuckle rumble in his ribs, and he squeezed me tighter. "Good to see you too," he said softer and gave me a final squeeze before drawing back. "You look good, girl. How have you been?"

"Oh, you know," I tried to laugh but the sound got caught in my throat. I cleared it once and brushed the escaping hairs from my face. "Fine."

"Just fine?"

I pressed my lips together and couldn't move my eyes from his dark, insightful gaze. I said nothing, but I blinked my eyes a few times, surprised to feel tears stinging the back of them.

He reached out and awkwardly brushed my shoulder once more with his hand but dropped it when Archie's door opened.

"You must be Archie and Grady!" I heard Andrew's voice over my shoulder, but I couldn't stop watching Archie.

Grady had the same cool, carefree charm I remembered from freshman year when we first met. It wasn't the electric type of charisma, but more of the soothing, comforting kind that meant instant friendship and kindness. "We've been called worse," he said. "Nice to meet you, man."

Andrew returned his firm grip and beamed. "I'm Andrew. Kathryn's husband." He shook Archie's hand as well.

"Where is that lovely lady of yours?" Grady asked.

"Hello, Grady," Kathryn said politely, still without looking up.

"There she is!" he announced, and in one graceful motion, Grady gripped the side of the truck bed and jumped into the makeshift fort, enveloping Kathryn in a bear hug I knew she would hate. But it was nice to see that, at least to Grady, time hadn't changed these old relationships. I envied his ability to pick things up right where they had been left.

Archie was fiddling with his hands in his pockets, not saying much.

Andrew cleared his throat. "How did you all meet?"

"College," Archie said, nondescript, at the same time I explained, "The campus parking lot."

I felt Archie's gaze flicker to mine. I wondered if he remembered the first time we had met. I hadn't forgotten.

Andrew laughed, politely, and that was all the conversation we had to make before Kathryn called to her husband, "Andrew, come here! Movie is about to start."

Andrew laughed. "Duty calls. Nice to meet you, Archie. Enjoy the show!"

"What are we watching?" Archie asked. It felt odd that it was the first thing he said to me all night.

I brushed past him, opening the back hatch of his van. *"The Princess Bride."*

"Really?"

I jumped into the back and sat on the edge, swinging my legs. "Have you seen it?"

"Long time ago," Archie said and sat beside me slowly. "With my mom and Addie once."

"It's a classic."

He ignored me and leaned forward. "Grady, are you coming back?"

"Nah, man." His voice floated to the car. "They have pillows and popcorn."

I shook my head. My friends really weren't the most subtle.

Archie shifted uncomfortably as the screen illuminated in front of us.

"We could put the back seat down," I offered, noticing he was doing his best to situate himself without touching me.

"It gets stuck sometimes," he said. "Won't fold all the way down."

I hopped out of the trunk and climbed into the back seat. "That's perfect actually. It can be like a movie theater recliner."

I tugged on the strap beside the seat belt, and sure enough, the entire back seat folded down to a nice forty-five-degree angle. I reached up and patted the back of the seat. "Here ya go."

"That works," Archie said.

He was taking up most of the space I had just created in the trunk, sitting exactly in the center. The speakers hooked up around the field crackled once before the movie started to play.

Archie simply held out his hand and propped up his feet, creating a space in front of him where he seemed to actually believe I was going to sit. Practically in his lap.

"Come here, Talia," he further directed, almost exasperated when I didn't immediately leap at his outstretched hand.

Now it was my turn to act like the awkward middle schooler. "You sure?" I asked, skeptical.

"Yes. I've solved every mathematical possibility of how to fit in here nicely, and nothing will change the fact that my legs are about 1.42 times the length of yours."

I sighed. "If you insist." And I took his hand, gripping it firmly, before pushing off the ground and letting him pull me into the car. I nearly fell onto him, and he steadied me, his hand against my hip.

"Sorry," I said. I knew my hair was in his face.

"S'okay," he whispered, and I eased myself down, wiggling a few times to get situated and facing forward.

I had been wrapped in Archie's arms before. The memory flooded me: his warm, solid, and surprisingly firm grip that night so long ago. Now his arms draped naturally over my shoulders, gently hugging me to his chest.

I tried to take a breath and wondered if he could feel the rattling of my heartbeat.

"You good?" he asked. His voice was so quiet, and his words were so close to my ear that his breath moved the wisps of hair at my neck.

"Mm-hmm," was all I could manage. I tried leaning back into him a bit deeper, trying to relax.

And we stayed that way for the first bit of the movie, neither one of us moving except for the necessary breathing, until Buttercup and Westley had fallen in love, been separated, and she was now betrothed to Prince Humperdinck.

Archie grumbled, "Who gives their kid the name Humperdinck?"

"Who gives their kid the first name Prince?"

"An avid music connoisseur."

I couldn't help but laugh.

Archie shifted once beneath me, adjusting his lower back. I tried to sit up and give him room, but his arms slid from my shoulders to my waist, and he tightened his grip. "You're fine. Don't move." He surprised me yet again with the husky quality of his voice.

I couldn't speak. I just took a deep, controlled breath, quieting the nerves that were on fire from his touch. What the hell were we doing?

What the hell was *I* doing?

He loosened his grip once he settled, but he didn't let go.

In the movie I was trying to watch very intently, Princess Buttercup was captured, and the masked man in black tailed her captors, besting each one of them, a feat that was entirely *inconceivable*.

"It's inconceivable that trope has prevailed—long past the eighties!," Archie said.

It was just like Archie to know what the half mask that Dread Pirate Roberts wore was actually called.

"Right!" I agreed anyway. "I mean, it's inconceivable that even if he had a *full* mask on, she wouldn't recognize his voice."

"It's inconceivable that after all this time, he managed to find her again, when Prince Humperdinck hadn't even looked for her yet."

"And they didn't even have smartphones."

"It's inconceivable that we're both here right now, after all this time," Archie said.

I froze and figured he felt it. Regaining as much composure as I could, I asked, "In the physical or metaphorical sense?"

"Both," he said simply and waited.

I diverted. "It's inconceivable that I've seen this movie maybe fifteen times and can't tell you that Prince Humperdinck was behind the kidnapping without ruining the romantic element for you. So he wasn't even searching for Buttercup. So of course Westley would find her first."

I felt Archie's light chuckle against my back. "Do you like the love story here?" he asked, amused.

"Yes and no."

"How so?"

"Yes, I like the movie. No, not because of the love story. Because it's not."

"Hmm." He made the sound slowly, a dull vibration in his chest. "How do you figure?"

"Are you watching?" I gestured at Westley and Buttercup as they entered the Fire Swamp. "It's an *adventure* story with romance as its propeller. But in real life, we don't always get the adventure unless we make one for ourselves."

He didn't miss a beat. "Some would argue that life is an adventure on its own."

"Yeah, but not like this." And as if on command, a Rodent of Unusual Size jumped out and attacked the couple. "See? They go on all these quests and check all these boxes to get to their final destination, which I guess is the altar quite literally here. But in real life, what happens when you finally get to the end? It doesn't just *end*, curtain closed, done."

Archie didn't have a rebuttal. I guessed he was thinking of one, choosing his next words carefully. Or he was entranced by ROUS costumes and fake blood.

"No. You have to keep doing it. Life, that is, without the propeller," I continued. "And quite frankly, it seems rather taxing, and this movie makes a happy ending entirely misleading."

"I thought you liked this movie."

"I love this movie. I'm just saying, it works because it's neat. And tidy. And life doesn't do that."

"It's entertainment."

"I'm looking for meaning."

"I thought you were spontaneous," Archie said and bumped his knee gently against mine. "When did you become so existential?"

I said nothing. Archie, oblivious to the internal crisis I was trying to articulate, continued, "I, for one, am enjoying this cautionary tale of getting lost in the forest with ROUSs and no GPS .... And I'm happy to be here with you."

"Hmm." It was my turn to vibrate the sound, and I gave up my argument. Instead, I leaned my head back and found a comfortable spot for it to lie in the crook of his neck.

Gently, he rested his jaw against my head, and his hands slid from my waist to my hips. It should have felt forced, or at least awkward. But instead it was natural, *right*, and terrifying how simple it was to cuddle up next to each other.

The worst part was that it was easy to be here, in the moment, with my former best friend, and ignore what I knew would have to come next.

Because like the movie, this adventure too would end. But I had to keep going.

And it was exhausting.

TALIA

SOPHOMORE YEAR

The hospital was a thirteen-minute drive from the college. It took an additional four minutes to retrieve my car from the parking lot, not to mention the time it took to jog from the diner back to campus. Every second that passed seemed entirely too long.

I knew then that I would never forget the look on Archie's face. It was blank, devoid of feeling, wiped clean of his usual dorky grin or confused eyebrows. I expected turmoil. But instead, he had schooled himself into a numb calm.

It scared me how quiet he had become.

I struggled to fill the silence that stretched and swallowed and consumed the car. "She's going to be okay," I said.

"You don't know that." His voice was monotone and even.

And I didn't argue. Because he was right. I didn't know. But for Archie's sake, I hoped I was right.

As I pulled up to the emergency room entrance, Archie unbuckled his seat belt, opened the passenger door, and spilled out before I had even stopped.

"You don't have to wait," he called as he jogged to the double door, not looking back.

"I'm parking, then coming in!" I yelled back, and he paused.

"Seriously though. You may not want to see this."

I reached over and grappled with the door he had left open. "I'd be a pretty shitty friend if I let you see it alone. Go. I'll find you."

He rocked once on the balls of his feet, debating. "Thank you" was all he said, and then he was gone.

I pulled into the open spot ahead, then got out of the car and ran for the hospital doors. I locked the car over my shoulder but didn't look back.

When I got to the front desk, Archie was nowhere to be seen.

"I'm here with a friend of mine visiting his sister," I said to the lady working the front desk. "Last name Morgan. First name Addie."

The woman didn't look up from her computer. "First name Adeline," she countered. "Your friend just ran through here. They're down the hall and through the third door on the left."

I managed a curt nod and left wordlessly, trudging my way toward *Adeline* and whatever disaster was brewing around the Morgan family. Each step I took grew heavier, and I wondered if Archie was right—maybe I shouldn't have come.

I understood the tone of Archie's voice well enough. I understood the fear lurking behind the faux-placid expression pasted on his face.

I had seen a version of it in my own mother's eyes once before.

The day of The Diagnosis.

What was strange, though, was the way Archie hadn't been compelled to explain anything that had been going on with his sister. I mean, I knew it was personal and a family thing, but in the moment when he cracked and let me drive, that slip of his facade hadn't required any explanation. I think he knew that I knew what we were walking into.

But I didn't have time to dwell on that. The heavy steel door was in front of me, and for a split second, I almost doubted the courage that had gotten me this far. Or maybe it wasn't courage at all. Perhaps it was stubbornness. My mom would agree with that.

But I knew the truth of my own cowardice. And it wasn't winning today. I was going to see.

I pushed open the door with my left shoulder.

The hospital was cold. Sterile. Goose bumps prickled my arms.

I recognized Archie's dad before I saw anyone else, mostly because I saw Archie's similar features in his worn expression. "Mr. Morgan," I said, warning him of my approach with a soft introduction.

He was standing outside the door to a recovery room, staring motionless through the skinny rectangular window. He startled at my voice before clearing his throat.

"Oh. Hi. You must be Archie's Talia." He cleared his throat, a choking sound, again. "He said you brought him. Thank you."

"Of course," I said, not bothering to correct the title he gave me. I guessed in this context I was *Archie's Talia*.

Mr. Morgan kept looking through the glass pane, so I looked around the barren hallway and found a sad-looking chair opposite Addie's room. I walked across and sat down, folding my hands in my lap, trying to look anywhere but the door.

"Do you know why we're here?" Archie's father asked while still looking in on, presumably, his daughter, son, and wife.

I debated the best approach to answer. I settled on "Because Addie is hurt?"

"Because Adeline hurt *herself*." He corrected me, softly. I doubted he'd even spoken the words until he turned toward me, a shine in his eyes.

"It's not your fault," I whispered back because some part of me just *knew*. I knew from the stories I had heard from Archie and the way he spoke of his parents with such fondness that there was nothing they could have done to cause this.

Mr. Morgan started pacing the length of the hallway. "I should've known," he mumbled.

I leaned back and finally settled into the uncomfortable chair, figuring I wasn't leaving anytime soon. I crossed my arms and said, "You couldn't have. Not if she didn't want you to."

"I think it's clear as day now that this was a cry for help." He paused at the door and resumed his staring contest with the scene in his daughter's room.

"At least you heard," I said without looking at him.

"It's pretty hard not to take note when your youngest tries to kill themself."

There it was. The crass, hoarse, sharp, bitter words out in the open. He turned his back to the door and slid down until he sat on the floor, as if speaking those words left him weak and despondent.

He started crying.

There was something weird about adults crying. Like the world tipped on its axis and shattered any predisposed illusion that parents were once superheroes. And as tears flowed from their eyes, you realized they were just as miserably human as you.

Watching Archie's father cry, my chest caved for a man I barely knew. I rose from my chair and sank beside him, patting his shoulder with an awkwardness he barely detected.

"But your daughter is alive," I said quietly.

"I don't know what would happen to us if she wasn't." And the sorrow that coated his words slid through the broken parts inside me and slicked my gut with a sadness that felt alien. I don't know if my parents would have said the same things about me.

I sat beside Archie's dad as his head remained in his hands, and we both waited for the door to open.

When the heavy door screeched across the linoleum, I sprang to my feet, wiping my hands together and backing away from the family that emerged.

Well, half the Morgan family. Archie's hands were protectively around his mother's shoulders as he steered her out of the room. Her eyes were glossy, unfocused. His father remained where I had left him on the floor.

The door closed behind them with a soft thud. Archie lifted his chin just slightly to meet my eye and gave me the faintest of smiles that was anything but happy.

To me, in the nicest way possible, Archie was like a stick-in-the-mud. He could be rooted in his ways, but with a gentle tug, he was like a sidekick who could be pried away and wielded expertly as a makeshift wand, or sword.

I'd never realized that in any context other than my life, Archie wasn't a stick. That small smile told me he was the whole damn tree, roots and all, holding his family's world together when the rest of them were trying to sink into the ground.

"We're going to go get a coffee," he told me and then turned to Mr. Morgan. "Dad? Will you come with us?"

"I don't really want to leave her," he said to no one in particular.

"I'll stay," I offered automatically. Then I offered my hand to Archie's father to help him stand.

He stared at it a beat, then grasped my palm surely, mumbling a small form of thanks.

I felt a hand land briefly on my shoulder, so soft I thought it was an accidental brush from someone behind me until Archie spoke. "She had fallen into a coma from the blood loss when they found her in her bathroom," he whispered. "We're supposed to call for a nurse when she wakes up."

I stared, dumbstruck at Archie's mature, calm demeanor. He looked the same. Still messy brown hair, still wide and *beautiful* hazel eyes, but at the same time, this was a different man altogether from my best friend I thought I knew.

I managed a nod and repeated, "I'll stay."

The small smile reappeared, then vanished once more as he led his parents into the attached café. "No use watching her sleep. We aren't Edward Cullen after all," he said to them, and on any other day I might have chuckled at his sad attempt at a *Twilight* reference. Instead, something drew me through the door, toward Addie.

My hand was hot, and the cold metal of the door handle bit into it. I gripped tighter and checked to make sure Archie and his parents were out of sight. When I confirmed no one else was in the hall, I took a deep breath and pushed open the door.

The first thing I saw were the bandages. They wound their way like vines around her slender wrists.

The second stark realization was the blinding white of the room, which to be honest, I should have noticed first. The white walls, the white hospital sheets, the white gown, the whiteness to Addie's cheeks. And the white mummifying *bandages*.

I stepped closer to her and rested my forearms on the back of a chair.

Even with Addie's eyelids closed, it was easy to see the resemblance between her and her older brother. The same slope of their noses, the fullness to their lips, the soft texture to their brown hair. Addie's was laid neatly around her head, like a perfect halo.

Her arms were crossed around her center, completing the almost angelic image.

Except for the *bandages*.

Something caught my eye at the edge of the gauze. I leaned in closer, over the edge of the chair. Just above where the gauze and tape ended and just below her elbows were several crosshatched thin red lines. They varied in degree of thickness and redness and continued along her arm until they slipped beneath the white wrap and disappeared.

"Practice."

Addie's hoarse, croaking whisper made me jump, then yelp. Her eyes were open now. Her hazel eyes.

She blinked lazily and drew a breath. "You were looking at my scars," she explained.

I took a breath of my own to quiet the rattle in my chest. "They look new," I said instead of denying it.

"Some of them are," she said and lifted one of her arms to inspect herself. "But a lot of them have been opened again."

And again, and again, and in a way that said she had been determined to prevent them from healing.

I cleared my throat. "I had specific instructions to notify an Important Person That Works Here if you woke up on my watch."

"I don't want to answer any of their questions," she grumbled.

I took another look at the girl who was watching her arms, staring at them as if they weren't attached to her own body.

She looked so young. She was so young.

I sat down in the chair beside her and sighed. "Just promise me you'll pretend to be asleep if your brother comes back before a nurse comes and checks on us."

Addie finally shifted her gaze to study me instead of her limbs. Her unblinking eyes made the stare seem alien. "You know my brother," she said rather than asked.

I tried to look elsewhere, but my eyes kept wandering to her hands. They were currently resting back in their previous, peaceful folded state. "Mm-hmm," I confirmed.

She rolled her eyes, then shook her head.

"Saint Archie," she muttered and stared out the only window in the room. Outside, the sunset colors of fall were clinging to the last few days of their life. Several of their fallen comrades were lining the windowsill of the hospital room, fading from fiery ruby to a crispy, dead brown.

"Archie and I are very different," Adeline finally said. "As if that wasn't clear enough already."

She fixed her eyes back on me, and their heavy pull drew mine back to her. Her stare was intent, her voice clear when she spoke. "And since you're the one in here pretending like you don't want to ask me questions, I think it's safe to say that he's going to be lonely in heaven when people like you and me are partying in hell."

ARCHIE

PRESENT DAY

I could've spent an eternity in the back of my van with Talia tucked snuggly against my body, listening to the slow, even rhythm of her breath, the scent of her orange blossom soap tickling the edge of my nostrils as her silky hair brushed my cheek.

The movie had ended, and the crowds had cheered. The parking lot was bustling as families gathered their belongings and ushered their children back into their car seats. Yet Talia hadn't shifted from her seat in my lap. And I didn't dare make the move to leave first.

I would've wondered if she had fallen asleep if it wasn't for the slightest movement of her jaw when she asked, "Do you still want to risk capital crime and punishment tonight?"

"Depends," I asked, my voice still low and my mouth still close to her ear. "Are you willing to post my bail?"

"I'd get caught too, dumbass."

"I think you run faster than me."

"I wouldn't leave you."

Maybe it was because she already *had*, but it was crazy that the prospect of the bare minimum had me so thrilled at the thought. Romance wasn't dead after all.

Talia rushed to cover what was becoming an awkward pause. "But, yeah, I do need some more help on the mural tonight."

I finally removed my hand from her body to check my watch. "Crazy to think that when we would play wingman, we wouldn't have even left campus yet."

Talia touched my wrist gently to check the time herself. "At 9:40? I don't think I would have even started pregaming yet."

I faked a loud, obnoxious yawn. "I don't know. It's getting close to my bedtime."

She slapped my knee and unceremoniously began extricating herself from my car. "Too bad, Grandpa. We've got work to do."

I followed after her and saw Grady, Andrew, and Kathryn making their way out of their truck bed.

"Thank you for joining us," Kathryn said politely as Andrew helped her down.

"Thank you for the offer. Talia," Grady said pointedly at her, and she returned a playful smile.

"Your company is always a welcome pleasure, my friend."

"Much appreciated, but I'm afraid this is where I depart. I've got some buddies downtown that I'm going to meet out," Grady said and looked down at his phone. "My ride is about ten out."

"Who are you meeting?" I asked without thinking.

Grady shrugged. "People."

Grady was like the mayor; he knew everyone in town, and everyone adored him. Although this time, I wondered if his story was indeed true or if he was just aptly showcasing his skills as my own wingman, forcing proximity between Talia and me. Either way, a part of me was grateful.

"You sure you don't need a ride, man?" Andrew asked. "We pass through the city on our way home."

"Nah, all good. Though you two are welcome to join if you'd like. We're starting at Banks Mill," Grady offered to Andrew and Kathryn.

I didn't miss Kathryn's dark eyes slant toward Talia. "What do you think, Talia?"

Heat wove its way through the crook of my arm as Talia wound hers through mine, and I instinctively tightened her hand against my side. "Would love to, but we've got nefarious plans that require our attention."

Grady chuckled. "I figured as much. Catch you later, friends." He held his hand up in a mock salute but was already backing away toward the exit.

"I'll see you later at home?" Kathryn asked, her focus still on her friend.

Talia nodded. "But don't wait up."

My heart leapt, which was stupid. It was going to be a late night of painting at this rate since we hadn't even started. Nothing else was happening.

But at the same time, I didn't mind. I just liked it when I shared the same space in the same vacuum of time as Talia.

Andrew crossed the space between the two couples (at least, that's what it would have looked like to anyone watching us) and held his hand out to shake mine. His grip was strong and friendly. "Great to meet you, Archie. Hopefully, we'll see you around more."

I nodded. "Sure. I'd love that." And I meant it. I needed to get out more. And if I was being honest with myself, being back together with Kathryn, Grady, and Talia made a small hollow pit in my stomach long for the times we used to be together in college. Things were different now, for a lot of us, but maybe we could find a way back to that simplicity of friendship we all shared at one point. Maybe this attempt at adulting didn't have to be so complicated.

Maybe this time around, Talia would want to linger a little longer.

Andrew clapped my shoulder, then opened the passenger side door for Kathryn. "Until next time. You kids don't get into too much trouble tonight."

Talia made a theatrical roll of her eyes. "Yes, Mom and Dad."

Kathryn gave Talia and me the briefest of hugs, so light it might have been a breeze that touched our jackets instead.

"Bye, Kathryn," I said with a smile I couldn't help but inject with a shot of adoration. She wasn't all that different.

"Goodnight," she said and climbed into the truck that Andrew already had running.

We waved as they pulled out, Talia's arm still folded neatly against mine.

Talia looked up at me when the red flash of their taillights finally disappeared. "I'm assuming you're driving?"

"A correct assumption since my car is the last one standing."

"I could always drive for you."

I gently untangled our arms from each other, feeling the instant loss. With a coy smirk, I opened the driver's side door. "As you wish."

Talia's driving sucked. Like, truly horrendous, and it only took about ten minutes to remember why I had always driven the getaway car.

"Talia," I began calmly as she swerved away from yet another curb, "do you even have a driver's license?"

"Everyone has a driver's license," she replied and tapped the brakes twice as we neared a red light. "You've seen it."

"I've seen a few fake IDs from when we were in college," I replied. "Not sure if I ever saw the real thing."

She stopped abruptly at the light and turned to me. "Chinese fire drill if you don't believe me."

"Would you lie to me?" I asked.

She considered this. "Depends on your definition of lying."

The light turned green, casting an eerie glow across her cheekbones. She stomped on the gas, only to hit the brakes once more as she rode the tail of the car in front of her who didn't jet off like a rocket at the intersection.

"Lying is not telling the truth," I said.

"But you see, in the phrase *telling the truth*"—she gestured around the steering wheel and we slowly eked forward once more—"is an implication of language used to convey meaning. And there is language that's nonverbal, so even if my words don't *tell* the truth, some part of my body is going to tell you otherwise. Therefore, if someone knows me well enough, I can never lie."

I stared at her openly. "So you're saying you're an unlicensed driver behind my steering wheel right now."

Her grin was sly. "And I thought you were ready to commit crimes."

"Chinese fire drill if we get pulled over for drunk driving when neither of us are even drunk."

She chuckled and made another turn. "I have a license."

"I figured."

"But it's always good to check."

"You're still a terrible driver."

"Good thing we're almost there."

And thank god we were. One more turn and Talia had us parallel parking on the road next to the giant brick wall that displayed our handiwork from the night before.

Weirdly, Talia could parallel park really well.

I didn't bother dwelling on the walking oxymoron she was. "Where are your supplies?" I asked. I hadn't even thought about where they ended up the previous night before we had gone to Blue Elixir.

She closed the door behind her loudly. "I stashed them inside. Wait here. I'll be back."

And she dashed off into the darkness. I stared at the paint we had smeared across the building. The vague suggestion of a face still emerged from the shadows, and I wondered what our next steps would be.

"What's the story behind this piece?" I asked Talia when she reemerged with buckets of paint, brushes balancing precariously on top. I made a move from my perch on the edge of the curb, but she shook her head. She had things handled. Obviously.

She set the cans down gently, but the brushes clattered everywhere. She didn't pick them up but rather dusted her hands on her pants and folded her arms. "It's rather personal."

I looked at her looking at her work. "Is that your way of saying you don't know what you're working on?"

"I mean, I know what I want it to look like, and I know the feeling I want to get from it." She turned her head to the side, chin jutting ever so slightly as she studied it. "But I'm still waiting for it to speak to me."

"Is that normal? For paintings to speak to you?"

"Usually. Sometimes they shout. Other times, they whisper." Her voice dropped several octaves, echoing the soft quality of the word.

She pulled out a Swiss Army knife I had no idea she was carrying on her, or when she had gotten her own, and started opening her paints. "I hope you aren't too partial to your outfit."

I gave my graphic tee, jeans, and flannel a once over. "What's wrong with my outfit?"

"Nothing. But things might get messy around here," she said as she stayed bent to pop another lid.

"I'll be careful," I promised, and she paused, pouting.

"That's no fun."

This. This was what I had missed. The constant pull of Talia. Gently tugging me further and further from the comfort I would have so easily remained in the entirety of my life had I never met her.

As if to prove I could be *fun*, I closed the distance to her and swiped a stray brush. "Put me in, coach."

In a sweet, adoring fashion, she gave me a smile and took the brush back from me. "You can get the ladder instead. It's right inside the doorway."

I tried to give her a puppy dog sad face, but the expression wouldn't quite stick whenever I was around her. "Side door?"

"Side door," she confirmed as she lined up orange next to yellow, purple next to blue, and green next to white just below what would become her next masterpiece.

I couldn't help but chuckle at the old times and how things didn't change all that much, yet everything was different. This time, I decided I wasn't going to be afraid of what *might* happen next. Now I was just going to be present and not dwell or plan.

When I went through the side door, I was surprised to see so much of the building's skeleton exposed. It had an industrial feel to it, with pipes and beams and a few wires still on display in the empty lobby.

The ladder was resting right against the doorway, but there was also a pile of what looked like older blankets, similar to the ones I had just seen in the back of Andrew's truck, next to it.

"Talia," I began as I backed out of the door, banging the metal of the ladder against the metal of the doorway.

"Yes, dear?" she answered without looking back.

"You're not sleeping here, are you?" I asked, trying to keep the traces of concern from my voice, but I figured it still bled through.

She looked up then, quizzical. "No? I told you, I'm with Kathryn." Then she seemed to remember the lair constructed inside. "Oh. I did come by earlier to look at the mural in the light. I took a nap too."

I propped the ladder open. "A nap? In an abandoned building in the city?"

"I'm nothing if not authentic and dedicated to my craft."

"I can think of far better places to nap," I said, leaning against the ladder while I watched her make long strokes of swirling orange just above the figure's brow.

"Bridgeport's iconic coed dorm room 307?" she suggested, still consumed with perfecting her orange curl.

My elbow slipped off the ladder, and I stumbled a bit. I thought I heard her faint chuckle, but my mind was whirling. She had to have been thinking about it too. That one night, the only night, Talia and I had ever come close to jumping headfirst, nose-diving across that friendship line we had wordlessly etched into our mutual existence.

I had been thinking about it. In my car, her in my lap, her body in my hands. I had been remembering that one time I had her that close before. Why else would she bring up my dorm room if she wasn't replaying that night too? Wondering what might have happened had we ever spoken of it again.

But we never did.

Or maybe that was giving her too much credit.

"Hand me the yellow?" she asked, wiping the edge of her brush against the tin of orange paint before pounding the lid back on with her fist. Hard.

I bent to retrieve the yellow and balanced it expertly without letting the contents drip down the side of the can. "I liked room 307 just fine," I said. Lame. That was so lame.

She threw me a dazzling smile over her shoulder, her dark hair framing her grin. "Me too." And without cleaning the orange from her brush, she dipped it into the yellow and started highlighting the swirls she had already created, blending the sunset colors together.

I racked my brain for something to say in response, but I came up with nothing. I stepped away from the artist and her work. "Let me know if you need me to do anything else." And I plopped myself down on the curb to wait for further instruction.

She proceeded to ignore me for several more minutes while she stepped up and down the ladder, brushing orange and yellow streaks seemingly haphazardly above the gray portrait.

"Can I have the green?" she finally asked, her back still to me.

I obliged, embarrassingly quickly, leaping to my feet to fetch it for her.

"Thank you," she said, and once again flourished the Swiss Army knife.

"Remind me not to meet you in a dark alley," I said, eyeing her weapon.

She looked down at the pocketknife in her hand. "This?" She popped the lid in an expert move. "I prefer a different weapon for my self-defense."

"And what might that be?" I asked as she found a new, clean brush to dip into the green paint.

She looked at me, an impish gleam in her eye. "This."

And she whipped the rich emerald-green paint across my chest.

My Led Zeppelin T-shirt—a band I didn't really listen to, if I'm being honest—now featured a streak of green across the letters.

"You did not—"

She immediately flung more paint, this time grazing my nose.

"Talia!"

"I thought you wanted to be in on the action," she said, looking uncharacteristically innocent.

I swiped the back of my hand across my face, and it came away green. I held it up for her to see. "I didn't need to be painted Grinch green."

"You've always looked good in green."

I let out a long drawn-out sigh and gave one more glance at my now-painted shirt. I moved a touch slower than she had, plenty of time for her to shy away if she wanted to. But when I lifted my hand to wipe the paint back onto her cheek, she didn't move.

"Not as good as you," I gave up and said to her.

She smiled. "Touché." She turned to her mural again.

"I do wonder though"—I picked up another brush—"how hard it might be to get green out of your hair."

She whipped back to me, her startling blue eyes widened. "You wouldn't," she whispered, but I already had my brush dipped and raised toward her.

"Archie!" she shrieked and ran away from the wall, but not before I caught her shoulder in a smear of green.

"This is war!" she cried as she ran a circle back to me.

"I'm ready this time," I said, laughing, and planted my feet wide to brace myself for her attack.

Paint brush raised high, she battle cried loudly for all the night to hear and catapulted into me. I caught her mid-leap around her waist and stumbled back, but we didn't fall. On the collision, her brush slid down the length of my arm.

"Biggest hit," she panted, her grin wild and so close to mine. One of her arms was still wrapped around my shoulder. "I think that means I win."

I tightened my grip around her waist and raised my own brush to the sliver of space between our rising chests. I dragged the tip of my brush slowly and deliberately to draw the letter X just under her left collarbone, above her heart. "Close," I murmured. "But I got the kill shot."

And the moment was so perfect, too good to ignore, though a thousand questions and a million doubts flickered through my mind. But right now, with Talia's open mouth staring up at mine, her body flush against my side, I knew I would regret moving away.

So instead, I dropped my paintbrush to the ground.

I brought my hand up to cup her cheek.

She stilled beneath my touch, but she didn't back away from it. I let my thumb drop to trace the edge of her bottom lip, watching my own movement rather than looking at her eyes, for fear that she was looking at me like I was crazy.

And then I lowered my mouth to hers.

TALIA

PRESENT DAY

A rchie was kissing me. Archie Morgan was *kissing* me.
And Archie Morgan could *kiss*.

He kissed with his whole body. And I let him.

I let his tongue coax my mouth open and sweep into mine. His lips pressed against mine with a pressure that took me by surprise, but then I welcomed it.

At some point I dropped my paintbrush, and both of my hands wound through his short crop of dark hair and tightened, holding his mouth to mine.

ARCHIE

PRESENT DAY

When Talia threaded her delicate fingers into my hair, the remainder of my questions obliterated themselves in an explosive fashion. I took my hand from her face and pressed the heels of both my hands into her hips. Without breaking the kiss, I turned her back to the brick wall and stepped into the space that still lingered between us, pushing her backward.

TALIA

PRESENT DAY

This was nothing like before. The only other time I had ever known what Archie's mouth felt like, it had been slow. Tentative. Cautious. *This* was hot.

My back hit the wall, and if there were any more rational thinking left in my body, it got rattled away. I *felt* the heat in my own chest explode, and I *heard* my own gasp as I wrenched my mouth free to catch my breath. I wanted to cry when I felt the fire of Archie's mouth below my jaw and then biting into my skin where my neck hit my shoulder.

My hands left the back of his head, skimmed over his shoulders, down his back, and found his belt loops on his jeans. In one swift move, I hooked a finger through each loop by his hips and gave them a sharp tug, pulling him into me.

ARCHIE

PRESENT DAY

My hips crashed into Talia's, and my teeth grazed her collar as I managed the words "Tell me you want me."

Her hands skimmed under the fabric of my shirt, her palms wide against my sides as she gripped me back. She turned her face back into mine and caught my mouth in a kiss that echoed the way I had been moving mine into hers.

"You know I do," she said against my mouth.

I kissed her back with a desperate fervor. "I need to hear you say it," I said. "I need to hear you say the words, Talia."

"I—" I caught her bottom lip with my teeth and tugged. She gave the smallest of moans, so quiet I would put money on the fact she didn't mean to make the sound.

I pressed my cheek against hers, and with my mouth at her ear, I said, "Tell me you want this."

TALIA

PRESENT DAY

Of course I wanted this.
I *needed* this.

Archie withdrew his face from mine, just enough so that our noses brushed each other. I could barely see what color his eyes were this close. "Tell me, Talia."

His voice was so low, quiet, pleading. *He* needed me to admit it.

"Archie," I said, "I want you."

I felt the relief flood through his body, and he sank back into me. "Side door?" he asked, the corner of his mouth pulling up into a smirk. *Goddamn. Archie was sexy.*

"Side door," I replied, suddenly breathless.

I don't know when or how his hands moved, but suddenly one was slipping into mine, and he gripped my fingers with a tenderness I hadn't expected.

And he led me toward the door, gently tugging me after him until we reached it and he turned toward me. He opened the door with his one free hand and backed into the building, eyes on me the entire time.

"You can still change your mind," he said.

I gently pushed him through the door, and we both tripped awkwardly as it closed behind us, plunging us into near darkness. His hand reached out to the wall and fumbled, presumably for a light, but I reached forward and grasped his wrist. "Leave it. I'm not changing my mind."

His arms went freely around me, my chest colliding once again with his. This kiss was a frenzy. Wild, consuming, *hungry*.

ARCHIE

PRESENT DAY

I moved my hands lower until they gripped the bottom of her shirt. "Can we get rid of this?"

Her mouth went to my neck, and I felt her smile grow against my skin. "Please."

I pulled it over her head in one clean movement.

Her body was unchanged and perfect. And I moved my mouth over her neck, down the slope of her collarbone, kissing the dried paint on her chest until I dipped my lips lower, over every inch I could find.

She pulled back and grasped the open buttons of my flannel and tugged it off my shoulders. "Your turn," she said.

I smiled in the dark.

She pulled my shirt all the way off, tossing it aside.

I gathered her close again and snaked my arm around her back to hook my fingers in the strap of her bra. "This too?"

She paused. She lifted her eyes cautiously to mine, and I sucked in a breath, wondering what happened, if I had done something wrong to make her still.

Ever so painfully slowly, she turned around and swept her hair from her back over one shoulder, baring her bra and her spine to me. And when she moved her hair to the side, my eyes had adjusted to the room enough to make out the shape of a small tattoo at the base of her neck. A delicate outline of a simple pair of wings.

I couldn't help it. My fingers seemed to have a mind of their own when they inched up and grazed the edge of the ink.

I didn't recognize the low, strained quality of my own voice when I rasped, "When did you get this?"

TALIA

PRESENT DAY

He was bound to see it at some point soon the way this evening was progressing. I shuddered underneath the whisper from the pads of his fingers as they caressed the tattoo. If he never stopped touching me like this, I could die happy.

"Right after I left," I said, equally as soft as the strokes his fingers traced on my back.

At that admission, his hands left my back, and his arms wrapped around my waist, pulling me flush against him in a sharp tug. I gasped.

His mouth was hot on my ear. "Why?" One hand left my waist and slipped up the space between us to unbuckle the clasp of my bra with one snap.

"Because"—his hands slid the straps down my shoulders, inch by slow miserable inch—"I wanted to remember."

I turned to him as my bra hit the floor. The chill of the air had goose bumps spreading across my back, and I pressed my chest into the heat emanating from his before leaning on the tips of my toes to kiss him again.

ARCHIE

PRESENT DAY

"Did you think I would be so easy to forget?" I asked before I thought better of it. I didn't want her to hear the potential truth behind her answer.

She dropped to her knees and tugged me down after her so that we were both kneeling on the blanket she had stowed in the building. "No," she said as she slipped her hands under my T-shirt and trailed them across my chest before I helped her take the shirt off over my head. "But I wasn't willing to take that chance."

My arms went around her once more, and gently, I leaned her onto her back so that I was straddled on top of her. I moved my lips from her chest, back up her throat until I caught her mouth once more.

Her hands traveled across my chest, over my shoulders, down my back, until they found the waistband of my jeans again. A small, guttural noise escaped my throat as she slipped a finger along the edge, teasing small movements as they dipped inside then retreated.

Until she brought them to the button resting between us.

"Fuck," I said and ripped my mouth away from Talia's, steadying myself with my hands on of her hips.

"What's wrong?"

"I—I don't have anything on me."

"What, Archie Morgan isn't the type of man to carry a condom in his wallet?" she joked.

I glared at her. "Really?"

She rolled her eyes in a dramatic fashion that rolled her whole head around on the blanket, spreading her hair even wider. She had never looked more beautiful. "Of course not. You're the perfect gentleman." She bit her lip and dropped her gaze to my chest once more before looking back up at me through her eyelashes. "I'm still on birth control."

It took me a few beats too long to register her words, but I didn't stop my thumb from moving circles on her hip as I digested what she had said. And what she was suggesting.

"And," she continued when my pause proved too long, "there hasn't been anyone in a while."

"Me neither," I whispered.

"Besides Lex," she said, which caught me off guard. I expected a sharp squint of her eye or a firm retort to the comment. But there was nothing. She said those two words with as little emotion as she could, a guard so thick I had an overwhelming, crazy sudden urge to comfort her.

I smoothed the hair from her face and bent to kiss her forehead.

"Talia," I said, slipping a hand behind her back, pulling her to me again. "There's never been anyone but you."

TALIA

PRESENT DAY

Kathryn was in the kitchen early Saturday morning making something for breakfast that smelled like pancakes. The scent sucker punched me with an extra dose of nostalgia, and here came the waterworks. Again.

My eyes had welled with entirely too many tears in the past few hours, and the thought of how weak I had been made me draw the couch comforter over my chin, burrowing deeper into the softness of Kathryn's cushions.

"I know you're awake," Kathryn said over the sizzle of her griddle. "Let me know when you want coffee."

"I don't want the life juice yet," I said through the covers, muffling my words. The mess I was currently making of my life seemed entirely too difficult to face coherently.

I had a burning regret deep in my core that kept me awake most of the night, staring at the ceiling, replaying last night with Archie as if it were on a repeat reel, a silent movie, just actors and bodies, no voice to say, *Stop. You're lying.*

But the worst part was, it wasn't entirely a lie. I hadn't lied to Archie when his eyes pleaded desperately as he asked if I wanted him. I wanted him with an ache so deep that my chest hurt at the thought of his lips on mine, leaving kisses all over my body. It hurt to think about the way he felt, the way he sounded, the way he made me feel like a firework exploded deep within me. The way he made me feel *alive*.

But last night made me realize just how hard it was to make *myself* feel like that.

Happiness is a choice was my mother's favorite line when I was in high school. *And you are choosing not to be, Natalia.* As if it were that easy of a concept. But what she didn't know, what *no one* knew, was how hard I fought to keep choosing, to keep trying, to get *just this much*.

And the worst part was, it wasn't enough.

And I was tired.

Last night with Archie stood in stark contrast to the *drowning* feeling in my gut as I sank lower into the couch, holding my arms around my center.

The Diagnosis was right. There was something deeply, inherently, and overwhelmingly wrong with me.

And I realized the unbearable truth that morning: I couldn't give Archie what he wanted. He wanted *me*; that part was clear. But in giving him that, I would be giving him something that was broken.

That thought split the dam inside me. It exploded in a horrible-sounding sob as I started to cry.

I cried in a way I hadn't let myself in years. Like all the sadness I had been carefully avoiding and replacing with numbness for too long erupted in a snotty, whining wail, and I couldn't stop it.

"Talia?" Kathryn's voice was laced with a note of sudden concern, a tone I'd never heard from her before. And then she was with me on the couch, kneeling in front of me, gathering my shoulders in her arms. "Hey. Hey, come here. It's okay."

I sat up and let her pull me into a hug. I buried my face into her shoulder and let the tears continue to flow, my back shaking from the weight of them.

"Whatever he did, I'm going to kill him," she muttered as one hand rubbed my back. Right under the tattoo she didn't know I had. Over and over again.

Through a series of hiccups, I managed, "He didn't—do any—thing."

"Oh yes," she said. "That's why you're currently a blubbering mess the morning after he dropped you back home."

"It's … me," I said miserably.

She continued to rub my back. "Well then, what did you do?"

"I came back!" I sat up and dragged the back of my hand across my nose. "I should've never … come back."

"I would beg to differ on that one."

"Kathryn," I whimpered and then paused. I had no idea where to start. It was all too much. Everything was too much. I settled with "I hooked up with Archie."

She nodded, as if this weren't earth-shattering news to her. "Okay. And this is a problem … why?"

I groaned and burrowed under the blankets once more, my crying turning less uncontrollable and tantrum-like. Just more pathetic. "Because. He deserves someone whole." Someone I didn't know how to be. Someone I simply *wasn't*. "I think there's something really wrong with me."

I looked at Kathryn then, my eyes swimming. Hers were laser focused, and for the first time since I'd known her, she looked worried. In a voice so small it couldn't have been mine, I said again, "Kathryn, something is wrong with me."

And instead of arguing the point like I expected she would, she stayed silent, that vigilant look still in her eye. Like she was looking back over all the years she had known me and reflecting on my statement.

And she didn't deny it.

NATALIA

THE DIAGNOSIS

I was seventeen when I was diagnosed with F33.1 major depressive disorder, recurrent, moderate. Or simply put: long-term, shitty depression.

It started with a simple college counseling appointment that was required for all seniors in my high school. I hadn't the faintest idea of where I wanted to go or what I wanted to study.

That's not entirely true. I knew what I would have liked to study. I knew the thing that I was most passionate about in the world.

"Have you thought about what you're going to write for your personal essay for your college application?" Ms. Mikayla asked. And yes, she went by her first name. It made her "relatable" and "approachable," or so she said upon our first introduction.

I shrugged. I had made the mistake of bringing up the whole *what should I major in* conversation with my parents over breakfast that morning.

"So I've been thinking," I had started as I poured my pancake batter onto the griddle I had gotten for myself for my birthday that month. "I think I really want to study art in college."

Like a character out of a cartoon, my father had spit his coffee out across the kitchen table. He coughed and sputtered, "Art? You want to doodle for your degree? Shouldn't you want to be a doctor?"

He was a doctor. And when I was younger, I swore off the job for myself because all I saw it bring home was anger and frustration when the hospital days wore on him. On those days I watched my mother take the brunt of his burnout. Or sometimes, he didn't come home at all.

"That's not my thing," I said.

"Well you better learn to make something of value your *thing*, Natalia. We've spent a lot of money on a private school education thus far; I don't intend for you to waste it."

As if that were the issue. Money was never the problem. My parents had plenty of it to go around. It was more what their country club friends would say if their daughter didn't rise to the title or rank expected of all the children in the neighborhood.

So when Ms. Mikayla, in her preppy Lilly Pulitzer sundress, asked me about my applications, the whole *what do you want to be when you grow up* thing soured in my stomach, and I couldn't give her an answer.

"Please tell me you at least know what a personal essay is," she said with a kind smile and a lifted eyebrow.

"I know what it is," I said as I sat across from her, drumming my fingers against the desk. *Tap, tap, tap. Tap, tap, tap.* "I just don't think I have anything noteworthy to write about."

"Why do you think that is?"

"Because my dad pretty much said that this morning."

"What exactly did he say?"

I sighed deeply and sat back in my seat, folding my arms. "It wasn't what he said, more how he said it. I don't know …. It just made me feel guilty for wanting something so much for myself. Like what I want is worthless. Does that make me worthless technically?"

I asked the question as a joke, but I realized too late how it must have sounded based on the look on Ms. Mikayla's face.

"Is this the only time you've felt this way?" she asked gently. "Or is this a recurring thought?"

That wasn't the first or the last time she had asked me something similar.

In another session, she asked me about my friends, or lack thereof, which I thought at the time was a rather personal interrogation for a counselor who was supposed to counsel me on my career, not my social calendar.

Another time, when I accidentally nodded off during the bit where we were researching medical schools, she asked if I had been getting enough sleep. It was an innocent enough question. But I told her sleep was hard for me. It came and went, and sometimes I just lay still in my bed, staring at the ceiling of my room until my vision would blur. I also made the mistake of saying I didn't mind when the world was blurry. It was easier to be a little bit numb sometimes, you know?

After about two months of meeting once a week, Ms. Mikayla called my house phone. I had been home sick with the flu, and I guessed no one had told Ms. Mikayla I was absent. I was sitting at the kitchen table wrapped in a blanket and could hear the static of her voice on the other end of the line when my mom answered the phone.

"Well, thank you for checking in on her, but I can assure you that Natalia will be perfectly fine in a few days. She looks forward to your next meeting," my mom said politely as she was chopping vegetables for chicken soup.

"While I have you, Mrs. Scott, there are a few things I would like to discuss with you about your daughter." I froze.

My mom laughed, a sound that was anything but humorous. "Have her test scores not been to standard? I can assure you the time spent with the SAT tutor after school has not been wasted."

"Natalia's test scores are fine," Ms. Mikayla said. "But a few behaviors from her have me concerned …."

I think I started to black out, but not before I heard the words *isolation*, *insomnia*, and *indecisiveness*, among other notes that I hadn't realized she had been making.

"Have you noticed any of this behavior before at home?" I heard her ask.

My mom's knife slipped off the carrot she was cutting with a loud thud against the cutting board. "Of course not. My child is fine."

"That may be, but in the event that is not the case, there are several mental health providers in the area who I think could benefit your daughter."

"Why would you think she needs that?" My mom's voice was rising, and I wanted to shrivel up on the spot.

"As I said, ma'am, she is showing behavioral signs that have me concerned ...."

"I'm going to stop you right there, Ms. Williams. You are out of line bringing this up to me in this manner."

I turned away from the eavesdropping and chose to actively ignore the phone call. I thought about retreating to my room, but that would probably make matters worse when my mom confronted me after the call.

It would look as though I had something to hide.

The voices continued back and forth until my mother finally said, "Okay fine, we will see a shrink, and she will prove to you there is nothing wrong. Good day, ma'am."

And then she hung up the phone.

She looked squarely at me. "Do you have anything you'd like to say about this?"

"I was having trouble with my personal essay," I mumbled.

My mother's voice rang shrill and clear as she spoke to me. "And who all did you tell about this? This ... supposed problem of yours?"

I suddenly felt a spike of anger. She wasn't worried about me in the slightest.

She was worried about what other people would think.

"We're settling this matter as soon as possible," she said as she started flurrying around the kitchen. "I'm getting you that appointment, and we'll never have to speak of this again. Understood?"

I bit the inside of my cheek hard until I drew blood. I nodded.

We went to a clinical mental health counselor two days later.

Apparently, I had the majority of the symptoms for major depressive disorder.

My mom was bitter and silent as we left the appointment with a diagnosis and a suggestion to return once more that week.

"We have to figure out what to tell your father. He's going to know we were here. Now, thankfully, insurance will cover this appointment, but he's not going to know what to do with this information."

"Because I'm officially broken?" I asked, staring out the window as she cranked the engine.

"You're not broken," she said calmly as she backed out of the parking spot, leaving the clinic behind. If I hadn't known better, I might've thought she intended some sort of comfort with that statement. But I knew my mother. She continued, "You can't be broken. He doesn't believe in all that psychobabble bullshit."

The explosion came out of nowhere. She slammed the steering wheel and yelled, "Damn it, Natalia! What is so bad in your life? Hmm? Tell me. Tell me what has made you *so* depressed?"

I knew better than to say anything.

She pressed on. "It really is such a selfish thing to do. And how dare you? Do you think this is funny? Do you think this is a joke? What is *so* bad that you can't handle?"

"N-nothing," I replied when it became clear she was looking for an actual answer.

"Damn right. Nothing." I could see her jaw clenched from my peripheral vision. "I've got way bigger problems than your childish mind could ever imagine. And if I can't fall apart, then neither can you."

Her words echoed into the deepest recesses of my mind. *If I can't fall apart, then neither can you .... I can't fall apart. Neither can you .... I can't fall apart .... Can't fall apart.*

And for the first time in my life, I was in my mother's shoes. I had heard every argument, every fight, every hateful word my parents had spat at each other when they thought I wasn't listening. But I never imagined the unpredictable rage or frustration directed squarely at me. My childhood had been like secondhand smoke exposure: I simply bore witness but still ended up with the cancer of mistrust and crippling independence. But I supposed I never felt the hit of the toxin quite as deeply as my mother and father took in. Not exactly.

And just like that, crumbling underneath the weight of my feelings was no longer an option.

We were quiet as we drove home, away from the clinic, away from the problem my mother couldn't solve by baking something Southern with an insane amount of sugar and spice and a smile so sickly sweet you have to look away before you get stuck.

I stared out the car window as we drove, looking at nothing. Feeling nothing.

I was seventeen when I made the mistake of listening to her.

I was seventeen when I chose to ignore The Diagnosis.

PART THREE

ARCHIE

JUNIOR YEAR

By the time I was legally allowed to drink, Blue Elixir stopped carding altogether, which quite frankly was a bit of a letdown to actually turning twenty-one.

The bigger letdown was that Talia had invited Boyfriend Justin to accompany us on what was supposed to be my twenty-first birthday and "The Grand Slam Wingman Event," per Talia. And yes, I was used to the ridicule from her—the burden that was my virginity was incredibly heavy on the both of us, or so she said.

It's not that I wasn't interested in sex. It's more that I had known the girls in my high school since second grade, having all grown up together. And then since college, I couldn't find anyone who compared to Talia in my eyes.

But as I watched Justin sling his arm over her shoulder from their side of the booth, I knew she was clearly off the table. And yes, since Justin had started joining our weekly wingman excursions, we had migrated from the bar to the corner booth, another unwelcome change to our routine.

"How's your sister doing, man?" Justin asked innocently enough as he took a deep drink from his bottle. Talia visibly stiffened beside him, but he didn't seem to notice. Talia, however, did notice when I went rigid and something in my jaw ticked tight. She looked uncomfortable.

"What do you mean?" I managed through gritted teeth.

This man was truly oblivious if he hadn't realized the abrupt shift in the atmosphere surrounding our trio. He continued, "Talia was telling me about her the other day and just got me thinking I don't know much about you. She said she went through a bit of a tough time last year?"

The pregnant pause that filled the table weighed down on us.

Justin continued, "I hope she's doing better."

Talia made a point of not looking at me, staring instead at the condensation on her glass. My voice was cold when I spoke, and weirdly, I didn't regret the words or the tone that came out of my mouth. "Well, I'm not sure why Talia thought that talking about private family matters was a good way to bring you and I closer together, Justin. But since you asked, yes. She seems to be doing better."

He really was stupid. He beamed. "That's great! Glad to hear it! Seems like that change of schools was all she needed then?"

I glared once more at the top of Talia's head, wondering what else she'd told him. "Yep," I said flatly. "Problem solved."

Justin raised his glass. "To Archie's little sister! Next round is on me then."

I gave a polite smile. "I'm afraid I'll have to leave the two of you for the next round. I'm going to go sit at the bar for a bit."

Justin reached across the table and thumped my shoulder in what I assumed was bro fashion. "Attaboy. Don't even need a wingman. Go get 'em, tiger."

I raised my glass to him in salute before chugging the remainder and slamming it down on the table. I didn't even bother to look at Talia before I stalked over to my usual seat at the bar. I only made it halfway there through the winding maze of pool tables before I heard the commotion of Talia bounding out of the booth behind me.

"Archie, wait up. Please."

"I'd rather not."

"Just stop, okay? Let me explain."

Not an apology. Not an *I'm sorry for spilling something that was incredibly personal to you to someone who is trying to sleep with me.* No, just an explanation. Or a justification.

I wheeled around to face her. "Talia, nothing about Addie is your story to tell."

She crossed her arms, defiant. "I wasn't trying to tell someone else's story."

"But you did."

"But I was there too."

"But Addie is the one who is sick!" I shouted, exasperated at her ignorance. "And it needs to be her choice who knows. No one else."

Talia's voice dropped, and she couldn't meet my eyes. "I never said she was sick."

My anger continued to rise. "So what exactly did you say?"

She opened and closed her mouth a few times, visibly fumbling for the words.

I pressed on. "More importantly, *why* did you say anything?"

"Because I was trying to talk to him about *me*," she said, and I could see a dampness start to form in her eyes. "Something about me I don't talk to anyone about."

I shook my head. "Typical."

"What did you say?" she asked, her voice rising.

I stood my ground and looked her square in the eye. "I said it was typical, Talia. Making this about you instead."

It wasn't fair of me to say, and part of me instantly regretted the hateful words that I knew would shut her down. But before I could say anything, or take them back, tears sprung from her lashes, and she angrily wiped them away.

"You know what, Archie? Go. Go on with yourself and go find a way to get laid. Lord knows you need it. I'm done for tonight." And then she spun away.

Unfortunately, a bigger part of me was still hurt and couldn't let her have the last word. "Good! Me too. Have fun with GQ."

The retort was lame, but I didn't give myself time to think about it. I turned and climbed the three steps to the bar and sat myself down, folding my arms in front of me.

A Michelob Ultra appeared, and I was grateful to the bartender. The look on his face was coy. "Trouble in paradise?"

I picked up the bottle graciously. "There would have to be a paradise in order for there to be trouble in it."

The bartender—I didn't know his name, even after years of serving us—nodded to himself as he started drying cups from the dishwasher. "Girls are all the same, aren't they?"

I sipped the beer. "What do you mean?"

He jutted his chin toward Talia and Justin in the corner. "You two obviously have feelings for each other. But that dude's with her now. Why is that?"

I tried to resist the urge to look over my shoulder. I knew what I would see. But for some reason I felt like torturing myself and stole a glance. Talia was tucked snugly against Justin's side, laughing at something he said. "Couldn't tell you."

"Because she's a chickenshit."

I looked up at him, surprised, figuring that if he were going to call anyone *chickenshit*, it would have to be me.

He continued, "You guys are friends, right?"

"Yeah." I figured that much was pretty obvious.

"*Best* friends?" he asked, and I knew he was poking fun, but for some reason I couldn't help but take it personally.

I bristled. "Well, yes."

He chuckled. "Guys and girls can't be best friends. Not without one of them getting feelings. And most often, it's the girl that freaks out and shuts down any potential budding relationship because they're afraid it would mess things up."

I thought about it from his outside perspective and wondered if he thought that was really true of Talia. I had always thought it was probably the other way around. But what if this bartender was right?

I shrugged. "I doubt it. Even if you were right at one point, it looks like I lost my chance."

"Give it time," he said and slid me one more bottle, even though the one I was still nursing had plenty left. "On the house. Go have some fun."

I harrumphed. "Thanks."

Like a scene from a movie, the beautiful redhead, Lex Carver—whom I had met freshman year, the very first time Talia pretended to be my wingman—sat down directly across from me.

I had seen Lex around campus a few times. Our interactions were polite and uneventful, but I hadn't seen her out at Blue Elixir in years. Lex was looking around the bar, trying to catch the bartender's eye to order a drink. I looked down at the brand new, just opened, untouched bottle sitting in front of me.

It seemed too good to be true. The Archie a few months ago would have let the opportunity slide. Tonight was different though. Drawing up whatever courage I had resting inside me, I picked up both bottles and walked over to the other side of the bar.

"This seat taken?" I asked Lex, cringing at the cheesy line but determined to forge ahead with my plan.

She jumped a little, surprised at my voice behind her. She spun to face me, and her expression warmed. "Archie! Hi, no it's all yours."

I gave her a smile that I hoped looked way more confident than I was feeling and slid the bottle in front of her. "For you."

She eyed the beer with gratitude. "You come prepared."

"I also come with an apology. For the last time we hung out here. And then ... after." I grimaced. I hated bringing up that night from freshman year where I made out with her and then ran away. But the elephant needed to be shoved out of the room if we were going to keep talking tonight. And I quite literally had nothing to lose.

She brushed it off. "Please, Archie, that was so long ago. Don't even worry about it." Her smile was kind, and I felt my shoulders relax on their own accord.

"Regardless, first round on me. Obviously. Then I can find us a pool table if you'd like to play?"

Her whole face lit up. "I've always wanted to play, but I didn't think I would be very good."

I raised my glass to her, and she lifted hers as well. With a light clink against her bottle, I said, "Well, fortunately for you, I happen to be a regular here, and I might be able to give you a few pointers so that you could reach my level of subpar."

Lex laughed, a sound strangely genuine and delicate. She took a drink from her beer, then stood. "You drive a hard bargain, Archie Morgan. Lead the way."

I felt Talia's eyes on my back when I played pool with Lex. Particularly the part where I corrected her stroke and, together, we successfully sank her eight ball and won her the game.

I chose to ignore Talia for once.

"You just helped me win," Lex said looking back at me.

I shrugged. "Maybe."

"That means you lost."

"Did I?" I asked with a half grin. I barely recognized myself in this interaction. "I guess you got my birthday luck instead of me."

Lex spun, mouth open and eyes wide. "It's your birthday? And you didn't say anything?"

I chuckled. "It's nothing special."

"How old are you?"

"Twenty-one."

"Archie!" She cried. "This is huge! I can't believe you didn't tell me."

I kept laughing at her outburst. "I'm sorry?"

"Oh my god, I have to make this up to you. Let's go to the bar."

And the next thing I knew, Lex was racking our cues and all but pushing me back up the stairs.

My bartender saw us coming and gave me a knowing smirk. "Ready for another?"

I opened my mouth to answer, but Lex jumped ahead, cutting me off. "We're here for a blowjob shot. One each. It's his birthday."

My eyebrows must have skyrocketed through my hairline based on the laugh I got from my new friend behind the bar. "Some birthday present she's giving you, buddy."

I felt my face turn a nice shade of tomato on Lex's account, but she didn't seem to notice. Rather, she told the bartender, "He's got no idea what's in store for him." And then she winked. She fucking winked.

He turned and started to mix the shots together for us, topped with a dollop of whipped cream on each one.

My face was still burning as I moved to pick up the shot glass in front of me. Lex gently stopped me with her slender fingers around my wrist.

"Uh-uh," she teased, and she moved my hand behind my back. "No hands."

I must have still looked confused, for she clasped her own hands behind her back and bent over the bar, wrapping her mouth around the glass. In one perfected maneuver, she gripped the glass with her lips and threw her head back, tipping the shot down her throat.

"Woo! Your turn!" Her grin was wild, and there was a bit of whipped cream left on the edge of her mouth. Her tongue flicked at it.

"I can't believe you're making me do this," I said, shaking my head, but I was already leaning down to the glass. I tipped it back with way less expertise and choked down the shot.

We were both laughing as she handed the bartender her credit card and suggested that we get out of the bar and go someplace together.

I didn't look in Talia's direction as Lex slipped her arm into mine, leading me out the front door. Instead of calling a taxi service, we walked the two miles back to campus, both of us warm with laughter.

This time, when we got back to her dorm room, I didn't stop her when we started kissing.

I didn't stop her when our clothes slowly started coming off, one article at a time.

In fact, I might have escalated the process when she reached for her jeans and I shimmied her out of them myself.

"I need to tell you something," I whispered between kisses against her skin.

"Hmm?" she asked the question as barely a moan.

"I haven't done this before." I could have been bashful about it. I could have made the statement apologetic. But Archie 2.0 was taking a page out of Talia's handbook and doing everything with confidence, even if it meant owning up to my own inexperience to one of the most stunning girls I had ever encountered.

And strangely, I think it worked. Her gaze turned endearing, and she placed her hand on my chest. With a gentle push, she said, "It's okay. I can show you."

ARCHIE

PRESENT DAY

Lunchtime on Saturday came and went, and I thought that, surely by now, I would have heard from Talia regarding the night before. I would have sworn she would reach out to lecture me about the work she still had to do at the building, paints abandoned for our other endeavor.

I sat on the couch with my family in the living room, watching some rerun of a show my dad loved and the rest of us tolerated. Saturday afternoons like these were becoming one of the only times during the week when all our schedules took a breath, and we could relax in the same space together.

But now that the show had ended, my mom and dad drifted toward their afternoon chores. I bounced my knee as I sat, agitated.

Addie walked from the kitchen into the living room and plopped down beside me. "What's got you so worked up?"

I flipped my phone over, face down on the cushion, hiding the nonexistent message. "Nothing."

Addie eyed the phone pointedly. "Waiting on a call?"

I grumbled and admitted, "I wish I wasn't."

"You were out pretty late last night," she pressed. "I'm assuming with our mutual friend?"

I didn't deny it but gave another disjointed grunt and folded my arms in front of me.

"You know, I don't think I ever actually asked her why she was even stopping back in town," Addie said.

The way she phrased the statement made my heart seize and fall down a few stories inside me. *Stopping back in town.* "She's committing a crime."

"Really?"

"Not sure honestly. She's working on a mural by the college."

"Like, graffiti?"

"Looks like it."

Addie pondered this. "Well, that's probably where she is now then. Should we go see her?"

"Probably not." She probably wasn't working in broad daylight, and even if she were, there was no way I was taking my little sister to the scene of the crime, where the memory of Talia's body was imprinted on my mind.

"You should go check it out and see if you can catch her."

Catch her. Like she could be blown away into the wind.

But I had quite literally nothing else to do. And to be fair, I didn't know what the mural looked like in the sunshine.

I could blame it on that curiosity, I thought, as I stood up to find my shoes.

"Tell her I said hi!" Addie said as she folded her legs underneath herself on the couch. "Or bye. Whichever it is this time."

"She's not leaving," I said abruptly, earning a lift of an eyebrow from my sister. But even as I said those words, I wondered whether they were true.

Talia was always poised for flight. She wasn't one to stay grounded. And me, I barely knew how to spread my own wings. I couldn't, even if I wanted to. And as I grabbed my keys and went for the door, I realized how scared I was of making a free fall without her.

TALIA

PRESENT DAY

I was behind schedule, which spurred panic. Before coming back, I rarely kept a schedule. The concept felt foreign. But I was supposed to be putting the finishing touches on the mural already. I left last night barely at the halfway point.

After the midmorning meltdown in Kathryn's arms, I put myself together and drove to the site, determined to make some headway on the vision in my mind that kept dancing rudely away.

I had been at it a few hours when I heard the familiar rumble of Archie's van rolling up to the curb. Honestly, I was shocked I hadn't heard from him sooner, but glad because I wasn't ready to face the aftermath of what we did last night—and the breakdown I had this morning.

But I knew this conversation was going to be inevitable. I stood and ran my hands down the front of my paint-splattered jeans as I heard Archie approach.

When I turned to him, he wasn't looking at me. Rather, he stood awestruck, if I dared describe his expression as that, as he looked up at the brick wall behind me.

"Wow," he said, staring.

I turned, too, really looking at my work for the first time since I had started today. The portrait was finally starting to come together, but the hair had taken up most of the day. Vibrant oranges and yellows were the base for long curls that looked like they were caught by an invisible wind. Lines of greens made the thick curls look *alive*. They twisted like vines through the existing colors and wrapped around the figure's left ear before trailing down its neck, over the exposed collarbone, and wrapping taut around its shoulder.

It looked like a wild woodland being. Feral. And it felt strangely personal.

"Looks good," he said, and I glanced over at him. He had his hands stuffed into his pockets and a weird little shy grin on his face. My heart sank even further at the sight. Even on the steps of an unknowing demise, he was still somehow both my weakness and strength. But I couldn't rely on him that way. Not again. Not anymore. Not ever.

"Thanks," I said simply, but the word was tight in my throat. I gripped my paintbrush with my entire fist and raised it once more to continue layering the wall.

"So what's the plan for tonight?" Archie asked from behind me, but he didn't come any closer. Maybe he felt the tension in the air, or maybe I was just imagining his caution. The space between us acted as a vacuum, pulling me back to last night. His body. His mouth. His words. *Tell me you want me.*

"I think I'm going to just keep working and try to get it all finished before then." I kept painting over the same line, blindly.

He paused. "Okay. Do you need any help?"

"I don't think so."

He got braver and slowly stepped forward until he was barely an arm's width behind me. I could feel his proximity in the air. "Do you want company?" he asked.

I sighed, and the tightness in my throat choked me a little harder. "Archie," I began, then turned to face him, dropping my brush.

He knew. The slap of trepidation hit his features and swung like an ax into my gut. He fell back a step at the look on my face. All bricks and sealed lips.

I was tired of trying to hide things. I was tired of the charade.

I hugged my arms around myself, finally letting the grief flow. "Archie." I tried starting over. "I need to talk to you."

"Is this about last night?" he asked, his voice hollow and taut.

I started to shake my head, then paused.

"Christ," he said, pacing with a hand sliding over his jaw. "Talia, I'm so incredibly sorry. If I did something to make you uncomfortable or overstepped—"

"You didn't."

"Then what? Was it—was I ...?" He was as awkward as a person could be, but the despair in his eyes didn't allow room for embarrassment.

"No, that's not it. You were ... are ... wonderful." And then I started crying. Again. "Damn it," I said, and angrily swiped at my eyes.

"Hey," he took both my arms in his hands, drawing me to him. "Talk to me. Just ... talk to me, Talia."

I shook my head, still angry at myself for allowing the tears to fall so publicly.

He dropped his forehead to mine and whispered, almost in a silent prayer: "Please."

I injected as much ice as I could into my next words in hopes of stopping the burning tears. "I'm leaving."

I watched him take a deep breath, but he didn't react. It was like he had been afraid the admission was coming, but not surprised. But instead of fighting or questioning, he simply poured his emotion into his heavy gaze and asked, "What can I do?"

I jerked away from him and folded my arms around my core, clutching my stomach. "There's nothing for you to do, okay? It's me. I can't keep doing this."

"And what exactly is *this*?" Archie asked. He stepped back, giving me space, and I wondered what we were referring to in particular. The unspoken weight of the balancing act that was our friendship? The way I waltzed haphazardly in and out of the comfort zone of his town? His life?

I grappled for words to come but they didn't. I didn't even know how to describe the turmoil rumbling inside me.

Archie finally broke the stillness and said, "You know running isn't the only option, Talia."

I immediately bristled. "I'm not running."

"Aren't you though?" He stepped closer to me. "The world got real at graduation. And you fled. This?" He gestured between the two of us. "Deny it all you want, but this, Talia, has always been real."

"Always?" I asked, skeptical.

"Yes." His eyes were molten.

I lowered both my voice and my gaze, looking away. "If that were true, you would have heard me, Archie."

"Heard what?"

My voice crackled. "That I'm broken."

"You're not broken," he said, like a reflex.

I turned his words on him with a sad smile. "Aren't I though?"

His eyes flashed, and he said in a low, barely there, gravelly whisper, "I've heard you Talia. I've always heard you. I *know* you."

"No, you don't," I said. "You know the version of me that I've shown you. But beneath that is someone that has a lot of broken parts that I … I don't know how to put back together."

"You haven't wanted to put them back together." He said it so fast, like the words left his mouth before he could think.

And the way he said it made me pause. He knew? Was it possible that, after all this time, he knew there was something *wrong* with me? After all these years, all the secret-keeping, all the hiding I thought I was doing, had he really seen right through it?

But he never said anything. He never said a word.

Some people might relish in the fact that they could be more than just their disease. That they could still be *themselves* without being reduced to the *thing* that crippled them. But for some reason, the fact that Archie may have known but done nothing made me angry.

"You know what?" I said, and the octave of my voice made him freeze. "You're right. You're so fucking right, Archie. Because you know what sucks?" My voice cracked. "I *like* her." I choked a sob. "I like the girl that you thought you knew. I liked that version of myself. And I wanted to be her. I wanted to be her so fucking badly."

"You're scared," he said, the realization evident in his voice. His body. The way he was suddenly reaching for me.

I spun away from him. "Of course I'm scared, Archie! It's all a lie. Everything has been a lie. I've been lying to you that I'm someone who is fearless and spontaneous and adventurous and ready to take the world and seize it, but I can't."

"You won't," he said firmly, finally regaining some ground to stand on. "There's a difference. You're choosing not to get help."

His words were sharp, sharper than I thought he could manage in that moment, but I spit back at him. "It's not that easy of a choice!"

"Talia, don't you think I know that?" he asked. "You're choosing to deal with this on your own. But the reality is you've never been alone."

Haven't I though? He'd never said anything.

"Yes," I replied. "I have been. And it's better that way."

"Talia," he said once again in that trained, calm voice. "I'm trying here, but you've got to meet me halfway and let me in. Please."

You're not trying! I wanted to scream the words, but some taunting voice in the back of my head stopped me by whispering, *It's not his job to fix you, you idiot.*

"I can't do that to you," I finally whispered back.

Archie started pacing the length of the curb again. He was quiet, hands stuffed firmly in his pockets, head down until he stopped and looked up at me. His expression was stony, but the pain in his eyes was torturous.

He finally said, "I want to keep fighting for this, our friendship, or whatever this is."

I put a hand to my temple, starting to feel the creeping edge of defeat. "And what do you want me to do?"

He stepped in closer to me again. "I want you to want to fight too."

For him? For us? Or simply for me? I couldn't look at him. "And what if I don't want to?" I asked, hushed, weak, soft.

In a whisper of a graze across my cheek, he gently tucked a wayward curl behind my ear. "I don't think that's true."

I returned his stare, studying the iron clasp he had put back on his emotions. "Why do you think you've stayed?" I finally asked. "After all of this, why have you stood by me?"

"Because I care. Obviously," he said. "How is that even a question?"

"No." I shook my head and pressed my lips together to keep them from wavering. "You've been waiting. You've been waiting for me to … get better."

He set his mouth in a line, much like mine.

I pushed on. "And that wait is going to be futile. I'm not going to simply *get better*. I can't."

"You're wrong, Talia."

I tried shaking my head to disagree, but he caught my chin and held me still, lifting my face to his. He stared into my eyes and seemingly through them, straight into my soul, as he spoke.

"You're wrong about me and what I've been waiting for," he said. I tried shrugging out of his grasp, but he pulled me toward him once more and continued. "I've been waiting for you to give yourself the chance to try. And to be there for you through it. I won't let you go through it alone."

Saint Archie, who was there for Adeline. Who was there for his family. Who *wanted* to be there for me.

But this was different. This time, I had some semblance of control. And I owed it to him to take charge and not let him be pulled under the tidal wave of my mind again.

Gently, I pulled away from his grip. "You're going to have to," I said, backing slowly away. "Because I'm not dragging you down with me." I bit my lip. "You're better than that."

He looked at me like I was something so much more than the shell of the girl he had once idolized. "So are you, Talia," he still said. "So are you."

"I think you should go."

He took a slow step backward toward his car, a slight retreat. "I'm calling you tomorrow. Give this a chance. Give yourself a chance. Stay."

The plea in his voice on his last syllable squeezed my heart out like a dirty, used-up dishrag.

One hand on his door, he said, "Promise me you'll think about it."

I clutched my hands behind my back and ran my thumbnail over my wrist, deep enough for the skin to break, and offered Archie Morgan one final lie: "Okay. I'll think about it."

ARCHIE

JUNIOR YEAR

My door opened, and I peered over my shoulder to see Talia leaning dramatically against the frame, one hand over her head, the other on her hip.

"Hello?" I said, and turned back to the game I was playing.

She strode into the room and picked up my spare controller before sitting down cross-legged beside me. She knocked her knee against mine. "What are you doing?"

"Plotting world domination," I mumbled, keeping my focus on the zombie I was currently hunting on my screen.

She nodded to herself, watching the screen too. "Fascinating."

Things between us were tense after my twenty-first birthday. Part of me stayed angry at Talia, and part of her stayed mad at me for being upset with her. That tension only escalated one day over lunch in the cafeteria when she sat herself down at my table with zero introduction and started hammering me with questions about Lex.

I had blown up at her and yelled, "Yes! We had sex!" Talia stared at me for maybe a full thirty seconds while I tried to go back to ignoring her, before she bolted from the table. Later that evening, she returned to my room with a giant cookie cake with *Congratulations! You're a man! Big dick energy!* written in red icing.

And just like that, she stopped avoiding me as had become the norm over the last week, and we picked right back up where we left off. Like that little blip in our friendship never happened.

Except for the fact that Justin kept coming to our Blue Elixir excursions.

And I was finally trying my hand at dating.

Not Lex. We were cool, and every once in a while, we would run into each other and have coffee, or sit together working in the library. But I didn't purposely seek her out, and she didn't seek me out either.

But I did try to keep that "big dick energy" rolling, and while Talia and Justin canoodled in Blue Elixir, I sat at the bar and "picked up chicks," as Justin had called it. But in reality, the whole talking-to-girls thing was getting easier and easier the more I practiced. (Shocker.) And the dates that followed seemed more and more natural too.

So for the most part, the first semester of junior year had gone swimmingly.

"It's almost Christmas," Talia said as if I wasn't aware.

"We *are* in the middle of finals," I said, continuing to tap on my controller.

"Precisely!" She slapped my knee in excitement, causing me to jump and get shot at in my video game.

I lost a life and gave her a hard glare, which she ignored. "Don't you think the poor students of Bridgeport could use some encouragement in this dark time?"

I glanced through my window. "The sun does set rather early."

"Now you're getting it. And darkness makes people sad right?"

"I guess so."

"So I had an idea."

"I figured you did."

She stood up and turned off my screen. I protested, but she plucked the controller from my hands, placing both on the desk beside my bed. "I want to spread some holiday cheer."

"I'm not singing Christmas carols with you."

She grinned and started braiding her long black hair. "We don't even have to serenade the other students."

I watched her hands work through her hair until she reached the bottom and tied off the braid. She pulled a hat from the pocket of her jacket and wrapped her hair underneath it, pulling it down tight over her ears. "Well, come on! Let's go."

"It's cold."

"Bring your gloves."

I grumbled but searched for my winter gear. She left the room in a flurry as I was still pulling on my boots. Instead of racing after her, I took my time, knowing she wasn't going to make it that far without me.

To prove my point, when I got to the bottom stairs of my dorm, she was sitting on the edge, with her arms wrapped around herself, hunched over. I gave her a playful slap on her shoulder. "Operation Holiday Cheer is underway."

Her smirk was impish. "Follow me."

It had snowed a few days prior, and the frozen, sparkling sheet still covered the campus. A few times as we made our trek, I spotted a patch of ice before she did and reached out to steady her arm.

"Thanks," she said, breathless as I caught her before she slipped.

"So what's the mission?" I asked.

Talia pulled us up in front of the fountain that was surprisingly still running despite the frozen temperatures outside. She reached down and scooped a handful of snow.

"Oh no. I'm not participating in a snowball fight for your entertainment," I said, backing away from her and her weapon.

She threw her head back and laughed openly. "You're ridiculous. I wasn't going to attack you. But now from your reaction, I feel like I should."

"Don't you dare."

She pressed her smile together. "Relax. Just watch. The concept is rather simple."

And I studied her hands again as they shaped the snow into two separate balls, one smaller than the other. With a flourish, Talia plopped the smaller one on top and set the miniature snowman on the ledge of the fountain. "Ta-da!"

"A snowman?" I asked. "That's the grand plan?"

"Not *a* snowman," she said as if I were the ridiculous one. The devilish smile returned to her lips. "An *army* of snowmen."

I chuckled. "All around the fountain?"

She jutted her chin toward the stairs to the cafeteria. "And lining the steps over there. That way everyone will see them in the morning and wonder who in their right mind would raise an army to guard their breakfast."

"I'm thinking the same thing," I said, but she paid me little attention, already forming her next snowman.

"I'll keep working here. You start on the stairs and make as many as you can until your hands stop working."

I looked down at hers. "Do you want my gloves?"

She gave me a look of adoring pity. "What a gentlemanly offer. But no. I'm fine. Get to work."

I shook my head at her but walked dutifully to the steps and started forming one icy ball at a time.

I never realized just how many steps there were on the cafeteria entranceway. And they wrapped all the way around the circular courtyard. Talia wasn't kidding when she said it would take an army of snowmen. I settled with leaving a few pathways available to the cafeteria and making the tiny soldiers guard each walkway. Snowman building was tiring, and even though I worked quickly, my hands were numb way before my sections were complete.

But I kept at it. I kept at it because I'd be damned if I weenied out before Talia gave in. I rushed through the snowmen collection, so some of them started to vary in size and shape. The intent was still there, and when I stepped back to look at a finished section, I had to admit that Talia was right. It was just ridiculous enough of a concept that it probably would elicit a smile from the students who came through here first thing in the morning.

I rubbed my hands together vigorously and then crouched back down to resume work, until I heard a splashing behind me.

I wheeled around, dropping the head of the snowman I was forming. Talia was in the fountain. Floating.

Talia was *floating* in the fountain.

"Talia!" I cried and jumped down the steps. My boots lost traction as I hit the snow, but I righted myself with an agility I didn't have time to marvel at as I ran to her. "Talia, are you okay?"

Her eyes were closed. Her arms hovered beside her body, fingertips slightly spread. Her mouth was gently parted, and her hair was freed from its braid and hat, floating around her head in wispy strands.

"Talia! Can you hear me?" I fell to my knees and reached for her, but her body was just out of my reach. She didn't respond.

"Oh my god," I said as the panic started to grip my throat. I sprang to my feet and swung a leg into the fountain. It splashed loudly, and Talia pursed her lips.

"You're disrupting my quiet current," she suddenly muttered.

I froze, overcome with anger. "Talia. Get. Out."

She opened one eye and peered at me. "Why?"

"Talia Scott!" I yelled at her. "It is quite literally freezing outside. Get the hell out of the water!"

She opened both eyes to roll them. She *rolled her eyes*!

"Fine," she said begrudgingly.

"Unbelievable," I murmured, fear still lodged between my ribs. If I wasn't here, I wouldn't have believed it if someone told me their best friend willingly climbed into the courtyard fountain in thirty-degree weather just to float around.

She was soaking wet, obviously, when she stood up and made the biggest show of sloshing her way over to the edge. She threw one leg over the fountain ledge and slung water everywhere. I jumped back, involuntarily. She tried to raise an eyebrow at me, but her teeth were already chattering.

I shrugged out of my coat and threw it over her shoulders when she climbed out. I ushered her back toward our dorm.

"Why the actual fuck did you get in the fountain?" I still couldn't wrap my head around the sheer stupidity of the stunt.

"It looked w-w-welcoming," she said, teeth already chattering.

"Welcoming!?" I cried. "It's practically *ice*, you idiot!"

She laughed. The girl fucking laughed.

"What is so funny?" I failed to see the humor in any of this.

Her laugh was punctuated by the clacking of her teeth and a sound that rumbled from somewhere in her chest. "You called me an idiot."

"Yeah," I said, steering her by the shoulders around the next turn. "I did. Because you are one. And you're probably going to get sick."

"T-t-too l-l-late," she said. I could barely make out what she said over the shivering of her entire body.

By the time we got to the door of our building, her lips were a scary shade of blue. I practically dragged her up the stairs. "Come on. We've got to get you out of those wet clothes."

"Archie, are you t-t-trying to get me n-n-naked?"

"As a matter of fact, yes," I grumbled as I dragged her up the last flight of stairs. "But if that's what you were after, I'm sure there were several less dramatic ways to go about it."

"Got your attention."

She quipped the response so quickly, I faltered and paused. "Is that what you were after? My attention?"

"No. I told you. The water looked nice." Her eyes, blue as the water she just bathed in, gave away nothing.

"You're impossible." I ripped my keys out of my pocket and opened the door in one clean movement. Grady had been holed up in the arts building the majority of this finals season, working on a series of several large sculptures. I swore he was nocturnal—he stayed out working all night and slept all day when I was gone. When I left for my accounting classes, he was returning, usually covered in some form of clay, plaster, or other medium.

I hoped tonight wouldn't change that trend. I practically shoved Talia into the room in front of me. I went first to the wall thermostat and cranked the heat as high as it would go. Then I went to my closet and found an extra pair of sweatpants and a sweatshirt. I threw them on my bed.

"Strip," I commanded.

"That's awfully forward," she responded.

"I'm not kidding, Talia," I grumbled as I rummaged for socks in the drawer next to my closet. I found three pairs of tall ones and tossed them into the pile, along with the towel on the back of my door.

"You have five minutes," I said and went to leave the room.

"Now look who's being dramatic. Just turn around," she said then dropped her voice. "Don't go."

She looked like a drowned mouse. Wet and sad with eyes too large for her face, wet hair stuck to her cheeks.

I sighed and folded my arms over my chest. "Fine. Tell me when you're done." And I turned to face the door.

I heard the rustle of the comforters on my bed before her small voice piped up. "D-d-done."

I looked back over my shoulder. She was in my bed, covers pulled above her chin so that only two blue eyes were visible underneath the hood that was also too large for her head. It would have been an adorable picture had I not been able to see her body still shaking underneath the blankets.

I ripped the blankets off Grady's bed and threw them over her as well.

"Thank you," she whispered, and her eyelids fluttered.

I smoothed the blanket over her body, running my hands over her arms repeatedly, trying to beat some warmth back into her body. Her eyes stayed closed.

I finally stepped away and sat down on Grady's bed, letting my head drop into my hands, trying to make sense of this latest performance.

Talia coughed once. Twice. I watched as she burrowed deeper into the blanket burrito I had made. That lasted about three seconds before she wiggled her chin free once more and spoke.

"Hold me?" she asked so quietly I didn't know if I heard her correctly. Her eyes looked glassy.

"Yeah," I whispered back, hesitantly. "Yeah. Sure."

I kicked off my shoes before quickly peeling back the covers and slipping in beside Talia.

I held out my arm, and she wasted no time in wrapping her body around mine like a koala. Her arms clutched at my back, trying to pull me closer.

And she fit against my body perfectly. Talia buried her head into the crook of my neck, her cold lips breathing onto my searing-hot skin. I let my chin rest on top of her head. Despite the frigidity of her hair on my cheek, I could have stayed there for an eternity. And the thought alone had me tightening my arms around her shoulders.

"I'm so cold," she muttered into my neck.

I gave a weak chuckle that rumbled in my chest. "I wonder whose fault that is."

She really was freezing. The air around us was warming up steadily, and underneath the weight of the extra blankets, I normally would have been a furnace of body heat right now. But anything in me was being absorbed into the ice that was Talia's skin pressed against my clothes, against my body.

"Justin and I broke up," she finally said.

My heart was hammering. I felt it in my eardrums. I wondered, with her head pressed against my chest, if she could hear it.

I ran through a list of potential things to say before settling with the unimpressive "Oh."

"Yeah," she said and nothing else. I was acutely aware of the rhythm of her breathing. The quickness of it. The shallow intakes.

"So ... is that why you were in the fountain?" I asked.

She made a sound that sounded like a snort laced with sarcasm, but it was so faint, it lost its impact. "He doesn't have anything to do with the fountain."

I doubted that was the case entirely, but I wasn't in the mood to argue.

I split my concentration into studying her breathing, waiting for it to slow, and on my own lung capacity to keep taking in air with her this close to me.

"Are you going to ask why we broke up?" Her mouth still hadn't moved from the skin at my neck.

"Only if you want to talk about it," I told her.

"I don't know."

I shifted and somehow managed to pull her closer. "I'm here if you do."

I felt her chest rise and fall against my side as she took a deep breath. "He just said something that hit a little too close to home."

Home. A word that was strictly off limits in the vocabulary of our conversations.

"Plus," Talia said. "I think he knew that he was just a good way to occupy ten minutes between classes."

"That's it?"

"That's it."

While I wasn't doubting the validity of her statement, I wondered how much of it was a deflection. For once, I decided to push her a little harder. I turned my face into her forehead. My mouth moved against the ice of her skin when I asked, "What did he say, Talia?"

She paused before she responded, and when she spoke, the disappointment rang clear in my ears. "It really was stupid, honestly."

"I'm sure it wasn't."

"I'm pretty sure I blew it up into something much bigger than it had to be."

I squeezed her. "Tell me what happened, Talia."

She let out a long shaking sigh. "It was last weekend. He wanted me to go out with him to one of his friends' parties. And I just didn't want to. I couldn't."

She sputtered a weak cough and cleared her throat before continuing. "There was no amount of willpower that I could muster to get myself dressed and walk myself to the apartment and drink the drinks and laugh at the jokes and smile at his friends. I couldn't do it. When he asked me to go with him, I felt like I was suddenly this dumb wooden puppet, and my brain refused to pull the strings to get me to play the part."

I felt the smallest shake of her head against my shoulder. She cleared her throat once more. "So I told him no."

The surface of my skin had gotten icy from the proximity of Talia's cold hands, but something heated and prickled inside me at those words. "He didn't like you saying *no?*"

"No, it wasn't like that. I mean, yeah, he was probably a little pissed, but I tried to explain this whole puppet metaphor to him, and obviously that sailed straight over his head."

"You've rehearsed the puppet metaphor?" I mused.

"It's something I think about."

"Hmm," I said. "And who decided it was a good idea to put the puppet in the fountain?"

She let out a deeper sigh. "I was tired of all the thinking about it. And I was tired of listening to his voice on repeat telling me to *suck it up*, and *it's not that bad*, and *come on, I'll promise you a good time.*"

My teeth clenched in the back of my jaw. "I knew I never liked him."

The shake of her head was much larger this time. "Honestly, he's fine. He's not a bad guy. He's just so … *surface.*"

She said the word as if it were something that hadn't entirely occurred to her before now. She repeated, "It's true. He's so surface. He's not wired to see deeper. And that's not his fault, not entirely I don't think."

"You can't change your hardwiring sometimes," I said, and for some reason, that made her look up at me.

"No," she mused softly, letting her eyes roam my face as if she had never truly seen it this close. Which she probably hadn't. "You can't change it."

She kept looking at me, this strange curious look flickering across her eyes and eyebrows. I stared back at her. Slowly, she lifted her hand from the clutches of the blanket burrito and drifted her fingertips to my cheek.

"Talia," I said slowly while she traced the line of my jaw. "What are you doing?"

She didn't respond, but her fingers continued their journey across my jaw and down my neck, resting above my pulse. "Your heart is racing," she murmured, watching her own fingers move.

"Um," I said, "I guess that's better than not running at all."

And as if we were suddenly sucked into a parallel universe, Talia placed her hand flat against my chest and used it as a balance to push herself up and press her lips against mine.

My arm tightened around her in surprise. The shock of her mouth on top of mine was enough to delay any other response. I should have pulled away. She was my friend. My *best* friend.

We should not be kissing.

But I didn't pull away. And I didn't stop her.

Instead, I kissed her back. Once. Twice. I moved my hand into her wet hair and cradled the nape of her neck.

She let out a sound that almost resembled a purr.

On the third kiss, I came to my senses. The overwhelming force that it took to wrench my mouth away from hers was almost embarrassing. "We can't," I said.

Her eyes were still closed, and a small smile played across those lips. "We *can* though."

"No," I said, gently unwrapping her arms from my torso. "We can't. I can't."

She opened her eyes, and the faintest flicker of hurt cracked like lightning across her expression. So brief before it was gone. "Okay."

"It's not like that," I blurted out.

"It's okay. I get it."

"No, you don't."

She looked up again, questioning me. I spoke again. "I can't kiss you right now. Trust me. I want to. But not … not like this." I reached out and gently lifted a damp piece of hair from her head, holding it between us.

She smiled with half her mouth and not her eyes. The gesture felt like a swift kick in the gut, but I couldn't change my mind. It wouldn't be right, kissing Talia in the state she was in.

"If you kiss me," I said, tucking the strand of hair behind her ear. "I'd want it to be because you want to, not because you're trying to … feel something else."

After two and a half years of knowing her but wondering what her lips might feel like, I never imagined the first time they might be pressed to mine would be as icicles. And even as I could feel the warmth from my body gently breathing life back into hers, it was all too much. To me, this moment was supposed to mean everything. To her … I didn't know what kissing me meant. All I knew was that her kiss tasted like deep layers of hurt I couldn't fathom on my own.

"I get it," she said again.

"Talia, I'm here for you, and I will always be here for you." I leaned down and pressed a kiss to her forehead. "But I don't want you like this. Not now."

She nodded and snuggled deeper into the blankets against my side, but her face was turned away.

The rock that had been lodged in my throat now settled down in my gut as I held her. I lifted my gaze to the ceiling and prayed to a silent god for the strength to do whatever the right thing might be. I only wished I knew more of what was happening behind her expression that had suddenly turned stony.

My focus flickered back to Talia as her breathing started to slow into a more regular rhythm. Her eyes remained closed, and I watched until the muscles around her eyes finally relaxed as she drifted into sleep.

As I resolved myself to the fact that I probably wouldn't be getting much sleep of my own, I wondered who else, if anyone else, would know about the puppet that nearly drowned in the fountain.

TALIA

PRESENT DAY

"No," I said. "No way."

"Yes," Kathryn said back.

"I don't want to."

"But you should."

"You can't make me."

"You're right," Kathryn said and rose from her seat on the couch Saturday night. "I can't make you do anything."

She left me in the living room, on the same couch I had cried on that morning, and wandered back into the kitchen to pour herself another cup of tea. "I can only tell you that I would be willing to go with you if you wanted to try therapy again."

ARCHIE

PRESENT DAY

I sat on the couch at home, still staring at my phone. Once again, I'd allowed my heart to go through the blender that is Talia Scott.

I told her I would give her the night.

She told me she would think about it.

And then I would call her tomorrow.

But my phone sat on the side table, face up, taunting me with its blank, dark screen. I stared up at the ceiling fan, the only sound in the quiet house as the rest of my family had long since fallen asleep.

Just then, an urgent buzzing. I literally leapt off the couch, and a few fumbles later, I saw a text from Grady flash across the screen. My stomach dropped a little, but I opened his message anyway.

Hey. You okay?

I tapped my thumbs across the screen a few times. **Why do you ask?**

Talia texted.

My stomach clenched. **What did she say?**

His typing bubbles flickered longer this time. **That it was good to see me again. And to look after her mural while she was gone. Assuming that meant she had left.**

I ignored the punch to my gut. **She told me she's leaving.**

Come take your lunch break with me at the school Monday. Then we can shoot a round of pool at my place after work.

He always knew exactly what to say, how to comfort, what to offer in a friendship. I was once again acutely aware of just how good a person Grady was.

I also realized how much I was going to need him, once more, when Talia inevitably left again. The thought made me want to take up permanent residence on the couch.

Thank you. I'll take you up on that.

TALIA

PRESENT DAY

Kathryn was a gem of a human being. And she made me completely, totally, and incredibly uncomfortable with the generosity of her offer to come with me.

"Really, it's fine. I don't need you to babysit me. I can be a grown up and take myself to my own appointment," I reassured her as I put on my coat Monday afternoon.

"One, I'm fully aware you don't need me," she said as she flitted around the kitchen. "But two, I hope you also realize that the reality of this appointment may have never come to fruition if I hadn't sat beside you while you made the phone call. Therefore, I think it's only fitting that I see this all the way through."

I bent to pull on my shoes; the movement felt robotic. I couldn't believe I had actually agreed to this. Kathryn had a way with words—she could be seriously convincing when she wanted to be.

"Who knows," she continued, "maybe you would just go for a drive around the block and come back saying that you went and it was fabulous."

"I wouldn't lie to you," I said. I was tired of not telling the truth. "And I doubt it's going to be fabulous."

"Exactly why I am coming with you," she said, closing the dishwasher and hitting the Start button. "Get your keys."

It had actually been Kathryn's idea to text Grady and ask for suggestions for a therapist. He sent a list over that night, and Kathryn sat with me on the couch Monday morning as I called down the list to see if anyone had any availability. Much to our surprise, Lacey Roberson had a late cancellation, and an appointment was available that same day.

"It's fate," Kathryn had said as I hung up the phone after accepting the time.

"It's a coincidence."

"It doesn't matter. We're going."

She followed me out the front door of her house.

The drive there was silent as I sat in the passenger seat and watched the neighborhood, then the city, fly by through the window.

Kathryn, to her credit, didn't try to fill the silence with any form of small talk, which was another thing that made me feel incredibly grateful.

Once we arrived at the counseling center, she did, however, put her hand gently on my knee. "I'm really proud of you, Talia," she said in a soft voice.

To my surprise, I felt a sting in my eyes and blinked at the tears forming rapidly. "You know, I don't think I've heard that expression that often."

"It's a good thing you're going to therapy then."

We got out of the car and closed the doors at the same time, then walked side by side, close but not touching, to the front door.

Lacey Roberson, LPC, MA, rented office space just outside of the downtown gridlock. I figured it was rented because I saw a faint outline of a family dentistry label that had previously occupied the window at the front. I pushed open the front door, and a soft chime rang out from above the frame.

A small lobby and a receptionist with glasses, graying hair, and a warm smile greeted us. "Hello," the woman said as Kathryn and I approached. "Are you Talia?"

"She is." Kathryn pointed first to me, then herself. "I'm moral support."

I grimaced, but the receptionist didn't seem to mind. "Wonderful. I just need you to fill out these forms, and Mrs. Roberson will be with you shortly."

Kathryn stepped back and plopped herself down on the floral couch, taking up exactly half the space. She crossed her legs neatly and folded her hands on her knees. Taking my clipboard and papers, I sat down beside her and started skimming their contents.

"Now the real question is … do I want to run this through my insurance or not?" I mused.

"Why wouldn't you?"

"I'm assuming since I'm still on my parents' insurance, they're going to see the statement and know I was here."

"Is that a bad thing?"

"It's probably not a good thing."

"You're a starving artist," Kathryn said. "And this is your health we're talking about. Nothing is more important. Use insurance."

The way she simplified my conundrum so matter-of-factly made me feel a little bit stupid for not realizing it sooner. I was also relieved. At least to Kathryn, this mattered. Being here mattered.

If I was being entirely honest, it mattered to Grady too. And Archie. It always had.

But until this moment, signing my name on the dotted line, I realized Archie had been right. I had never *let* it matter to me.

I signed my full legal name on both the insurance form and the professional disclosure statement: *Natalia Scott.*

Lacey Roberson was young. The diamond on her left hand and the photograph on her desk of her with her husband said she was happily married, and the overall glow she exuded made me doubt she could sympathize with any of my woes.

Not that I necessarily had a reason for them.

That was the problem.

"Talia! Hi, it's so nice to meet you. My name is Lacey Roberson." She rose from her desk and stepped forward to shake my hand. Her grip was sure and confident.

"Hi," I answered meekly, then looked around the room.

"Please, take a seat." She gestured to the green velvet armchair in front of her wooden desk. The entire office had a woodland feel to it, complete with twinkly lights and ivy strung throughout the walls.

"Now," Lacey said as she sat once more, this time in the armchair directly across from me. She leaned in, intently. "Can you tell me a little bit about what brought you in today?"

I looked anywhere but at her face, struggling for an answer. I finally admitted, "I'm afraid I don't have a good enough reason."

"Well. You're here. Why don't we start there? How did you get here?"

"I drove."

She smiled. "You're funny."

"I've been called worse."

"Is this your first time seeing a counselor?"

I thought about lying. I really did. And I wasn't proud of the thought. Ultimately, I conceded to the truth. "No."

"Can we talk about what that was like for you?"

No. "I suppose so." I drew a breath. "I guess it started with a few mandatory visits with the college counselor. And then it escalated."

"What do you mean by that?"

"I had to graduate to an actual clinical mental health counselor, per the college counselor's recommendation. That didn't go over well."

"With you?"

"My family."

"How so?"

At some point during the conversation, my thumb had found my wrist again, the thin line my thumbnail traced across the skin. Over and over and over. "They were against the idea that something could be wrong with me."

Lacey's eyes dipped to my hands, watching. I unfolded my hands from each other and sat on them instead.

"You know, Talia," she began, "in my professional opinion, the people coming to see me don't have anything wrong with them. They just need help navigating the challenges that come with life."

I looked away.

There was a heavy pause while Lacey waited for me to respond. I didn't know how.

After several moments, she continued, "Was this a recurring thing? Going to the counselor?"

"No," I said. "I only went to the clinical mental health counselor once."

"And what happened at the one appointment?"

"I got a diagnosis."

"That sounds intense. Was it terminal?" she asked with a sly smirk, and surprisingly, I softened.

With a chuckle that indicated anything but humor, I said, "I don't know, you tell me. Major depressive disorder. Recurrent. Moderate. F33.1."

"Quite the label you put on yourself."

"I didn't. Therapy did."

"I'm going to let you in on a little industry secret," Lacey said, crossing her legs and leaning back in her chair. "A diagnosis is used for two major reasons. The first is for insurance as a way of getting companies to help pay for your visits. The second is to provide a sense of normalcy for those experiencing various concerns. A diagnosis doesn't define you. But it might help you feel like you're not alone."

"That's all it's done," I said. "All it has done is define me. And alienate me. I can't be me without depression. I don't even know who that would be."

Surprisingly, against every prediction I could have made about this appointment, Lacey Roberson smiled. "Well then, Talia, I think we've found a great place to start."

TALIA

JUNIOR YEAR

I loved Saint Patrick's Day. As a kid, I had loved the greenery of the holiday and the pinching repercussions if you weren't wearing any of it. As a fledgling adult, with drinking-age acquaintances, I quickly decided that Bridgeport's annual St. Patty's Bar Crawl topped my list of reasons for loving the holiday.

It was actually Grady's idea to go this year. One night I had been working late in the art studio, and he came barging through the door with two coffees in his hands and a giant grin.

"Thought I might find you here," he said and gave me the cup that was a nice beige color, keeping the dark one for himself.

"Thanks," I said, putting down my brush and accepting the cup graciously.

"It's not free," he said, shrugging off his backpack. "This is my formal notice that I expect you to return the drink favor when we go out in a few weeks for the bar crawl."

"Bar crawl?" I asked.

"The seventeenth."

"What's the seventeenth?"

"The day we celebrate the life of Saint Patrick on the day of his death."

"St. Patrick's Day?"

"That would be the one, yes."

"I guess I never realized we drank on his death date."

Grady shrugged. "A celebration of life. But anyway, I digress. You're coming on the bar crawl."

"Cool," I said and put my cup down, picking up my paintbrush once more. "You realize I'm still using a fake ID, right?" Even though the rest of my friends had turned twenty-one already during our junior year, my birthday wasn't until the beginning of September, and I wouldn't hit that monumental milestone until senior year.

"It'll be fine. We can have safety in numbers. Let's get a group to go."

That group ended up being our roommates. Both Archie and Kathryn reluctantly agreed to attend—Kathryn because I promised it got her out of any more societal obligations with me for the remainder of the semester, and Archie because there was a free T-shirt involved with the purchase of a ticket.

Regardless of the bribery it took, the four of us were on the downtown streets a few short weeks later. I had managed to find a full green suit at a local thrift store, complete with a green shamrock tie. I had on a white button-down underneath the too-large jacket. The pants were a little long but worked fine once I rolled the cuffs three times. Kathryn let me tie a green scarf in her long hair. Grady had a large green cowboy hat and green paint streaking across his face. "We raided the art supplies. Don't tell Joe," he said with a sly wink when he walked up to us.

Archie must have been roped into the face paint as well, as there were remnants of what had once been a shamrock on his cheek.

"Where's your costume?" I asked Archie as I looked him up and down. The gym shorts he'd chosen had a green stripe on them, but the overall *grayness* of his outfit was not very festive.

"Don't worry," he said and then shrugged out of his sweatshirt to reveal the bar crawl's T-shirt underneath. It looked like it had been attacked with a Sharpie. "Grady already defiled my souvenir to rectify the situation."

I leaned closer to Archie's torso to read the slanted letters that read *Kiss me like I'm Irish.*

I laughed. "I guess that will have to work."

Archie grumbled and pulled his sweatshirt back down over his body.

"All right, people! Let's move out," Grady said, leading our pack to the first destination on the bar crawl's list.

By the time we hit the halfway point, we had stopped at The Kitchen Sink, Hastings Pub, and Greg's Bucket Shop. We also lost Grady's cowboy hat and the tie around my neck at one of those destinations, but I couldn't say where.

When we entered Al's Tavern, there was a steady buzzing in my ears and a lightness in my step.

"Hey," I tapped Archie's shoulder.

He turned to me, and by now, he had been drinking enough that the scowl he had attempted to hold on to had vanished and he was grinning. My heart did this weird little leap at the sight.

"Yeah?" he asked, smile still lopsided.

"Wanna do a round of wingman?" I asked.

He shrugged. "Sure. I don't know who's up to bat though."

"You're up," I said, knowing full well that I had sat out the previous rounds we played. I hadn't really tried to see anyone since the breakup.

Since the night Archie and I had made an army of snowmen.

And the fountain.

But that was months ago. I just hadn't had it in me to be the front-runner once again for our usual antics.

Either Archie was way more drunk than I thought, or he was just being his usual gentlemanly self, but he nodded and said, "Okay. Who's our target?"

I looked around the sports bar, packed with cozy booths and long communal tables. The bar itself stretched underneath the long row of TVs.

I found a group of girls presumably on the bar crawl as well in their matching T-shirts, high-waisted jeans, and green plaid flannel shirts. I jutted my chin forward. "Any one of those would work."

Archie looked over to where I was staring and then back at me. "Raise the stakes. I can get every one of their numbers in twenty minutes."

"Wow, someone has grown some confidence this year."

"I've learned from the best," he said and winked at me.

Archie Morgan just winked at me.

Grady and Kathryn had already pushed through the crowd and managed to find seats at the bar, but Archie gave me a friendly pat on the back before striding off toward the group of girls.

"Do you need your wingman?" I called after him.

He turned to me but kept walking backward. "I'll holler if I do." He still had that crooked smile on his face.

"Cheeky bastard," I said under my breath and went to find my friends.

Kathryn had sprawled her and Grady's jackets across two seats next to theirs at the bar, but I scooped them up and handed them to her. "Just me. Our sweet baby Archie is on the prowl."

"Look at him spreading those wings," Grady mused, an affectionate tone in his voice. "We should be so proud."

As I sat down next to Grady, I allowed myself one glance at the high-top table in the back of Al's. The group of girls—it looked like five in total—had all welcomed Archie into their circle and were laughing and talking. He looked rather pleased with himself.

I turned back and ordered another round of beer for Grady and cider for Kathryn and me. "I would like to take all the credit for bringing the little hermit out of his shell."

"Took you long enough."

"No credit to you."

The bartender set down our drinks, and Grady lifted his glass to mine. "Touché," he said with a nod.

Kathryn struck up a conversation with the bargoer who had taken Archie's vacant seat.

I drummed my fingers against the cool glass a few times. *Tap, tap, tap. Tap, tap, tap. Tap, tap*—"Hey, Grady."

"Hey, Talia."

I dropped my voice to a lower octave. "Can I tell you a secret?"

"Depends," he said and turned his body to face me, turning his back to Kathryn and the spirited debate she was currently occupied with. "Do I have to keep it?"

"I would prefer it if you did."

He considered this. "Okay, I will. What's up?"

I took a deep breath and couldn't meet his eye. If I did, I would probably chicken out of what I was about to say. "I did something recently."

"What kind of something? Are we talking criminal or petty crime? Do I need to start saving for your bail?"

I let out a weak little laugh. "Neither. But I appreciate you being willing to post my bail, should I ever need to call in that favor."

He stayed silent, waiting patiently for me to continue my confession.

I took in more air and held it there a few seconds before I rushed out an exhale and said, "I tried going to the campus therapist."

I figured Grady was a safe person to confide in because, to my knowledge, he wasn't aware of any of my past slipups in covering up The Diagnosis that I had shoved somewhere deep, *deep* down inside me. And if he didn't know the depth, then he wouldn't judge. Or worry. Or applaud. He might just listen.

Archie might do all of the above. And I didn't know if Kathryn would understand.

Out of the corner of my eye, Grady nodded, slowly. "I think therapy is a good idea for everyone. Thought about it myself."

"Well, if you are considering, don't go to the campus site. They said the waiting period is two to three months, and they weren't going to help me unless I was experiencing suicidal ideation."

"They told you that?"

"I think the intern was working the front desk that day."

"And have you?" Grady asked. "Ever experienced suicidal ideation?"

It was a blunt question, which sounded weird coupled with the softness in his voice. But for some reason, I appreciated him not shying away from it.

I decided to answer truthfully. "It hasn't been that bad in a bit. I'd say I've only felt the edge of that particular brand of darkness a small handful of times in my life. Therefore, I'm probably lucky."

"Poetic."

"I'm an artist."

"I'm aware," he was smiling as he said it, that same affection coming through that he had reserved for Archie. "Just promise me one thing."

My heart squeezed, anticipating what he was going to ask next. "Yeah?" I breathed the question.

"You call me, Talia Scott," he said, his eyes darkening and seeming to stare through my soul as he spoke, "If you ever get close to that edge."

ARCHIE

PRESENT DAY

"I brought the goods," I said, dropping a chicken sandwich combo on Grady's desk Monday afternoon.

"Oh, man," he said, leaning forward in his seat to open the bag. "How did you get through security with this loot?"

I sat on the couch across from him and took a sip from my lemonade. "Didn't even get asked to make myself a visitor name tag."

"They let anyone in here nowadays."

"They let me in because they've seen me drop Addie off in the mornings. Plenty." I took the extra sandwich he handed me. "Thanks for the invite, Grady."

"Thanks for the food," he said as he popped a fry into his mouth. "It's a suitable payment for my companionship."

"How's Addie doing?" I asked.

"You know I can't talk about her. Confidentiality in the school and all."

"She's not your client. She's your boss's client. And my sister."

Grady nodded. "She's been good. But I think you know that. So why do you ask?"

"I don't know," I said. I chewed my food slowly before adding, "There's just something I haven't been quite able to get off my mind lately."

Grady put down his sandwich and leaned in. "What's going on?"

I chuckled. "You don't have to therapize me."

He remained silent, waiting for me to continue, like a therapist would.

I sighed. "I've just been wondering … what if we hadn't been there? Like, what if Addie had gone through some of the dark shit without anyone? And what that outcome might have been."

"You're talking about people being alone with their mental illness?"

"Yeah. I guess. And what happens then?"

"You're worried about her?" He eyed me intently. "Or Talia?"

I looked at him, incredulous. "You know?" After all this time, I thought I was the only one that harbored her secrets. And here was Grady, speaking so openly as if it were common knowledge.

"Of course I know. I'm a trained professional at this point. It's my job to watch and know."

I considered this. Maybe I wasn't the only one who'd seen the signs. Maybe she had once cracked so deeply that she'd opened up to others too.

And yet, the other day, she chose to withdraw and push away once more.

"How did you know?" I asked. "Not about Talia—you don't have to tell me that. That's between you two. But … how did you know that this"—I gestured to the office space around us—"was what you wanted to do?"

"Counseling?" Grady asked, following my gaze around his office. It was covered in art: some originals, some prints, some signed with names I recognized from other students from Bridgeport. But many were unframed, posted on the walls with a simple thumbtack. Student artwork, I assumed.

I turned my attention back to Grady. "Yeah. Counseling. Expressive arts therapy. How did you find this path where you were able to combine all the things you loved into one? Art … helping people … talking …"

He gave a little smile at the last item on my list. "Well, first I found what I was passionate about."

"What do you mean by that?"

"Archie, you know I love you, man, but if you're asking me for help to figure out what you want to be when you grow up, you're going to have to find some passion."

I bristled immediately. "That's not fair. I have passion."

He gave me a pointed stare, and in the silence, I was forced to look at myself as well. Of course I had things I was passionate about …. Right?

Grady started again, cautiously. "As long as I've known you, you've spent all these years consumed by this idea you've had of Talia, and this whirlwind romance story that may or may not have led to you simply following her as her shadow."

"I'm not her shadow," I argued, but the weight of what Grady had just spoken into the universe started to press on my chest.

He gave me a sympathetic smile. "Haven't you though? As your outside-perspective friend, not your counselor, it kind of seems like you've done an awful lot of waiting."

Waiting. *You've been waiting …. And that wait is going to be futile,* Talia had said.

"I think it's time you figure out what you want next, Arch," Grady said softly.

I looked down at my lunch, suddenly not very hungry. I set the remains in the paper wrapping and crossed my ankles. I became very interested in my shoes. "I haven't been the most able to spring forward," I finally grumbled. "I've had more than Talia to be thinking about."

"Your family?" Grady prompted.

I nodded. "Talia may have taught me to be the guy that waits. But my family taught me to be there. Or … here."

And it wasn't just Addie. It took her a long time after her attempt to talk to our parents. She came to me first. With an apology. And it nearly broke me, split my heart straight down the middle to hear the words come out of her mouth: "I'm so sorry, Archie. I'm so sorry I put you through that. I just didn't know what else to do."

"Come to me. You could have come to me," I told her.

She got angry at that. Angry at me. Angry at herself. "You wouldn't understand. Every day was this overwhelming darkness, and I didn't know how to get out of it. I felt small. I felt empty. I felt this numbness where every step of every day felt heavy and exhausting, and I didn't want to be like that anymore. I didn't know how to pull myself out of it. And when I bled, I saw light and clarity and control, and I thought it would help me get better …. But I cut too deep."

That gut-wrenching perspective into the workings of my little sister's mind was bad enough. It was almost worse to see the tears in the corners of my mother's eyes every time I told her I was leaving the house.

"Just … come home safe, okay?" she'd say. "Just come home."

And so I did. I came home. Often. And even after graduation, I hadn't ever truly left. Because I couldn't stand the guilt that would come from it. The thought of it squeezed my stomach into coils.

And then there was my father. The man who always had a plan, who always took the lead, who always took care of our family in a way I would probably never fully comprehend. The vacancy that had taken up residence on his face that day in the hospital still haunted me. I had never seen the man so … *vulnerable*. And more than that, I had seen for the first and only time that my father was utterly terrified.

And if a rock like my father could splinter into fragments, what hope did the rest of us have?

Grady had been silent, presumably waiting for me to further explain, but I kept a few of these secrets for myself. Instead, I sighed and just said, "My family needs me. I haven't been able to move on. I haven't been able to … even have any problem myself. It's been easier to decide to just be content."

At that, Grady finally started talking. "You can't settle in your own life," he said. "Or spend it scared that the other people in life aren't responsible for themselves. You can only control yourself and what you do."

I started to interject something along the lines of *they are my responsibility*, but he held up a hand and continued, "I'm not saying that you shouldn't be the support system you want to be for those you care about, but that's what you are. Support. In their stories. It's time for you to start living your own life and be a little more of a protagonist."

I considered this and felt defeated. "I wouldn't even know how to do that."

"Maybe it's not about *how*. Maybe it's about *where*. Your field of vision is a little pinpoint on a map called Bridgeport, and that's about it, my friend. You need to get out there and go see what else you might like."

"What, like travel?"

"It wouldn't be the worst thing for you to get out a little."

I shook my head. "I don't think it's realistic that I would just up and go backpacking around Europe."

Grady rose to throw out his trash. On the way, he gave my shoulder a little pat. "We can find a starting place though."

ARCHIE

SENIOR YEAR

Talia had very specific orders for how she wanted her twenty-first birthday to go down:

1. She didn't like her birthday.
2. Don't ask why she didn't like her birthday.
3. But if you did ask (Grady made the mistake the week prior), be prepared for a lecture on how her family *loved* her birthday and threw the *biggest* parties and made it a huge social engagement at the country club, and she hated every second of it because there was usually an obscene amount of pink things and the affair involved people she didn't even like.
4. This year was going to be different.

Talia's twenty-first birthday happened to fall on a Thursday, which meant it fell on an obligatory wingman-excursion night.

"We aren't going to Blue Elixir tonight," Talia announced when she barged into my room and flopped herself down on my bed.

By senior year, Grady and I finally agreed that it was probably time to have some separation from each other. We had lived so well together for the first three years of college, but when he got the opportunity to move into an apartment complex with a few of the other art students, I told him to go for it. I wasn't going to hold him back. I stayed on campus but switched dorm buildings to an available single room.

Talia and Kathryn decided to split up senior year too, as Kathryn had started dating someone outside of school, and Talia was … not dating. It was a mutual agreement for them both to find new housing, except Talia didn't like her new roommate, Gabriella. Gabriella's sorority friends were always over, so more often than not, Talia was with me.

"Why aren't we going to Blue Elixir?" I asked without looking up from my economics homework.

"Because," Talia said, exasperated, "it's my birthday, and I want to do something else."

I looked over at her, surprised she even mentioned the holiday. "Happy birthday?" I offered.

"Ugh, don't say it again," she said and propped herself up. "I just wanted to guilt you into listening to me for once."

"I always listen to you."

"Debatable," Talia said and stood up. "I'll drive. Be ready in an hour."

"You're surprising me for your birthday?" I asked, setting down my pen.

"Don't say it," she repeated. "See you soon."

Talia took us to a strip mall on the other side of the city.

"I feel like you're driving me to a dark corner of town to murder me or something."

"Please," Talia said as she pulled into a mostly empty parking lot. "If I wanted to be rid of you, I would have found way more creative ways before now."

She parked the car underneath a glowing sign: THE TATTOO BAR.

"Are you serious?" I asked, eyeing the glowing signage. "You're getting a tattoo?"

"No," she said as she turned the car off and unbuckled her seat belt. "*We're* getting tattoos."

"Oh no," I said, keeping my seat belt firmly locked and crossing my arms, defiant. "I am not getting a tattoo. No way in hell."

"Come on," Talia whined. "It would be such good bonding though!"

"I'm going to work in a corporation!"

"Everyone has tattoos nowadays."

"Not in corporate!"

"Get it somewhere no one will see!"

"My parents will kill me!"

"Archie, you are almost twenty-two years old. Keep a secret from your parents. No one will know but me." She got out of the car as she lectured me. Before she closed the door, though, she turned back and said, "But only if you use cash. There's probably an ATM inside."

I muttered a string of curses as her door closed and then scrambled to undo my seat belt and get out of the car. I jogged after her to the door. "I'm not getting a tattoo, Talia," I said again.

She didn't even glance back at me as she raised her keys above her head and locked her car with a loud chirp. "You can admit you're nervous about it. I am too. It's okay."

"There's nothing to be nervous about if I'm not planning on getting one!"

"Hi, welcome to The Tattoo Bar," said the woman working behind the front counter as Talia wrenched open the door, silencing me with a death stare.

Unsurprisingly, the woman was covered in tattoos that looked both beautiful and rather painful. There was a steady hum in the air of the small lobby that I quickly placed as the sound of whirring needles. I shuddered.

"I love your artwork," Talia said, gesturing to the woman's sleeve. It was floral and spread from the tips of her fingers to the top of her shoulder, disappearing under the neckline of her tank top at her collarbone.

The woman held out her arm, looking at the ink. "Thank you! Jason does fantastic work here."

"Is he available?" Talia asked excitedly. "Or do you guys take walk-ins?"

I wanted to sucker punch her for not knowing the answer to that question considering we just *walked in* to The Tattoo Bar, clearly without an appointment.

"We do take walk-ins," the front desk woman said, "but Jason doesn't work Thursdays."

"Looks like we might have to leave," I whispered over Talia's shoulder, and she shushed me.

"But Rachel is available and doesn't have another client scheduled for the evening."

Talia flashed me a devilish grin over her shoulder before placing both her hands on the counter. Leaning in, she told the woman, "That's perfect. Does she have a book?"

The woman reached under the counter and provided a portfolio of Rachel's work, along with another book full of small design options "if we needed inspiration."

Talia took both graciously and plopped herself down on one of the sofas in the lobby to peruse. I gave the woman a polite nod, then sat next to Talia tentatively.

"What kind of tattoo do you want?" I asked Talia, looking over her shoulder at the open books.

She sighed. "Correction: What kind of tattoo do we want?"

"I'm not getting a tattoo."

"Even if I get a matching one?"

"You want to get matching tattoos?"

"That is the reason I brought you here, yes."

I paused. "You want to get matching tattoos with me?"

"Yes," she said and pointed at a pair of delicate wings in the book. "You are my wingman for life. Might as well commemorate it."

I swear my heart stuttered a beat at the look in her eyes when she lifted her gaze to mine, but she didn't lift her finger from the page. I glanced once more at the design, and once more at the open expression in her wide blue eyes, clear and vulnerable.

Something about the bareness of her gaze made me forget all my resolve, replacing my original apprehension with pure desire to see Talia happy in life.

I glanced around the room and found an ATM lurking in the corner. "Okay," I sighed. "I'll get a tattoo with you."

Talia made me sit in the chair first, claiming she wanted to see the process before confirming where she wanted hers to be. I thought that meant she was actually more scared than she let on, but I wasn't about to show her how nervous I was either.

I'm not sure what I imagined our tattoo artist, Rachel, would look like, but when we were led back to her room, I didn't think we'd be getting stabbed with needles by an elderly woman with graying, frizzy hair and purple cat-eye glasses. And not a single tattoo to be seen on her exposed wrists, ankles, neck, or hands. She only wore baggy jeans and a chunky sweater.

"What are we doing today, dears?" she asked in a voice as soft and kind as my grandmother's. I half expected fresh baked cookies in the room.

Talia handed her the book and pointed to the pair of lightly feathered angel wings. "We both want something like this, ma'am."

I was surprised to hear the slip of the Southern drawl come from Talia's lips at the request, but I didn't say anything. Maybe it was a nervous habit I had yet to hear, based on the way her eyes kept shifting uncomfortably around the room.

Rachel examined the symbol. "I can do that, easily. Any modifications?"

Talia shook her head. "No, I think it's perfect the way you have it drawn already."

Rachel beamed. "Wonderful. Let me go get a stencil set up for you two."

She left the room, leaving Talia and me to glance awkwardly around her setup. I moved over to the corkboard Rachel had set up by the window. Several sketches of potential tattoos were tacked to the board. Lots of flowers and cats.

I chose to ignore the display of needles and ink next to the large chair in the center of the room. It seemed like Talia was avoiding it as well, for she had taken a liking to the prints and paintings on the other side of the window opposite from where I stood.

"Now I have to ask," Rachel said as she entered the room again, causing us both to jump. "Do either of you have tattoos? Or will this be your first?"

"First," Talia and I said together and quickly. We glanced at each other.

"Wonderful!" Rachel beamed as she sat down on her stool next to the chair still looming in the center. To make the stage even more daunting, she reached up to flick on an overhead light, illuminating the seat in a spotlight glow. "Who's up first?"

I cast one more wayward glance at Talia, but she wasn't looking at me. Instead, her stare wasn't moving from the chair. Or the needle that Rachel picked up.

I tilted my head to the side and closed my eyes for a half second. Letting out a sigh, I said, "I think it's me."

Rachel patted the seat. "Well, don't be shy. Up you go, dear." She set down the needle she was prepping and picked up the stencil. "Now where were you thinking of placing these wings?"

"I was thinking on the back of my shoulder," I said as I sat in the chair and reached behind my head to tap the first inconspicuous spot that came to mind.

Unfortunately, I spoke up about the same time Talia came back to life and proclaimed, "His left ass cheek."

Rachel chuckled in an adoring fashion. "A bit racy for your first tattoo," she said, winking at Talia. Then she leaned in closer to me with a smile. "I have a few there myself, though. Excellent spot if you don't want it seen."

I glared at Talia. She had a hand over her mouth, stifling a chuckle. "It's true," she finally said. "No one will see it there. Well, maybe not no one. But it sure would make for a great story whenever you got your pants off."

My glare stiffened.

"It's up to you, dear," Rachel said and lifted the stencil, holding it out in front of her.

I looked back and forth between Rachel, Talia, and the tattoo stencil.
I gave up. "Fine. Okay. Ass cheek." It would be less noticeable there
anyway. And it was small.

"Yes!" Talia cheered.

I ignored her and swung my legs back over the chair and unbuttoned
my jeans.

"We can just do a little shimmy with your pants and boxers. Don't
need too much real estate." Rachel was a little too cheery as I flipped over
onto my stomach.

"Okay," I said, willing my pants a little farther down. "Let's get this
over with."

Rachel's hands were cold, and I flinched.

"Easy, dear," she said, with a light laugh. "We haven't even gotten to
the fun part yet."

I closed my eyes and tried to ignore the commentary as Rachel and
Talia picked the "perfect" placement for the wings.

I found myself thinking maybe this wouldn't be that bad after all, until
the vibration of the needle started purring in the air and the bite of the
first line seared into my skin.

"Holy shit!" I cried and jerked back. Rachel calmly turned off the
buzzing torture device and looked at me patiently.

"You get used to it after the first few strokes," she said. "But we can
take our time."

I looked over at Talia, confirming we were indeed going to continue
this ridiculous spectacle of hers, but nothing in her expression told me
whether or not she expected to continue.

I sighed. "I guess it would look pretty ridiculous to leave it how it is."

"Like a toddler took a Sharpie to your butt?" Rachel asked, deadpan.
"Yes, probably a little silly."

"Okay," I said, taking another breath, and situated myself down on
the chair, face down. "I can do this. Keep going."

Rachel obliged, and in my head, I cursed Talia in new and creative ways. The pain was like a hive of bees steadily stabbing me in the ass, marching one by one with their little stingers zapping me in a constant stream. I ground my teeth together and bit back any noise that could resemble a whimper.

The torture lasted about fifteen minutes based on the way the clock hands had moved around their circle, but it felt like an eternity when Rachel gave my cheek one final wipe and announced that she was finished.

I glanced at Talia to find her peering on her tiptoes to get a glance at the ink. Or my ass. Or both. I slid off the chair and shuffled awkwardly to the mirror, clutching the front of my boxers as I twisted around to look at my tattoo.

The line work was thin and precise on the outline of the feathered pair of wings. The design was simple and not too big, small enough to stay concealed, but etched permanently in my memory and body.

I pulled my pants up. "All right, wingman extraordinaire, you're up next. Where are you putting yours?"

Talia was quiet, staring at the needles once again.

"Are you okay?" Rachel asked her.

Talia stayed silent, still staring. "Hey." I finished buckling my pants and moved toward her. She looked shell-shocked and didn't even flinch when I took her hands in mine. "Talia?"

Her eyes flickered toward mine ever so briefly. "I can't," she whispered.

"Why?" I cocked my head slightly. "The needles?"

She pressed her lips together and shook her head.

I lowered my voice and squeezed her hands. "Then what is it?"

Her mouth quivered once, and I thought this might have been the only time I had ever seen Talia truly afraid. "It's forever," she whispered.

"Yes," I said. "That is the point of a tattoo. It'll never go away."

Her eyes were shining wide and unblinking as she turned them on me. "But what if I do?"

My heart leapt and wrapped its fist around my throat at the thought of her ... ever not being around. I thought for maybe the first time about what would happen after college, where our lives might go, at the possibility of our paths ever potentially diverting from each other. "Are you planning on it?"

"I ... I can't," she whimpered and gave me one more sidelong glance. She gave Rachel an apologetic wave, and I was shocked to see her eyes turn glassy. "I'm sorry."

She turned to the door, leaving me dumbstruck with my jaw open. She paused once more. "Archie ... I'm so sorry."

I stared at her dumbfounded as she left The Tattoo Bar. This whole excursion had been her idea and she just ... bailed? It was so uncharacteristic. And the fear lodged in her expression—I had never seen anything like it before.

What if I do? Was she planning something I didn't know about? Something about ... leaving?

I turned to Rachel and muttered something along the lines of a thank you and an apology before paying for the matching tattoo I suddenly had no match for. And as I pulled cash from my wallet, that thought alone sent a neat little fissure through my heart, cracking it just slightly, almost undetectably, but still pulsing and a little bit broken.

TALIA

PRESENT DAY

I went back for my second therapy session that same week. I stayed mostly in Kathryn's house until then, only venturing outside for the necessities, biding my time until Lacey could see me again.

I hadn't heard from Grady, and I ignored the few texts from Archie that promised to "check on me." I didn't want either of them, or anyone else for that matter, to know I was still lingering in town.

This time, I drove by myself to the therapy office.

"So we spent a little time last time talking about who you were and how you came to be here," Lacey said as she made us both a cup of tea. I hadn't noticed it, but behind her desk she had a small bookshelf full of different and seemingly random mugs she had collected, with an electric kettle on the middle shelf.

She offered me the cat-shaped mug, and I took it with both hands, holding the warmth of it tight in my palms.

"And I think I got the short version of your family," Lacey said as she sat with her legs crossed in the oversize armchair across from mine.

I let a weak little laugh escape. She just smiled kindly at me and said, "I want to hear more about your people."

I took a tentative sip from the mug. It had to be some sort of English breakfast tea, and she made it sweet with milk and sugar. "My people?" I asked.

"Yes. One of the most crucial steps as we find a way to move forward in assuming your identity as someone who can and will continue to live with depression is to have a circle around you."

I considered this. "I think I have a triangle. Or a square. Depends on if I'm included in the head count."

"I don't discriminate against shapes."

I returned her smile and tucked my feet underneath me. Lacey waited for me to continue.

I took a deep breath and told her the first name that came to mind. "Grady Mitchell."

"Boyfriend?"

"Hardly."

"Friend?"

I thought about it. "Yes. Not particularly the closest. But we had a lot of classes together in college."

"Do you guys still talk?"

"Some." I bit my lip and drummed my fingers against the mug. *Tap, tap, tap. Tap, tap, tap. Tap … tap.* "There was this one time … I don't know, maybe a year or so ago now? I … he …"

I tripped, fumbled, and fell over the words I had never dared to voice aloud. I took a breath—long and slow and deep enough to fill my lungs and chest—and I tried again. "He was essentially my suicide hotline phone call." I exhaled.

A burning shame flamed my cheeks at the admission I hadn't dared think of since that night. I had been staying in Charlotte, North Carolina, visiting the arts district on the edge of the city. It didn't take long to find a part-time nanny job on the local social media pages. I had even picked up work at one of the cafés in the area. And in a short time, I found a cute apartment from someone who was subletting, also from local social media. It was too perfect to turn down, and every day that I walked through town to the café, I thought harder and harder about staying longer and longer.

Unfortunately, I ran into someone from high school who had moved up from South Carolina and taken a corporate banking position in Charlotte. Turned out they told their parents they saw me, who in turn told my parents, and the whole telephone charade ended in a surprise visit from my mom when she stopped in at the coffee shop a few days later.

"Natalia," she said. I thought a ghost had said my old name based on the sudden chill it elicited.

I turned my whole body around, slowly, my eyes frozen in the shock of hearing, then *seeing* her. My mother folded her arms in front of her chest, the purse at her shoulder nearly slipping off. Her nose was lifted in the air as she said, "I don't need to know where you've been, but this little game of yours has gone on long enough. It's time for you to come home."

I opened my mouth to speak, but no sound came out. My lips just opened and closed, like a fish that flopped out of water, desperate for its lungs to be filled with something, *anything*, that may give life back to its dying body.

"I don't know where you're staying," my mother continued, "but I'm willing to come with you to pack your things. Then we are going back home. Together."

"No." I finally managed the one syllable in a hoarse, croaking sound.

My mother tilted her head slightly. "No?" she repeated, this time in an amused question.

"I ... I can't go home," I said, setting down the cup I had been clutching. A crease lined the cup where my grip had choked it. "I won't. I want to be an artist. And I can't ... there." The thought of being back in my hometown made me feel like I was suffocating. I felt a burning sensation behind my eyes.

"And what is it that you're doing now, hmm?" She looked almost smug as she glanced around the café. "You're pouring coffee, living off who knows what cash—not to mention how you've come by it. Your father and I have let you play out this childish, whirlwind fantasy, but enough is enough. It's time for you to grow up. We're leaving tonight."

"No," I said again, still unable to produce much volume when faced with my mother.

"Yes," my mother hissed. "I want to know where you're staying. I can either help you pack or wait in the lot. But this ends. Today."

I lied about my shift and gave myself an extra hour to prepare. It didn't take long to pack my things. I didn't know where I was heading when I got on the highway, but it was dark and had started raining at some point, just to add insult to injury.

I don't know when I started crying, but by the time a few exits had passed, my tears were flowing, and sobs wracked my body in violent tremors. Somewhere between my aching heart and the empty spaces between my ribs, I held on to a faint recollection of a promise I'd once made.

I fumbled with my phone. I would only make one call, I promised myself. If he didn't pick up, I wouldn't call back.

Grady answered on the third ring with his usual carefree lilt. "Talia Scott. Long time not to hear from you."

"You told me to call." The words came out in an awkward, whiny rush, and I swiped at my nose with the sleeve on my elbow. "You told me to call if I ever got close, right?"

He paused, and I thought I could hear him shuffling around on his end of the line. When he spoke again, his voice had taken on a much lower tone than I had ever heard. "Talia," he said again, "are you all right? Where are you?"

"You told me to call," I repeated. "If I ever felt that ... darkness." I hiccupped and said stupidly, "Well, it's dark. Outside. And I guess inside too."

The lights from the other cars were streaking by me; I left their red taillights in laser-like streams behind as my foot laid its deadweight on the gas pedal.

"Where are you?" he asked again, this time with more urgency.

"I don't know. Somewhere in North Carolina? And hopefully farther north."

"Goddamn it, you're behind a fucking steering wheel, aren't you?"

"It's raining," I said in a quiet, pathetic whine.

"Yeah. Yeah, I'm sure it is. Can you tell me what happened? Why are you driving … in the *dark*?"

I hiccupped again, and my foot jerked on the pedal, causing the car to leap forward. "My mom found me and wants me to come back. But I didn't want to be found." The one hand that wasn't clutching the phone to my ear loosened its grip on the steering wheel until just my fingertips were grazing the bottom of the wheel.

"You've been hiding."

"I thought I was exploring."

"So why are you running now?"

Running. I took my fingers away from the wheel, testing how long it would take for the wheels to drift to the left, toward the concrete median, before I touched the wheel to straighten the car.

"I shouldn't be," I finally whispered. "She's right. It does end. This all ends. It has to. I can't go back."

"Talia," Grady said firmly and chose his next words carefully. "You don't have to go back. But you have to look ahead."

I lifted my gaze from watching my hands to staring at the blur of the white highway lanes. I turned off my windshield wipers. "To what? I'm going to fail, and she knows it. I'm already failing. I've always been a failure."

"No," he said, his voice full of kindness. "No, you're not. Please listen to me, Talia, when I say that you have to pull over so we can talk—right now."

I reached forward and flicked my headlights off, saying nothing, but pressed the gas pedal just another millimeter farther. I checked the speedometer and watched as it ticked a notch over one hundred.

"Talia," Grady pleaded again through the phone. "Pull. Over."

I said nothing. I stared at the road, refusing to blink, letting my eyes slip in and out of focus.

The sound of a siren behind me made my chin jerk from the blurred lines to the blinding lights in my rear-view mirror.

"Talia!" Grady yelled through the phone. "Talia, talk to me. What is that siren?"

I eased my foot off the gas. The energy to keep pressing faster dissipated, and my eyes focused on the road once more. I saw the police officer flashing his lights behind me, signaling for me to pull over.

"Just the cops," I said miserably. "I'm getting pulled over."

"Send me your location," Grady said. "I'll find a way to get to you."

I finally took my foot off the gas and watched the speedometer ease back down before pulling into the right lane to stop the car. "It's okay. I'm okay," I said, and a sudden clarity washed over me at what I had almost done. I started crying, even more violently than before, as I stopped the car.

"Leave me on the line and talk to the cops," said Grady. "I'm coming for you, Talia. Hold on."

And he did. Grady met me a few days later somewhere near the North Carolina and Virginia border, and we talked openly about that night. To be fair, the reckless driving ticket did a good amount of sobering with the fine I had to pay.

But that night etched Grady as a permanent fixture in my life. I felt indebted to him.

I told Lacey every part of the story. I had never uttered a word of it before to anyone else; even Grady and I didn't speak of it. It stayed underneath the surface of our every interaction though and flashed in his eyes at times when he looked at me.

My thumb found its way to the thin skin of my wrist as I spoke to Lacey. Instinctively, my knuckle had curled so my nail could run its routine track. I paused and resisted the urge to glance down at my hands. Instead, I made my thumb flatten and pressed the pad of it to the thin scar, holding it there lightly.

"I'm lucky," I finally said after a heavy pause on the conclusion. "It's never been that bad since then, but I'm lucky I had Grady to call."

"Is he the only one you could have called?"

I shook my head. "I don't think so. I think I can see that now. I have others. I have Kathryn. Kathryn Sullivan. Or Walker now. She's married."

"And who is Kathryn to you?"

"My roommate from college. We lived together for a few years. She was always one of those people who didn't say much, but she didn't need to because she saw everything. And I never realized how much she probably understood until recently."

"Why is that?"

"She's who I'm staying with right now. She was the one who helped me find you. And she ... she didn't judge."

"I think you'll find that most people don't judge if you give them the chance. Especially those closest to you."

I bit my lip. "I also have Archie."

"Who's Archie?"

The tea in my mug was starting to get cold. I set it down on the coffee table in front of us and took a wavering breath. "Archie Morgan is my best friend in the entire universe and quite possibly the great love of my life. He's like ... my person."

Lacey offered a soft chuckle. "Why didn't we start with him?"

I said in a low voice, "Because I was scared to finally admit it."

"That's good."

"Why's that?"

"Because that means you care. Tell me the origin story of Archie. How did he come to be such an important fixture in your life?"

I reminded myself to breathe once more, and then I started at the beginning. "It started with a game. We met at the start of freshman year, and we would go out every week to this local dive bar together. We called it playing wingman, where we would each take turns picking a target for the night and then help the other score, whether it was getting a girl's number or a quick make-out session or simply just a good conversation with someone else for the night. It was fun.

"But over the years, it became more than that. For me, at least. And if I'm being honest, it always was more for him too. It became a ritual that we both looked forward to, I think just because we were together. Everything in my head seemed better when I was around him. I think I always knew that, too, even if I couldn't admit it. And I knew that I couldn't do that to him forever."

"What do you mean?" Lacey asked.

"I couldn't let him be my crutch. I'd always been a loner, and for the first time, I felt *better* when I was with someone. And when I realized it, it made me feel selfish. Senior year, I told myself I couldn't do that to him anymore. So ... I left."

"You just left?"

"Yes," I said. "I left. I wanted, still want, to be an artist, so I took myself on a tour visiting art districts across the country. But more than that, I think I got scared. And then I got weak."

"Why do you say *weak*?"

"Because I came back," I said, as if it were obvious. "I came back here. To this town. Where our college was, where it all started, back to where Archie is. I reached out to one of my old professors about wanting to work on a mural. I thought after all the street art I had studied, I was ready for one of my own. And Joe gave me a workspace and a few days to pull it off."

"And did you do it? Pull it off that is?"

I nodded. "Yeah. Yeah, it's finished."

"What about talking to Archie?"

"What do you mean?" Instinctively, I reached up and rubbed the spot at the back of my neck where I had my tattoo.

"I'm assuming you've seen Archie since you've been back?"

His lips, his hands, his body. The hurt in his eyes when he thought I was leaving him once more. "Yes. I've seen him. We've spoken."

"Have you shared with him some of the things you've told me?"

"Not all of it," I admitted. "It's not his job to fix me. I don't want that for him."

And then Lacey said the same thing I had heard come out of Archie's mouth. "You're right," she said. "You've got to want to help yourself." She reached forward and gave my knee a gentle pat before standing up to go pour another cup of tea. "And by the looks of it, you're on the right track."

ARCHIE

PRESENT DAY

A few days after my lunch with Grady, I sent a couple more texts to Talia that remained unanswered. Then my father stopped by the front desk and promised "big exciting news" that night over dinner. I told him with a dutiful smile that I was excited to hear what it was, and then I continued to file papers for Stacey.

By the time the clock hit 5 p.m., I took off my glasses and rubbed my eyes. The pressure in my head was growing as Grady's voice continued to ring in my ears. *What are you passionate about?*

This wasn't the first time. The question had been pulsing in and out of my every thought since Grady had first asked it. Especially when I realized that I didn't know the answer.

He was right. I had accepted so much of my life as mundane and routine. And while my reasons for never changing seemed valid, I couldn't stop wondering what something different might look like.

Hence the headache.

"Clocked out yet?" my dad asked as he came out of his office.

I lifted my head out of my hands and watched him slide his arms through his jacket. Absently, I shuffled the loose papers in front of me into neater stacks to finish filing tomorrow. "Just about," I said.

"Sounds good, son. I'll see you at home."

I nodded to him and was putting things away when he stopped at the front door. "Archie?"

I looked up to see him offer a small, simple smile at me over his shoulder. "I don't think I tell you enough. But you're doing a good job around here."

The affirmation felt warm, but not as rewarding as maybe it should have. "Thanks, Dad. I appreciate it."

"Keep up the good work," he said and shouldered the door open. "See you at home."

Home. "Yeah," I said. "I'll see you there."

"How was everyone's day today?" my mom queried as she set down the last plate at the table for family dinner before seating herself at the head.

Adeline piped up: "I got my literary essay back for my AP English class. A-plus."

"That's wonderful, honey," my mom gushed, and they started up a conversation about *Madame Bovary* and literary realism and rejection of Romanticism and all things bookish that I tried to keep up with, but I kept getting lost.

Eventually, as their conversation started to subside, my dad cleared his throat. "So I told Archie today at work that I had some exciting news for him, but I wanted to wait until tonight when I could share it with all of you."

My mom's face was full of pride as she set down her utensils on her plate and folded her hands in front of her. "What is it, Roger?"

From his seat beside me, my dad slapped my knee and gave it a firm shake. "I've been talking with my partner. We've both been watching you over the past several months."

"Two years," Addie said with a nearly undetectable eye roll.

My mom cut her a chastising glance, but my dad marched right on with his speech. "We've taken notice of the hard work you've put into the company."

"The front desk is high-level stuff," I said, looking down at my plate.

"Regardless," my dad said, "we've both decided that it's time for you to start to take on more for the company. We'd like to give you the opportunity to shadow some of the accounting in action."

I swallowed. "I don't have a CPA."

"We can call it an internship. And I've found a good online program we can get you enrolled in."

I stared at him, not quite making sense of what he was saying. Neither Addie nor my mom offered to fill in the gaps either. "What would be the point of all this?" I asked.

My dad sighed. "I want you to take over the family business one day."

I stopped breathing.

"Not now, we've got quite a few years until then. But I trust you and your judgment and your work ethic in the field." He was beaming, his chest puffed out with pride.

I was dumbstruck. The pause around the table grew until it was too large to ignore, and I realized it was my job to fill it. I cleared my throat. "Wow. Um … Dad. I don't even know what to say."

"Well, it's simple," he said with a laugh. "Just say thank you!"

Once again, Grady's voice of reason chimed from somewhere in my ear. *It's time for you to start living your own life.*

"I—yes. Thank you," I managed. "But … can I think about it? A little bit?"

My dad's smile flickered, and his left eye twitched. He composed himself in record time and said, "Yes. Yes, of course. Take your time." He slapped my knee once more. "It is a big decision, after all."

"Yeah. Yeah, it is." I stabbed a brussels sprout with my fork. "Uh … Mom. How's the yoga studio been this week?"

And the conversation shifted away from me and my supposed future. I pictured Grady shaking his head at me. Until my dad had voiced his wish for my future, I hadn't realized how much I knew that taking over the family business wasn't what I wanted to do.

But right then, faced with that moment of clarity and expectation, I couldn't bring myself to voice it. Not without inciting major familial disappointment over dinner. Not yet.

I kept eating. My family kept talking.

Grady was right.

TALIA

SENIOR YEAR

There wasn't much worse than feeling like a middle schooler all over again when the guidance counselor sits your class down and gives the "Let's think about what you want to be when you grow up" speech.

I had done a whole study on that already in eighth grade. I was well versed in the sad statistics and the likelihood that you couldn't survive off the nonexistent income of a wannabe artist. Apparently, some sadist of an academic organizer thought that, as college seniors, we needed a repeat of this discussion, which in my opinion, was a little late.

The whole gang was together. And I mean the *whole* gang. The entire senior class took up the majority of the Constance L. Weber Auditorium as the director of the career center gave us all a nice reminder (lecture) that we were approaching our last semester of our undergraduate program and emphasized the importance of internships and how it was never too early to start job hunting. My phone was incredibly entertaining for the bulk of the one-sided conversation.

"You should be paying attention," Archie said the fourth time I checked my email. "I don't think you've completed a single step to 'furthering your career post-academia.'"

"How do you know that?"

We got a shush from a blonde girl in the row in front of us who delivered a swift death glare and obviously took this lecture very seriously.

Archie leaned over and dropped his voice to whisper directly in my ear, "Because if you're not in the art studio with Grady, you're lounging in my room—not writing a résumé or network profile."

I closed my email abruptly. "That's just rude."

Archie smirked and sat up tall once more in his seat. "Just saying. You should probably be paying attention."

I sighed. "I think we should just leave. You obviously don't need any more tips or tricks. You already have a job waiting for you when you graduate."

He looked over at me with only his eyes and a lift of his brow. "Jealous?"

"No. I couldn't stand the torture of being trapped behind a desk from the hours of nine to five. I'd rather gouge my eyeballs out with a mechanical pencil."

Archie folded his arms in front of his chest. "You *are* jealous," he said incredulously.

"No," I repeated. "I think I'd keel over if I had to work with my family the way you're going to."

Lucky for Archie though, his father owned a successful accounting firm with a guaranteed job that had been waiting for Archie since he started excelling in his math classes. So he was set for the foreseeable future. No *what-ifs*.

But still. There was no way in hell I could live the life he already had outlined for himself.

The speaker was still droning on. I checked my phone—there were at least twenty more minutes of this. "Please," I whined, which earned me another shush from the girl in front of us. I ignored her and wrapped both of my arms around Archie's bicep. "Can we please leave? My senior art show portfolio isn't anywhere close to being done, and it needs my undivided attention."

"Your art show isn't until April."

"How do you know that?"

"Because it's usually the only thing you're talking about when you're not writing a résumé or network profile in my room."

"I'm leaving. You can come or you can stay."

"Where are you going?"

"Away."

"More specifically?"

"I told you. Art." I got up and didn't wait for him. "I'll see you later. Probably in your room. Probably not writing résumés or networking."

I heard Archie's chuckle behind me, and he wished me luck with my endeavors. No one tried to stop me as I picked my way through the crowd to the double doors.

The air was cold as I exited the auditorium, and I made the swift decision to stop by the coffee shop on campus before going to the studio. I left one hand buried in my jacket pocket but started to scroll through my email once more, refreshing it twice on the way to get my coffee.

A new unread email sat at the top of my inbox as I reached for the door handle. Sender: THE DIGITAL ART SHOW. My heart leapt into my throat, and I took a step back on the concrete stairs, one foot teetering on the edge.

I had been waiting for a response from the blog for what felt like an eternity but was, in reality, only a few weeks. *The Digital Art Show* had started doing routine posts every Friday to showcase both local and new artists across the country. And one night, one of the only nights I was in my room without a roommate but stocked with copious amounts of alcoholic seltzers, I had downed enough liquid courage to submit a piece of my own.

With shaky fingers, I opened the email.

Dear Talia Scott,

Thank you for your interest in The Digital Art Show. We greatly appreciate your time and submission. After careful evaluation, however, our team has decided that your piece, *Self-Portrait in Acrylic and My Parent's Disappointment*, may not be the best fit for our online platform at this time ….

I barely registered the remainder of the email.

Rejection. I had gotten my first rejection.

I knew it was to be expected at some point, but somehow, reading those words attached to my name, with my work, made the inevitable sting feel like a whole damn hive had been dropped on my head. And the bees were swarming like a thousand tiny sucker punches.

Every statistic, every warning from my parents that I might not succeed, and every annoying one-liner the career center could dish out suddenly rang in my ears.

I abandoned the coffee I hadn't even ordered and went straight to the studio.

It was empty when I opened the heavy door; the squeak of it across the floor drowned out my shallow breaths that came quicker and quicker. I found the canvas I had photographed and scanned for my submission to the online platform. It was tucked behind several of the other students' self-portraits. I would say it had been hiding, but I had chosen the largest canvas to paint.

I wriggled it free and carried it over to the sink, studying it as I marched. The grayness of the mouth and skin, the bright orange and yellow of the wild hair that spread around the figure and covered the majority of her features. The hand that reached ahead, neither pleading for help nor reaching out. Just … outstretched. I fumbled around above the sink and found the lighter I knew Joe kept with his candles stored in the shelving.

I brought the lighter to the palm of that hand first and flicked it on.

The flame licked the edges of the canvas, slowly teasing its way around the lines of the painting. The heat spread until the fire ate its way across the mouth of the figure and wrapped its way through the brazen color of the curls on her head.

I moved my own fingers out of the way, lightly holding the wooden frame of the canvas until that was starting to be swallowed too. I felt the prickle of heat around my hands and thought about what it might feel like to hold that fire as well, but ultimately dropped the remainder of my portrait into the metal basin of the sink and turned on the water, letting the flames sizzle and swallow what was left of the ragged canvas.

You're throwing away your education, Natalia.

No. I was doing worse. I was burning it.

TALIA

PRESENT DAY

My third therapy session revolved around art.

"Tell me what you do," Lacey said. Once again, she sipped her tea.

I gripped my own mug. "Usually I'm a bartender or a barista. Nothing now though," I said.

"I didn't mean your job," Lacey said. "That's not what makes you *you*. Unless you identify as a career bartender and that's your entire personality trait, which if so, kudos to you. I can't remember that many drinks."

I lifted one corner of my mouth into a smile. "I had a cheat sheet," I admitted. "But I've told you before. I do art."

"When did you pick it up?"

"Middle school? I picked it as my elective all three years, which apparently you weren't supposed to do. We were supposed to be exploring all the things we could possibly be interested in. But for me, it's always been art."

"And what do you want to do with it?"

I tried to refrain from rolling my eyes and failed. "Be an artist."

"What qualifies someone as an artist?"

"Someone who makes art."

Lacey paused. "And are you someone who makes art for themselves or someone who makes art to be seen?"

"I'd like to be someone who makes art to be seen …." I looked down at my mug and mumbled, "I had this mission, I guess."

"Which is?"

"I wanted—*want*—to leave my mark on the world. That's why I traveled so much, studying a ton of street art in different cities. I was trying to learn as much as I could, so I could do it myself. And it made sense in my head to paint my first mural here, where I first studied art in college."

Lacey smiled at me over her mug, and her face glowed with something warm that I thought looked like pride. "I love that."

"A lot of days, it sounded pretty stupid, even to me."

"I think," Lacey said, "that without even realizing it, you were finding ways to use art as a form of healing."

"Funny enough," I said, putting down my mug and tucking my legs up to my chest, "you're not the first person to have suggested that."

"Who else?"

"Joe."

At the raise of Lacey's eyebrow, I voiced the answer before she could ask it. "My art professor."

"What did he say?"

I took a deep breath. "He said it during a conference we had on one of our bigger projects. It was on color theory. And I did a study of the color red, and on accident, mostly, I used my own blood as part of the landscape. And before you say anything, I realize how morbid it sounds."

"I wasn't going to say anything," Lacey said and took a sip from her mug. "Yet."

"I thought I was going to be in a lot of trouble," I began.

When he had called me into his office, I had an irrational fear that I was going to be suspended. I later found out everyone had a conference on their projects, but I was the lucky one who got to go first and be scared.

"Tell me about your project," Joe said when I sat down in his office, which was, essentially, the back corner of the arts studio where he kept all of his own current works in progress stashed.

"Well," I started, my eyes flickering back and forth from his curious expression to my canvas that sat propped on an easel for both of us to view, "it's a landscape portrait of the field next to my elementary school."

"From back home?"

There was a lump in my throat. "Yes."

"I had gotten the impression you didn't like home very much. I'm surprised you chose a landscape from there," Joe mused, gazing at the canvas.

I looked back at it, too, and spoke to the memories that bled on it. "I was surprised too. But there were some good memories with a few friends I had when I was younger. The school was small, and every once in a while, our teachers would take us to the field and let us play in the woods for our recess instead of the playground."

We had built forts out of sticks and our imaginations were the captains of our adventures.

"Anyway. I followed the rubric," I said. "And all of the materials were found in nature. Or the grocery store. It's like a giant fruit salad threw up on there."

"Does that include the blood?" Joe asked candidly.

His question warmed my cheeks, flushing my skin. "Yes," I said. "It was mine though. And I wasn't really planning on it. I cut myself by accident and ... it was just there. So I decided to use it."

"What does that mean, do you think?" Joe asked, still looking at my canvas. "That some part of you decided to use it? What does it symbolize?"

I sighed. "I don't know .... It's probably on par for the destruction that field later saw. It got bulldozed."

"I'm asking about you," he said, turning to me. "What does it symbolize for you?"

"Chaos? Loss?" I paused, contemplating my next thought. I almost checked over my shoulder to make sure no one else was listening. "Inner turmoil?"

"That's the easy answer, Talia. Surface level." And as if to emphasize his point, he reached out and grazed his fingers across the surface of the trees. "If what you're saying is true, you gave blood to this project, quite literally. You gave a part of yourself for something else. That could be considered healing for some."

I told Lacey this, and how Joe's perspective on my project must have meant he thought I could be an awesome blood donor for a worthy cause .... Or something.

She was quiet, in her listening way, which was only one of two reactions she ever had. The second was questioning.

"Have you ever heard of expressive arts therapy?" she asked.

I gave a dry chuckle. "Funny enough, that's what Grady does."

"Have you considered it?"

"I think I probably need it more than I could give it." I finally unfolded my knees from my chest. "I thought about teaching though."

"Why didn't you pursue that?"

"I wanted to prove to myself that I could do it first. I didn't think I'd be qualified if not."

"And have you?" Lacey asked. "Proved it?"

I shrugged. "Joe called and said my mural is being unveiled tomorrow."

"Congratulations! Who's going?"

"It's open to the public."

"Yes, but who in your triangle, or square, of people is going?"

"Kathryn," I said. "She actually seems really excited. I think Grady will be there too."

"And Archie? The possible great love of your life."

"I haven't told him," I said simply, leaving out the detail that he didn't even know I was still in town. "I assumed Grady would tell him."

"Do you want Archie there?"

Yes. "I don't know."

"What about your parents?"

"The ones on the other side of the country who don't approve of me choosing to abandon their mold of what a perfectly unbroken daughter would do? I don't think they're interested."

"You're making an awful lot of assumptions about people rather than communicating clearly your own thoughts and feelings. And, Talia," Lacey said, setting down her cup and putting a hand on my knee. "Listen to me when I say this. You. Aren't. Broken. And you don't have to be healed. What defines you is how you move forward."

She withdrew her hand, but the spot on my jeans remained warm.

"But I've found that the only way to do that," Lacey said, "is to make peace with the past too."

ARCHIE

PRESENT DAY

The morning after my dad pronounced his faith and confidence in me as a future accounting wizard, I volunteered to drive Addie to school. Even though she was seventeen and nearly done with her junior year, we still only had two cars in the family.

I knocked on her door a few minutes early to make sure she was up and getting ready because I wanted to stop for a coffee on the way. She obliged sleepily, and I waited until she had a mocha in her hands before starting my conversation.

"Hey, Addie?" I asked as I pulled away from the drive-through window.

"Hmm?" She made the sound as her lips were pressed to the plastic of her coffee cup lid.

I kept my eyes trained on the road as I took a breath, steadying the words that were waiting to spill from my mouth. "So you know how Dad was talking last night about … wanting to promote me? Or whatever."

"Yes," she said simply. "I thought it was pretty comical."

I bristled, figuring she was going to continue to poke fun at the snail's pace I had been working through at the company so far, no matter how intentional. "Why did you think it was comical?"

"Because you're obviously not happy doing the job."

I turned at the stop sign back onto the main road to drive toward the school. "How do you know that? Maybe I really like spreadsheets and typing in numbers."

"You file papers and schedule meetings. And aside from the fact I think no one actually enjoys doing either job, I know you, Archie," Addie said. "And contrary to popular belief, you're actually really smart. You could have moved on from the front desk a long time ago. So I think the bigger question is, why haven't you? Or better yet, why haven't Mom or Dad asked why you haven't?"

"Why haven't you asked?"

She stared at her paper cup. "Because even though you've never said it, I think you stay because of me."

I didn't know what to say to that. I let the hum of my van fill the air instead.

Addie continued. "My therapist said a while ago that instead of apologizing for things in the past that I can't change, a healthier way of moving forward is to simply express gratitude."

"That sounds well rehearsed, Adeline."

"It's called practice," she said with a little smirk. "Regardless, I appreciate you always being around to keep an eye on everyone. Including me."

I nodded, my throat weirdly tight. "You're welcome."

"But you don't have to, you know."

I glanced over at her. She was still watching the road. "How do you figure?" I asked.

Addie sighed. "It's not your job to take care of me. Or Mom. Or even Dad and the family business. It's kind of similar to what I've been told the past few years. My own body, health, life, is my job. And you've been neglecting yours."

I opened my mouth to argue, but my little sister cut me off again. "Seriously. You need to do you. I want you to go and do you. Get out of the house. Get a real job that you actually like. You deserve it."

My hands tightened on the steering wheel. "You mean that?"

"Yes," Addie said, exasperated. "I want you to pretend like you're actually twenty-four years old."

I chuckled at the thinly veiled insult underneath the endearing sentiment. I reached over and ruffled her hair, earning a shriek in response as she smoothed her layers back in place. "I've been thinking about it too," I said. "About trying to pretend like I'm twenty-four years old, as you put it."

"Oh yeah? And what does that first step look like?"

I grumbled. "Telling Dad I don't want to be an accountant and take over the business."

"Are you going to give him the whole 'It's not my dream, it's yours' speech?"

"Sounds lame when you put it that way."

"It might be easier to follow up with a plan for what you'd like to do instead."

"I'm working on it," I said as we pulled into her school parking lot. I drove up to the front door and idled.

Addie gathered her bag from her feet and opened her door to get out of my van. As she rustled around, she added, "And you might as well get the girl while you're at it."

I stilled. "What do you mean?"

"Talia, dumbass."

"Talia left days ago."

"Talia *told* you she was leaving, but did she ever say when? There's a distinct possibility she hasn't actually left yet," Addie said, climbing out of the car.

My heart leapt. "How do you know that?"

She shrugged and put her hand on the door handle. Before closing it, she said, "There's also talk that Bridgeport College is revealing a groundbreaking mural tomorrow by an artist called T/S, whose identity remains anonymous. But legend has it she's a Bridgeport alum."

The mural. *Talia's* mural.

"Don't ask," Addie said. "I just listen, and I know things." Then she closed the door, taking the stairs two at a time to the school, leaving me dumbstruck.

The email came twenty minutes after I dropped Addie off at her school. I had just finished making my second coffee of the day in the office. I sat down behind my desk, the front desk, to check my email.

Bridgeport Alumni,

You are invited today to the unveiling of a new mural by new artist…

I tabbed over on my phone to send Grady a text with zero context: Are you going tomorrow?

He responded quickly. I can pop over during lunch. You?

I typed, I don't know. I feel like if she wanted me to be there, she would have asked.

His response was swift again. Since when has Talia ever asked for anyone to look at her work?

I thought of all the times she came up to my room during college, assuming I would join her in a quest of some sorts. She asked for company like that all the time. But something about her art? A glimpse into the inner workings of her mind that stayed secured behind bars and bricks and daggers to keep people out? I had seen a collection of hers exactly once, during senior year. And she had been tense, on edge, and agitated the entire time.

So no, she never asked anyone to venture that close.

But that didn't mean she wouldn't want the encouragement this time around.

On the off chance I was right, I typed, I'm going to go see it.

And her.

Addie just popped in and told me she's skipping counseling to come see it. Sounds like we'll both be there.

"Hey there," my dad said as he strolled by the front and leaned against the desk.

I startled and dropped my phone into my lap with a squeak.

He looked amused. "How's that schedule looking?"

"I just got an invite for something over lunch tomorrow," I said. "But you've got a pretty light morning, it looks like."

He nodded and tapped his knuckles once against the wood, leaving to get back to work.

"Hey, Dad?" I asked tentatively, and before any of the spontaneity could leave my chest, I huffed out the words, "Do you want to go out to lunch together today? I'd like to talk a little more."

We sat down a few hours later, both with our sandwiches and another cup of coffee steaming on the table between us at Millie's Deli.

My dad finally broke the silence. As he wiped the corner of his mouth with a napkin, he said, "Have you thought more about my proposition?"

"The one about the kid who rose from secretary to owner in an example of accounting-world domination?"

He laughed. "That's one creative title."

I looked at the sandwich between my hands and then set it down back on my tray. Brushing my hands clean, I said, "I have. Been thinking."

I cleared my throat and tried again. "I've been thinking that I want to move out."

My dad looked at me as if I had grown another head from my shoulders, but I held his gaze.

When he finally spoke, he said, "Okay. That doesn't have much to do with your work environment, but let's talk about it."

I exhaled. "I've been saving money living at home, but I think it's time for me to get a place of my own."

"You moved out for college."

"I moved around the corner."

"Where are you planning on moving to this time?"

"I was thinking maybe Grady's apartment complex."

"Which is where?"

"Um, around the other corner."

My dad laughed. He actually laughed. And I thought he found the whole idea ridiculous. My cheeks heated, and I folded my hands in my lap.

He finally said, "It's about damn time, son."

I looked at him quizzically.

He continued. "Your mother and I were actually talking about how to bring it up with you, that you might want to start standing on your own two feet at some point."

I bristled. "I can stand. I know how to stand."

"I'm sure you do," my dad said, still chuckling. "In theory. But I support you learning how to in practice."

"Okay," I started slowly, waiting for the catch. "So … you'd be okay if I stopped by the leasing office and got some information?"

"It's your life, Archie. I'm not going to stand in your way."

I made the split-second decision to keep the ball rolling. "Okay. Well, that being said, I don't know if I want to be an accountant the rest of my life."

Once again, he paused. This time, he folded his arms over his chest. "What else would you like to do?"

Now I sighed. "That part I don't know. But I … want to try to figure that out."

My dad looked at his sandwich, nodding to himself. He finally looked up at me, and I saw a fondness that made my heart swell and feel heavy in a way that took the weight off my shoulders.

"I want you to figure it out too, son," he said and reached out to put a hand on my arm. "It's time to move forward."

TALIA

PRESENT DAY

I tugged at the bottom of my black dress, the same one I had worn at Joe's art show a few weeks ago. This time, I paired it with a light-green sweater Kathryn let me borrow. The soft material hugged my neck with warm comfort, and I had to refrain from tucking my chin inside.

But I kept my chin high. I wouldn't hide behind a barrier any longer. Not today.

"Ready?" Joe asked as he walked up to the riser that the college had put in front of my mural to give me a small stage of sorts. His baseball hat was backward on his head, and the exposed lines around his eyes and mouth were crinkled in a smile that glowed with pride.

I returned his smile with one of my own. "It still feels surreal," I said, looking back at the brick wall behind me, etched with my signature at the bottom right corner in black Sharpie: *T/S.*

Joe was looking at my work too. "You did a good job, kid."

A lump formed in my throat at the words. "Couldn't have done it without you," I said. And I meant it: the education, the wall space, and the support to keep trying.

"Yeah, you could've," Joe said and fished a microphone from the back pocket of his jeans. Handing it to me, he said, "Just might have taken you a few more years."

I chuckled and took the mic from his outstretched hand. It was strangely heavy as I gripped it in both of mine. "Thank you. Regardless."

"Don't mention it," he said. "I'll be back in a second to introduce you to the crowd. And then you can introduce your artwork."

I took a deep breath, and as he disappeared, I lifted my gaze to the sea of people that had steadily grown around my little stage. Kathryn was right in front of me, Andrew at her side, and they both gave me encouraging thumbs-up when I met the excitement in their eyes.

I returned a small thumbs-up of my own before continuing my scan. It looked like mostly local people on their lunch breaks who had stumbled upon my setup, but I wasn't going to complain as they lingered. I also saw what had to be Bridgeport students; Joe had told me attendance wasn't mandatory, but almost all the art club students were waiting "with bated breath to see a real live artist that wasn't their teacher or already dead." (Or so he had quoted.)

I realized as I surveyed the faces in the crowd that I wasn't just looking. I was searching. Which was ridiculous. I hadn't invited him.

But it was hard to ignore the void Archie left when his presence lingered in the brushstrokes on the wall behind me and in the memory of his body on mine pressed against the bricks.

"It's go time!" Joe said, and I jumped at the sound when he leapt on the stage next to me. Flourishing his own microphone, he tapped it twice with his palm.

"Good afternoon, friends!" His voice boomed through the throng of people that started to drift closer to his voice. "On behalf of Bridgeport College and the Visual Arts Department, thank you for coming out today. For a little background on what gathers us here now, the town of Bridgeport reached out to our program with an opportunity."

He pointed to the wall behind him and said, "These bricks on this new building needed some paint on them!"

There was a unanimous chuckle beneath us, and I blushed while Joe continued, "And Bridgeport College is proud to announce its new

Community Outreach Initiative with the opening of this newly painted building, which should serve several purposes. It will be a new studio for the college's art students to utilize, complete with theater space, musical rehearsal areas, and several galleries. But more so, it is Bridgeport's hope that the community will visit this space, as the main gallery level will feature artists both local and renowned, and the theaters will be used by other local schools and organizations as well."

Joe paused politely as applause sprung up all around us. While he waited, I caught movement at the far corner of the crowd. I blinked twice at the sight. Grady was there, along with Adeline ... and Archie.

My whole square was here.

For me.

"But with plans for art that speaks volumes," Joe continued, "it was only fitting that the outside reflected the beauty to be held within. And we had an alumna of our own up for the job. As a previous student of mine, now an emerging artist in her own right, I'm thrilled to introduce you to Talia Scott!"

The crowd cheered even louder, and my vision turned watery as I saw Grady lift his hands to his mouth to let out a whistle. Adeline, almost too short for the back of the pack, had clambered up onto Archie and was gripping him piggyback style as she maneuvered her phone sideways, presumably taking a video.

The smile in Archie's eyes as he cheered made a tear spill from the corner of my eye. I laughed as I swiped it away and lifted the mic to my mouth.

"Hi," I said, breathless. I cleared my throat, steadying the racing of my heart, before starting my speech. "So this piece is called *Self-Portrait in Latex Paint and Inner Turmoil*. And it's personal to me because it is a concept I started a few years ago, but I thought that something so close to me didn't have a chance of success. So I burned the first draft."

I might have imagined the shocked hiss in the crowd as I paused, letting my words sear in. I felt the press of the notecards on my hip in the pocket of my skirt, but I left them there. Instead of reading the bullet points I had prepared, I kept my eyes on my friends as I spoke. "Flash forward to now, a few of the visual aspects have shifted, but the core meaning of the painting remains. The words on the piece symbolize an attempted censorship." I glanced back at the two white strikes I'd added last night with the bold black letters, one through one of the eyes, that read: **SIT**. And the other through the mouth: **STILL, LOOK PRETTY**.

I took a breath before continuing. "This was a message I received a lot growing up. Not directly, but the meaning was implied. I couldn't speak up. I couldn't speak up about the things I wanted or the things that were wrong. I was expected to be something I couldn't be. And I couldn't stand up for what I wanted to be. I was expected to sit down and smile through it."

I drummed my fingers against the bottom of the microphone. *Tap, tap, tap. Tap, tap, tap.* "I have clinical depression," I calmly enunciated. "And it's not something I'm proud of. In fact, it was something I was ashamed to admit for too long. But denying it to myself meant I had been living a lie. And I think I hurt a lot of people by doing that. Myself included."

My gaze focused on Archie, and I waited to see if there was a reaction to the truth I finally spoke out loud. By microphone, no less. But he didn't flinch, he didn't cower, and above all, he didn't pity. The encouraging smile made my heart feel like it was soaring.

"This mural is the first in a planned series of portraits I want to paint on buildings all over the country," I said as I stepped back and put a hand on a painted brick. "This first one is supposed to be a piece of my story, but I want the rest of the series to tell the stories of others as well. I want to tell the stories of those who were told stories about themselves, and how they learned to break them and tell their own truth instead."

I stepped aside and reached for the ladder. I tucked the microphone under my arm and started to climb to the point where I could reach the white strike, the censor on the painting. Using my fingers, I clawed at the edge until the tape pulled loose. In one swift tug, I ripped away the message **SIT**. One more scrape and tug, and I ripped away **STILL, LOOK PRETTY**.

I pulled at one more piece of tape hidden just above my signature and removed it to reveal a new, longer message: **SHOUT ... or at least whisper. Someone wants to listen.**

I rolled the tape into a large ball and stepped down off the ladder as the crowd cheered.

No. They didn't just cheer. They roared. And as my feet hit the floor of the stage, I felt like I was floating. I lifted the microphone to say one last acknowledgement. "Thank you. Thank you all so much for coming out. And for listening."

The noise elevated once more as Joe came back beside me and gave me a hug. Dropping his voice so that the mic couldn't pick it up, he said, "Nicely done. I love the conclusion."

"Thanks," I said, pulling away. My eyes involuntarily flickered back to where Archie had stood. He was walking toward me, a grin reaching toward his hazel eyes.

I turned to Joe once more and said, "I think it's a better ending than the one I thought I was going to give it."

ARCHIE

PRESENT DAY

Talia's mural was beautiful. *Talia* was beautiful. And I felt magnetized, drawn to her, as Grady, Addie, and I moved through the lingering crowd toward the stage.

Her face erupted into the biggest smile I'd ever seen, her blue eyes squinting at the edges from the pull of her lips toward her ears. "You guys came," she said, her voice thick with emotion as she hopped down off the riser.

Grady was the first to reach her, and his arms went around her center, lifting her by the waist to spin her. The sound of her laughter rang in my ears and, somewhere deep inside me, reverberated like a Ping-Pong ball between my ribs.

"Congratulations!" Addie said when Grady set Talia back on her feet.

Talia pressed her lips together and gave my little sister a small knowing smile before reaching toward her, wrapping her small frame in her own arms, drawing Addie to her chest. Addie went willingly with a smile of her own, and ever so softly, I heard Talia's whisper, "Thank you."

Addie returned the same look Talia had given her and squeezed her wrists once before stepping back.

When Talia finally settled her crystal eyes squarely on mine, the clarity in them was so striking my words faltered. "H-hi," I said.

She gave me an amused little laugh. "Hi."

I finally was able to slide my eyes off hers to glance once more back at the brick wall. "It looks good. You know, finished. And in the daylight."

She dipped her head to look at her boots as she nodded bashfully. "I probably should have given you credit somewhere in that speech."

I shook my head. "No. It was all you."

She tilted her chin and peered at me from underneath her dark curls. She rocked once on the balls of her feet, then gave up the debate and threw her arms around my shoulders. I smiled into her hair as I held her tight. She still smelled like oranges and flowers.

"Can we get dinner tonight?" The question was so soft it tickled my ear as she spoke next to it.

I nodded against the crook of her neck. "I'd love to."

For old times' sake, we agreed to meet at the diner next to campus that night.

While we waited for our pancakes to arrive, Talia filled me in on the past week. She was still staying with Kathryn, she had started seeing "some chick named Lacey" (whom she later admitted was her therapist), and she visited the mural site a few more times to make the changes and additions I hadn't known about.

"So I guess the painting finally spoke to you," I said as a waitress brought out our breakfast for dinner.

Talia thanked her, then started pouring an ungodly amount of syrup. "Not exactly. I think I just finally figured out what I wanted to say. Because it was something I had chosen not to hear." She passed the syrup to me and folded her hands neatly in her lap. "Archie. I'm sorry. There were so many times I accused you of not hearing what I wasn't saying, which obviously wasn't fair. But it was really me who wouldn't listen to you."

I recalled the words on her portrait. *Shout ... or at least whisper. Someone wants to listen.*

"It's okay," I said, out of habit.

"No, it's not," she said firmly.

I paused and looked up to find the piercing blue of her eyes boring into mine as she leaned toward me. "I mean it," she whispered.

I set down my fork and reached for her hand on the table. She stiffened slightly at the touch but then relaxed. "I mean it too," I said, watching our hands rest on the table together. "As long as you're okay, it's okay. I made my own choices too. And I chose, and will continue to choose, to stand by you. As long as you let me."

She was looking at our fingers woven together like vines. Her eyes were downcast when she said, "I don't think I ever really told you why I left South Carolina."

I was quiet for a moment, and then even quieter, I said, "No. I don't think you did."

"You've probably pieced together the most important parts of the story," Talia said. She gave my hand a little squeeze before untangling our fingers from one another and folding her hands in her lap. "But you were right. I was running. I've been running. And for so long, I wore the shame of who I was, not even fully understanding that identity."

"I don't think I ever fully knew how much you were running from yourself," I admitted.

"I'm done running." She picked up her knife and fork, starting to cut into her pancakes. "I'm turning around, facing my past and myself head-on."

I picked up my own utensils. "Interesting enough, I was thinking about starting to run. And maybe try finally looking ahead to something. Funny how timing works out."

"Or doesn't."

I met her gaze once more. It was heavy and full of feelings that I'm not sure either one of us knew how to voice properly. "So you're still planning on leaving?" I asked.

"Yes." She stabbed her pancakes and ate a large bite. "And no. I'm not entirely sure."

I had no idea what she wanted me to say. Not even quite sure what I wanted to say.

"I was thinking about calling in one more favor from Joe," she said.

I glanced up at her. "Oh yeah?"

"I mean," she continued in a rush, "I still want to travel. And I still want to work on my mural projects. But I was thinking .... I don't know .... Maybe a home base would be nice. And some steady income."

"These are all reasonable things," I said cautiously, waiting for further explanation.

She chewed on her bottom lip. "I may not be very good at it."

"Good at what?"

"God, are you going to make me spell it out?"

"Or paint it."

She cracked a smile. A real one. One that crinkled the corners of her eyes. "I'd like to try to get a teaching job. I can start as an assistant, or a substitute, take some classes to learn how to become a real one. I don't know, but I think there would be a way to do work both in and out of the classroom. Some of my best memories with art are in the classroom, and I'd like to try to give that feeling to someone else."

I felt a stiff flutter in my chest. Just for confirmation's sake, I said, "And to clarify, you're considering trying to find a job ... here?"

"Well"—she smirked—"not as in this diner here. But here as in Bridgeport, yes. I'm considering it. If I could work out a class schedule that was heavy in the beginning of the week, I could do most of my traveling and painting over long weekends."

And suddenly, the answer was so simple. The things I had started to mull over for myself, Talia wanted as well.

"Well," I said, "conveniently, I'd like to see a few more places too. And I've been known to wield a paintbrush with average skill. Or just be the brute strength lookout."

She peered up at me quizzically. When she registered the conviction of my voice and expression, and that it just so happened that our goals were aligning, she smiled once more. "Are you saying that you want to come with me?"

I shrugged. "I'm saying that I do need to get out of Bridgeport. I need to see new things. *Try* new things. And figure out what I want to do next. So it makes sense to travel as a pair, don't you think? We can go somewhere new every weekend, and you can work on your murals, and I can explore."

"Explore?" she questioned, but her smile was glowing.

"Explore," I confirmed. "I don't even know what I don't know yet. But I'd like to learn."

Talia's smile was contagious, and I returned her grin with one of my own. Taking a bite of my pancakes, I asked, "Where are we going first?"

TALIA

PRESENT DAY

"I'm so excited to hear that things went well at your mural!" Lacey said when I sat in her office the following Monday. It was the perfect segue into the conversation about setting goals and looking into the future. She was even more pleased when I came prepared with a few ideas of my own.

I didn't love her bit about learning how to recognize self-sabotaging habits and changing that pattern, but I listened regardless.

I guessed that showed progress in itself.

The sun was shining high above the city when I left Lacey's office and started to drive toward the college. Joe seemed excited when I had emailed him and threw out the idea of trying to get into a classroom again. He wrote back that same day with a request to come into the arts department office for a meeting with the chair to "further discuss our options."

I knew it would be a long journey, one foot in front of the other, but it felt *good* to have something like this to be stepping toward.

And Archie's question echoed in my mind: *Where are we going first?*

Archie. And his new eagerness to see the world, or at least the country, by my side.

After my session, I noticed the sleeves of the blazer Kathryn had let me borrow were long at my wrists. I tugged at the cuff while I idled at a red light, and I accidentally brushed the bandage I had started wearing on my wrist. It was a small act of rebellion against my own brain, but it was working. Since covering my wrist in the thin fabric, my skin had remained unbroken.

And I felt the burning desire to dig into it less and less. I think that was progress too.

As I pulled into the main parking lot of Bridgeport College, my phone started buzzing in the pocket of my slacks. (Also borrowed. Also too long.)

On the very last ring, I managed to slide the button to answer Grady's call. "Hey."

"Have you been on your phone at all?" he asked with zero introduction or context.

"Um," I said, "no, I just pulled into the college. I have a meeting with the arts department to figure out a way to become an adjunct teacher."

"Don't you need a master's for that?"

"Probably," I admitted. "But I'm just trying to get all the information I can."

"Good for you," Grady said, and he sounded proud. "So … you haven't checked your phone yet?"

I turned off the ignition and put the call on speaker so I could check my messages. "No. I haven't gotten any calls or texts. Well, besides yours. Why? What's wrong?"

"I doubt that this shockingly new revelation would be present in a simple text message." Grady sighed. "You might want to check *The Digital Art Show*."

My heart was a bowling ball that plummeted straight through the cavern of my chest and thudded onto the floor of my car. "The … what?"

I could also hear the grin that seeped between his words as he said, "You heard me. Go look at it. They just made a new post."

How had I missed it? Today was Friday after all, and I stalked the new weekly blog posts religiously. Wild to think I had forgotten to look this morning.

I scrambled to type in the website, and when it loaded, right there on the home page was a link to the new post titled "One to Watch: Emerging Street Artist."

With shaky hands, I clicked the post to open it. A video with a short caption sprang to life on my phone. The caption read: "This week's submission was sent in by an anonymous spectator at a local mural-unveiling ceremony for new artist Talia Scott, who is better known by her pseudonym T/S. We look forward to the next installment of her project."

I could hardly breathe as I clicked on the video—just to be sure that I wasn't hallucinating or there wasn't another street artist sharing my name out there.

But when I saw my own face and heard my own voice start reciting my own speech, I actually squealed with delight. "Oh my god!"

Grady chuckled on the line, and I had completely forgotten I was still on the call with him. "Grady!" I said, as the video continued to play. "This is real! This is really happening!"

"Technically it already happened."

"Oh, just shut up. Don't ruin this moment with logic. I'm so excited."

"Good," he said, the pride evident in his voice. "You should be."

I reread the caption again. "I'm 'one to watch.' Which means they're going to keep watching!"

"Only if you keep creating."

"I have to," I said with conviction. "I'm an artist. It's part of the job description."

Grady chuckled once more. "It's about time you admitted it."

I finally closed the video and took my phone off the speaker. Pressing it back close to my ear, I said to Grady, "Thank you. Thank you for everything."

"Don't thank me," he said. "I didn't submit the video."

I cocked my head. "Then who did?"

"You probably know already."

"Archie?"

"Adeline."

I faintly recalled her perched on Archie's back, recording the speech with her phone. I pressed my lips together in a tight upward smile that held much more warmth than I thought possible. "I guess I have another phone call to make."

"There's no need to thank us," Grady said, simply. "Just remember the little people when you make it big one day."

"I could never forget you. Any of you. Or what you've done for me over the years," I said, hoping that the weighted truth of my gratitude bled through the words.

"I'm getting off the phone before you're late for your meeting," Grady replied. "Good luck, Natalia."

I didn't correct him. Instead, I thanked him once more and hung up the phone. But before I exited the car, I opened the blog post one more time, if only to confirm it was still there and hadn't disappeared when the phone call ended.

My mural, my *voice* was still there on the screen. I glanced at the clock on the dashboard of my car and promised myself I would only use one more minute to scroll through the comments before heading inside. There was a healthy collection of emojis, positive one-word adjectives, and overall impressed reactions flooding the feed.

One username stuck out, and my thumb paused on its own accord, hovering over the comment: *Well done, Talia.* The username was *CristinaScott.*

My hands worked robotically as they tabbed out of the blog and typed a quick text to a number I hadn't pulled up in years: How long have you followed The Digital Art Show?

She started typing immediately, then stopped. Finally, those three dots popped up once more before her message came through. Your college professor sent your father and me the link this morning.

My next message flew out before I could stop the question. Joe?
Mr. Conrad.

I took a deep breath. **Yes. Joe Conrad. He sent you the link?** And before I could stop myself, I sent a double text. **Why?**

He said we might want to see what you were up to.

There was a pause before her next message came through. **He was right. It was good to see you in the video. And hear your voice.**

It was the third message that put a nice little crack in the armor I had built around myself when it came to me and my past: **I'm happy for you, Talia.**

I hovered over my keypad, debating on how to respond. I finally settled with the truth: **Thank you, Mom. I think I needed to hear that, more than you know.**

She was typing again, then deleting and rewriting by the looks of the dots that flickered on the bottom of the screen. When the message came through, that crack in my armor exploded, shattering my preconceived barrier: **I'm glad you are doing what makes you happy.**

Happy. My mother had once told me, and she always firmly believed, that happiness was a choice. In my case, it was a bit more complicated than that, but I doubted she would ever fully understand.

But she wasn't entirely wrong. For the first time, I was doing what made me happy, no matter the consequences. And I was actively making choices to keep moving in that direction by surrounding myself with people who brought out the best for me and my mental health.

That word *happy* used to hang above me, taunting and just out of reach, but now I chose to look at it as an opener. With the gloves seemingly off, I asked the question I had never dared utter before. I marched straight into the trenches and typed, **What about you? Are you choosing to be happy yet?**

Once again those dots flashed repeatedly while I held my breath, recalling the fateful words my mother had said to me so many years ago on the drive home from the mental health clinic: *If I can't fall apart, then neither can you.*

My mother's response was a cold shock of honesty. **I'm not sure how.**

I took a deep breath with a new resolve I was mildly surprised to feel. My mother and I may never see eye to eye, but I could choose to listen.

I'm sure my art tour is going to take me back south at some point. Maybe we can grab a coffee and talk about it.

My mom typed out her final message: I would be grateful. Best of luck with your tour.

I didn't respond. I didn't need to. The door I had slammed shut between us when I left home now had a slight crack in it that might shed some light on why we both were the way we were. But until then, these simple texts were enough.

I clicked off my phone and got out of my car. As I walked toward the campus entrance for a future that didn't exist just a few months ago, I told myself that this was enough for my next chapter.

And I made a vow that tomorrow, and for the foreseeable tomorrows after, I would keep finding ways to be enough for myself.

ARCHIE

EPILOGUE

"On to the next adventure!" Talia said as the train came to a screeching halt, and we both stepped onto the platform set squarely in the heart of Boston, the one place we could both agree on to start. Kathryn had vouched for her hometown as well.

"It's not quite time to adventure," I said as I grasped Talia's hand firmly in mine, leading her through the throng of people. "I've got to take you on a date first."

"A date?" Talia laughed out loud. "What do you mean? I'm here for a work trip. You're here *exploring*."

"Correction," I said. "I think these next three days can qualify as both work and pleasure. But we're starting with the latter. I'm taking you out first."

"But—" Talia started to protest, surely thinking about the itinerary she had planned thoroughly and described in detail on the flight here. I had taken mental notes the entire time of the lapses in her schedule to throw in a few plans of my own.

"No buts. We'll make sure your next mural gets done in time. But first, we need food. And we're going to go play tourist," I said as I continued to lead her from the train station out into the heart of downtown Boston.

Talia stopped abruptly, jerking my arm to halt beside her.

"You okay?" I asked as I searched her face. The look in her blue eyes was one that I hadn't seen before: a mixture of gratitude and deep adoration. But she didn't give me long to study it before her mouth broke into a wide smile and she tugged me close to her.

"You're pretty awesome. You know that, right?" she asked me.

I put my arms around her and held her body close. "What makes you say that?"

Talia shook her head. "I just appreciate that you would think of planning something for me."

"A nice change from letting your schemes lead the way for us."

She went to playfully punch my chest, but I held her close by her wrist. "Talia," I whispered.

"Archie." She looked at me and grinned. "Kiss me."

A strand of hair had come loose from her ponytail. I tucked it behind her ear and didn't protest the request. The rest of the world—people, commotion, the past, and what came next—all slipped away. There was just Talia, and her kiss, and the overwhelming satisfaction of being in the present.

I regretted finally breaking the kiss, but the words I whispered when I let my forehead rest against hers had no remorse. "I love you."

Her breath hitched in her chest at the admission I had finally dared to say out loud, but it was a truth we had both always known.

"I know," she whispered back. And my own heart sang when she said, "And I love you for that, and love you back."

The walk from the downtown train station to Newbury Street was longer than I'd anticipated, but we dutifully followed the directions on my phone and arrived at a bustling cityscape that looked not entirely unlike Bridgeport back home. The buildings were taller, and the streets were wider, but the energy and atmosphere of people eating, shopping, resting, playing, working, and living felt familiar.

Talia's hand found mine once more. "You're right. I am hungry. Where are we going for lunch?"

I checked my phone once more and made one final turn. "Here, actually."

The sign above a small side door read MAX'S: American Bar and Grill.

Talia flicked an eyebrow at me. "Impressive. You managed to find it on the first try."

I'm not sure if it was being in a new place where we had no rules or personal history, or the gentle electricity humming between our intertwined hands, or maybe it was finally vocalizing our love for each other. Regardless of the reason, I got a little braver and leaned my mouth down to her ear to say in a low voice, "I think you know there are lots of things I can find on the first try."

The tips of her ears turned a bright shade of pink, and I chuckled, giving her hand a gentle tug.

The hostess greeted us and showed us to our seats out on the patio. Talia had regained her composure by the time a waitress had delivered glasses of ice water.

"First paintings, now *dates*," Talia said with a coy smile as she sipped her water. "And the actual reason you're accompanying me on these trips? What are you going to explore while we're in Boston?"

I leaned back in my chair and folded my arms in front of my chest. "I think I like cities."

She laughed, and I had to chuckle too at how strange the phrase had sounded coming from my lips. "I mean it though," I said. "I really do like cities. Like, I like Bridgeport—don't get me wrong. I like the idea of how people move in and out of the architecture and the green space, but now I'm excited to see it on a larger scale. It's kind of cool to think about the layout and how different spaces work and how humans come together in them. And I like that people like you want to decorate them and give them more life."

Talia blushed at that last bit, but I was still thinking of the landscapes we had passed on our way to the restaurant. "I think we take it for granted when we slip into the mundane routine of everyday life," I continued. "I'm guilty of it. Head down, headphones in, walk to work, sit at a desk, go home, do it again the next day."

"So you're going to people-watch instead?" she asked as she picked up the menu.

I reached for my own and opened it. "And study. Might do a little research on urban development."

"Sounds like you may have already started."

I skimmed the contents on the menu. "I may have looked up some of Boston's history on the plane. It's pretty well known for its smart urban planning. Did you know Boston is home to the first public park, first public school, and first public transportation?"

"Maybe you'll be a history professor or a city architect."

"Good thing I've got time to figure it out."

We both perused the menus for a few moments longer until the waitress came back. I almost ordered a Reuben, the same sandwich I would always get at Millie's, but instead I picked something else. Just to try something different.

After we handed the waitress our menus, I asked Talia, "So what's your plan for this mural? Do I get to know? Or is it a surprise?"

She placed her hands gently in her lap. "It's another portrait."

"Self-portrait?" I raised an eyebrow.

"No," she said with a small smile. "Not this time."

"Then who are you memorializing forever in history on the side of a building in Boston?" I asked as I reached for my water glass.

"It would make sense to be Kathryn since she's the local," Talia mused. "But I'm starting with Adeline."

My pinkie finger twitched against the edge of my glass as I paused. "Addie?"

Talia nodded.

"Why's that?"

Talia chewed on her straw while she contemplated her answer. She took a deep breath before saying, "Because she's the bravest person I know. She showed me that it's possible to get through the hardest times. She gave me hope."

My chest got weirdly tight. I reached my hand out across the table for hers, which she willingly slid into mine. The words came out small and strained when I managed to say "Thank you."

Talia gave my hand a firm squeeze back before letting our hands just rest there on the table, gently entwined together. I cleared my throat before changing the subject. "You know, you never told me why you got the tattoo."

"The wings?" she asked, her other hand subconsciously flicking to the tattoo at the back of her neck to touch them lightly.

I nodded.

"I think it's pretty obvious." She laughed and withdrew her hand from mine.

"Enlighten me."

"Archie," Talia said with a smile that shattered any resolve I had left in me not to trip and fall anymore head over heels. "You're my wingman. It's always been you," she said. "And as you put it, that was worth memorializing. Forever. In history."

"And future?" The question slipped from my lips so automatically that I had no regret in uttering it.

She smirked. "Well, it's not going away anytime soon."

"Me neither," I said.

"Me neither," she said. And it sounded like a promise we both intended to keep.

ACKNOWLEDGMENTS

One of the closing themes of this book—the sense of community that Talia finds—wouldn't have come alive in your hands without my little community and its support.

The biggest thanks go out to Avery Morgan, whose horse, Wingman, otherwise known as Archie in the barn, was the inspiration for Archie Morgan's name in the book. Aside from your naming suggestions, you were just as close to these characters as I was while they were formed. Through every scene, every draft, thanks for never begrudging me talking about what Talia and Archie were up to. I can wholeheartedly say this book would have never been drafted without you pestering my word count goal of one thousand words a day. For that, I am grateful.

To Rylee Rosenthal, thank you for being the second person to read the draft in its entirety and willingly stepping in to guide media and marketing with your expertise from Rylee Rose Photography. (Special shoutout to Avery Johnson and Sydney Koenig for modeling Archie and Talia!) Seeing these characters brought to real life after living for so long in my head made publishing even more special.

To Mike Alessandro, I still have the text saved you sent me when I first told you I got the contract for this book. Thank you for the constant, unwavering support. You are my rock.

Other early beta-reader shoutouts to Sydney Pifer, Macy Koziel, Mikayla Sengle, Christie Heuman, Quinn Larimer, Carly Alessandro, and Nicole Mandracchia. Thank you for the revisions and encouragement to tell Talia and Archie's story.

To Rennie Dyball, my first editor and continual hype girl, thank you for polishing the story until it gleamed and was ready for publisher eyes to see.

To Lauren Cassidy, thank you for taking a leap of faith and working through the whirlwind of ideas for the cover! The art you provided perfectly captured Archie, Talia, and their little Bridgeport town.

To the team at Warren Publishing:

Thank you, Lacey Cope, for reaching out after reading my debut, wanting to know if I had written anything new recently. Without that email, *The Wingman* may not have made it to your inbox.

To my editors Melisa Graham and Danielle Lange, thank you for the fine-tooth combing over the story and finishing touches that made it complete.

To Amy Ashby and Mindy Kuhn, thank you for taking the chance on a manuscript that means so much to me. It's a joy to be a part of the Warren family.

And to those who happen to be reading this now, thank you for sticking with the journey this far. It means more than you know.

PLAYLIST FOR THE WINGMAN

- "Everywhere, Everything" by Noah Kahan
- "This is me trying" by Taylor Swift
- "Mess It Up" by Gracie Abrams
- "You'd Never Know" by BLÜ EYES
- "Caffeine" by Fly by Midnight (featuring Shoffy)
- "I Love You, I'm Sorry" by Gracie Abrams
- "Striptease" by carwash
- "All My Love" by Noah Kahan
- "Kiss Me" by Dermot Kennedy
- "Ready to Love" by CVBZ
- "The Archer" by Taylor Swift
- "Numb" by David Archuleta

DISCUSSION QUESTIONS

1. On its surface, *The Wingman* is considered a love story. But it also serves as a conversation piece for what can sometimes be a stigmatized discourse surrounding mental health. In what ways have you seen or experienced conversations around mental health changing over the years?

2. In many ways, Talia and Archie's story on how they prepare to face the world with their new perspectives could just be the beginning. What further work do you think needs done for them to continue their healing journeys?

3. What setbacks might they face as a result? And how might they cope in healthy ways? What about unhealthy ways?

4. This book utilizes the expression of visual art as a medium for healing. Other expressive arts that can be used therapeutically are writing, music, etc. Why do you think it's easier for society to accept these discussions more so than traditional conversations?

5. Adeline's parents and Talia's parents are portrayed as very different in their level of support with their children's mental health, yet both daughters are affected. How do these two characters foil each other?

6. Furthermore, how much of mental health struggles can be attributed to nature versus nurture?

7. Which side character(s) would you want to get to know better and why?

Also by Meg Rosenthal:

The Right Words